E.

Evelyn James has always been fascinated by history and the work of writers such as Agatha Christie. She began writing the Clara Fitzgerald series one hot summer, when a friend challenged her to write her own historical murder mystery. Clara Fitzgerald has gone on to feature in over thirteen novels, with many more in the pipeline. Evelyn enjoys conjuring up new plots, dastardly villains and horrible crimes to keep her readers entertained and plans on doing so for as long as possible.

Other Books in
The Clara Fitzgerald Series

Memories of the Dead

Flight of Fancy

Murder in Mink

Carnival of Criminals

Mistletoe and Murder

The Poison Pen

Grave Suspicions of Murder

The Woman Died Thrice

Murder and Mascara

The Green Jade Dragon

The Monster at the Window

Murder Aboard Mary Jane

The Missing Wife

The Green Jade Dragon

by
Evelyn James

A Clara Fitzgerald Mystery
Book 10

Red Raven Publications
2018

Chapter One

It was a fine early September day. The sort where the weather is trying to pretend that summer is not really over and that autumn is just a figment of the imagination. Clara Fitzgerald, Brighton's first female private detective, sat in her office and contemplated some paperwork from a case involving suspected embezzlement of the church flower fund. It had proved a simple problem to solve. There was no thief, no naughty Christian helping themselves to the pot of donations. It all boiled down to an error in the accounting system. As it turned out, the fund was surprisingly healthy with surplus in it rather than any loss.

Clara was finishing up her report on the case to be handed to the little committee that controlled, among other things, the flower fund. She was relieved for once to be able to report that no one had died or been found to be a dastardly criminal. It was just the sort of case she had started out on, in those early days of her work when life seemed a lot simpler. Now many of her cases revolved around murder or other such sinister crimes and, though the work paid well, it had a tendency to leave a bad taste in the mouth, very unlike these quiet, mundane affairs.

She was just signing her name to the report when she

heard the bell ring at her front door. Clara rose and stretched, then headed downstairs to see who had come calling. Clara rented a set of rooms above a haberdashery shop, and these served as her working space, though invariably her work would also find her at home. As much as she liked to keep her business and domestic lives separate, her clients often had other ideas. She walked down the tight staircase to the front door and opened it. Before her stood Mrs Wilton.

Clara's heart sank a little. Mrs Wilton had given Clara her first murder case and set her on a new path in her career. She should really be grateful to her, but Mrs Wilton had a habit of frustrating people and annoying them. She was interfering, slightly eccentric and often silly. Since she had hired Clara that first time, she had felt it her duty to find work for poor Clara and was always pressing her friends upon her – not that her friends seemed to appreciate the situation either. After all, does someone really want to hire a private detective just to discover who picked the daffodils from their front garden? Or why the postman had been replaced by a new man? Or to learn who had been knocking over the bins and scattering the contents? The answer was of course no, but all these matters had been dragged before Clara, along with the unfortunate friend or neighbour who had been foolish enough to mention them to Mrs Wilton in the first place. Remarkably, Mrs Wilton always had new friends to impose upon. She was that sort of woman.

"Clara!" Mrs Wilton declared, looking to all the world as if a great calamity had just befallen her and the world were about to end. She was a woman of middle years, with the sort of wiry hair that reminded Clara of a terrier. It had been black once, but was now going very grey and was determinedly swept back into a bun. Mrs Wilton wore black, she was a widow and was perpetually in mourning for her husband who died in the war. She stood before Clara and wrung her hands. "We must talk at once! It is dreadfully urgent!"

Many things were urgent to Mrs Wilton and Clara had long ago learned to take such statements with a pinch of salt. Probably the paperboy had forgotten to deliver her magazine and she was perceiving this as something dire, perhaps a terrible conspiracy within the publishing industry to deprive her of information. That was the way Mrs Wilton's mind worked. Nothing was simply a fluke of fate, everything was part of a sinister and dastardly plot to destroy her life. Clara did have some sympathy for the woman, after all, she had been told by the War Office that her son was dead only to have Clara discover him alive. And she had been briefly accused of murdering a fraudulent clairvoyant. All this made her a little prone to overreacting.

"Why don't you come upstairs?" Clara said reluctantly.

Fortunately, she had nothing else to do and if she could settle Mrs Wilton and send her home feeling more herself that would benefit them both. What Clara did not want was to become embroiled in another of Mrs Wilton's wild goose chases.

They retreated upstairs and Mrs Wilton gave a respectful nod to the portrait of Clara's father hanging on the wall. It was a habit Mrs Wilton seemed unable to break. She acted as if the eyes of the portrait were really looking down upon her. Clara offered her a chair and then sat down in her own behind the desk. The September sun still had power and beamed onto Clara's back warming her shoulders.

"Now, Mrs Wilton, what is the problem?"

Mrs Wilton took a long, deep breath and then exhaled it as a sigh of relief.

"I am most distressed with my neighbour, Mrs Butterworth," she explained. "But I need to go backwards a little and explain myself. Mrs Butterworth has suffered the misfortune of her husband absconding from the marital home."

"Oh dear," Clara said without enthusiasm, cases involving adultery or abandonment were always messy

3

and emotionally draining. She tried to avoid them as they never had happy endings.

"It is even worse than that," Mrs Wilton persisted. "Mr Butterworth took Agamemnon with him when he left."

"Agamemnon?" Clara asked with a touch of concern.

"The cat. A Persian, I believe, and rather expensive, or so you would think the way Mrs Butterworth goes on. Anyway, Mr Butterworth disappeared three weeks ago, with the cat, and his wife is now beside herself."

"I can imagine," Clara said politely, still trying to keep the case at arm's length.

"She came to me for advice," Mrs Wilton plumped herself up, as if this gave her a new aura of importance. Clara had to wonder why anyone would go to Mrs Wilton for advice. "I suggested she hire a private detective and I gave her your name."

"Oh," Clara said, wondering now if the matter was not that Mrs Wilton had a case for her, but rather that somehow the affair with Mrs Butterworth had slipped her attention and she was to be accused of negligence. "I haven't heard anything from Mrs Butterworth, as far as I am aware."

"Well you wouldn't have!" Mrs Wilton declared. "That's the problem! She only went and hired another private detective!"

"Oh," Clara repeated herself, this time because she was truly surprised by the information. As far as Clara was aware there were no other detectives operating in Brighton but, of course, there was no reason someone should not start up their own business.

"You don't understand the implication!" Mrs Wilton persisted, almost bouncing in her chair with ire. "She went and hired a female private detective!"

Now Clara was interested. Another woman had set herself up in the detective business? Well, why not, there was no restriction upon it, even if it did give Clara a pang of concern.

"I do not have a monopoly on the detective business," Clara said carefully to Mrs Wilton. "Nor can I deny another woman the opportunity to set herself up as a private detective if she wishes."

"But... but you are Brighton's first female private detective!" Mrs Wilton insisted. "It isn't on, it just isn't!"

"I don't know what you wish me to do about it," Clara smiled at her gently. "I can't stop this woman, no more than the greengrocer can stop another person opening a greengrocer's shop."

"Surely you can investigate her?" Mrs Wilton leaned forward, her tone now urgent and a little desperate. "She could be a troublemaker!"

"Or she could be someone wishing to make their way in the world independently," Clara countered. "I suppose, considering the successes I have had, it was inevitable that someone would eventually decide to copy me."

Mrs Wilton pursed her lips, this was clearly not the response she had either anticipated or desired. She wanted Clara to be as outraged as she was. She was affronted that after comforting Mrs Butterworth in her despair and offering Clara's name when it was asked for, the woman had then gone off and done her own thing, including hiring this new detective, this usurper on Clara's home turf. Mrs Wilton thought the whole matter was underhand and disloyal.

"Her name is Sarah Butler," she said, her tone surly since Clara was not as upset as she was. "I have no idea who she is. Seems to have popped up out of thin air."

"People do," Clara shrugged. "The name is not familiar to me, either."

"And after all you have done for this town, Clara. All the help you have given and the cases you have solved. Why, I consider it most ungrateful of Mrs Butterworth to go with this new person instead."

Clara was rather relieved she had not been given the case and thought Miss Butler could have it. She would soon discover how disagreeable marital cases were. It was no real skin off Clara's nose.

"Never mind Mrs Wilton," she attempted to appease the woman. "I am sure there will still be plenty of work for me. If I can cope with having a rival private detective in Brighton, I am sure you can."

Mrs Wilton gave a slight huff. She was hardly mollified, but she realised she was not going to get any further. She rose and picked up her handbag.

"You are too nice, Clara. I just hope your generosity will not come back to bite you."

"Even if I wanted to do something about Miss Butler, I hardly could," Clara replied, as she showed Mrs Wilton downstairs. "She is doing nothing illegal."

"Yet!" Mrs Wilton held up a warning finger, then she made her farewells and disappeared off.

Clara returned to the flower fund report she had just finished and placed it in an envelope and addressed it. She neatened her desk and emptied the teapot she kept by the fire. With a final glance at her father, who had been gone now these last five years, she departed for home.

Supper was waiting for her. Annie, her friend and housekeeper, had prepared a simple meal using cold meat from the leftovers of the roast they had had the day before. Clara's brother Tommy was sitting at the dining table perusing the newspaper, and just to his left was Captain O'Harris. O'Harris had recently experienced a most horrific accident in an aeroplane, which resulted in him being missing for a year. He had suffered terrible shock and was still not mentally fit to go home and live alone. He was currently staying with the local doctor while he recovered, but spent a great deal of time at the Fitzgerald household as well. He was friends with both Tommy and Clara, and their company was of enormous help to him.

He smiled at Clara as she entered the dining room. Tommy mumbled a greeting without looking up from the article he was engrossed in.

"A message was left for you," O'Harris said. "I

answered the door."

He pointed out a folded piece of paper that he had placed beside the chair Clara usually sat in.

"I told the gentleman about your office, but he chose to leave a message here. He was a servant, a butler or valet, I think."

Clara picked up the piece of paper without unfolding it.

"I had the delight of Mrs Wilton's company today," she sighed. "A shame this other fellow could not have called upon me as a distraction."

Clara twisted the paper in her fingers. There was a worry nagging at her, something she had to mention to the others to get it off her chest. Despite her words to Mrs Wilton, she had been lying when she said it did not matter that there was a new private detective in Brighton. It did matter. It worried her; it stirred up anxieties about her ability to maintain her livelihood. While the investments her father had made before his death could sustain his children, they were not substantial enough to do anything more than keep them ticking over. Clara had started working to provide the extra income the household needed. Tommy had come back from the war a cripple, and while he was slowly recovering, he was not yet fit to work. Clara was the breadwinner in the house and it scared her, just a little, to imagine a time when she could not provide them with what they needed. What if, for instance, this other private detective took all her work? It was an over-dramatic thought, but that did not make it any less troubling.

"Mrs Wilton was telling me that another woman has started a detective business in Brighton," Clara blurted out.

Tommy now did look up from the newspaper.

"Another private detective?" he said, testing out the idea. "That's interesting."

"Mrs Wilton was most appalled by the idea," Clara shrugged. "Perhaps I should be appalled too. Should I be worried?"

"That you have a rival?" Tommy asked. He pondered his answer. "Only if she is as good as you, and that would be unlikely."

"Your loyalty is impeccable," Clara said, amused. "But, in all seriousness, what if this woman was to take my business away from me?"

"Rivals come and go," Captain O'Harris now spoke. He held Clara with his dark eyes, boring into her. "The only way to beat them is to be the best at what you do. Then people will want to hire you instead of them. Sure, some will drift to the opposition, but the ones that matter, they will stick with you. In my time I have had plenty of rival pilots pushing for the same records and achievements. The only way I defied them was by being better than them."

Clara nodded. She understood, she just wasn't confident enough to declare herself the best at anything.

"I won't let it worry me," she said firmly, as much to herself as to the men. "Now, what is this note?"

She unfolded the slip of paper and found it an invitation to call upon a gentleman named Mr Jacobs at her earliest convenience. It stated that he would be most grateful for her advice in a matter that was causing him concern. Another case. Just what Clara needed to take her mind off things. She scanned the address and recognised the road name as one of the better ones in Brighton.

"I think he was a butler," O'Harris mused to himself. "The fellow who gave that to me. Now I consider it, I am certain he was. He had that sort of appearance to him."

Clara folded up the note. She would push worries about this new detective to one side. She had a case to work on and she would do as O'Harris had suggested and be the best she could be. She would prove that she was Brighton's foremost private detective, even if she was not its only one anymore.

Chapter Two

Mr Jacobs lived in a Victorian extravagance masquerading as a house. It was the sort of thing you could not imagine anyone building in post-war England, but which had seemed such a natural thing to the Victorians. It was built over three floors and included a basement. The windows were mock-Tudor, but the walls were red brick. There was a porch over the front door which might have come from a country cottage and on the left-hand corner, as Clara walked up the gravel drive, there was an octagonal tower that finished in a conical spire roof. On the very top was a weathervane in the shape of a Welsh dragon. There was something both garish and enticing about this hodgepodge of designs and styles. It was rather like someone had gone through a catalogue of architecture, picked out all the bits they liked, and then insisted they were put together in a semi-homogenous form. It was too early for Clara to say whether the result worked or not.

Mr Jacobs was a retired antiquities expert. He had worked at various prestigious auction houses in London, valuing and assessing lots. He had picked out more than one fake in his time, and had also been responsible for authenticating some significant finds. He had always come from money and his work had not been necessary from a financial point-of-view, but it kept him busy and amused. The house belonged to his parents and he had retained it after their deaths, intending to retire to Brighton eventually. This he had done just after the war, though he still kept busy, often travelling about the country to offer his expert insight on objects in other peoples' collections.

He was also constantly updating his personal collection and could regularly be found at sales with his eye on some exquisite and undervalued piece that his fellow 'experts' had failed to recognise for what it was.

Clara was shown into Mr Jacobs' personal sitting room. It happened to be the room with the tower at its corner. Clara glanced over curiously and could see how the builders had affixed the octagonal structure to the side of the house, knocking through the walls so that it was possible to step straight into the tower with its three windows. There was an armchair in the awkward space, next to a pile of books sitting on a small table. It appeared to be Mr Jacobs' reading spot, but he was not there for the moment. Instead he was sitting on a long sofa before a large Tudor style window, with its glass arranged into little diamonds by strips of lead.

Mr Jacobs was dressed in brown tweed and had a little red bowtie at the collar of his white shirt. He looked well turned out for greeting his guest, down to the purple silk handkerchief carefully arranged in his top pocket. He was bald, except for a rim of hair about his ears. This was a light brown with no hint of grey. He was well-fed, but not to the point of being fat, rather he looked well-nurtured like a solid carthorse. Clara noted a ring on his finger, but it was not a wedding band.

"Welcome Miss Fitzgerald, I am delighted you could come so swiftly," Mr Jacobs rose and indicated that she should sit on the sofa beside him. Clara obeyed.

"Your note indicated you required my help?" Clara said as she sat down. The room was warm and filled with the evening sunshine that cast glowing lines across the floor.

"Well, the police have failed me and I am forced back upon my own resources. I had hoped you could assist me."

"What has precisely happened?" Clara asked.

"Just over a week ago my property was burgled," Mr Jacobs said sadly. He looked a tad embarrassed at admitting his misfortune. "Only one item was stolen, a very specific item, which leads me to imagine that the burglary was a professional undertaking. I have been in the antiques business a long time and I have seen things like this happen before, though I never imagined it would happen to me. I always thought my security precautions adequate."

Mr Jacobs looked abashed, clearly feeling ashamed that he had allowed such a thing to occur. A thin gloss of sweat was forming on his bald pate as he flushed with indignation.

"What was stolen?" Clara asked to distract him.

"A relatively small item. Very specific," Mr Jacobs rose and showed Clara to what looked like a table, but which was in fact a box with a glass top – a display case for small items. Inside the case were a series of individual compartments, all divided by wooden sections. Mr Jacobs lifted the lid of the cabinet and showed Clara the trinkets inside. "These are Japanese netsukes. They were used to hold objects together, serving as a toggle, if you will on a string. Originally they were just practical little beads, but over time they became most exquisite. They became an art form."

Mr Jacobs lifted out one of the objects. It was white and carved into the form of several hares leaping in a circle. Each hare was tiny, but precisely carved with detailed fur and even a seeming expression on each face.

"I am an expert on Japanese antiquities, one of the foremost in England. I even have Japanese collectors asking my opinion on objects they have bought. Naturally, I have my own collection. These netsuke are my most precious items, not that all of them have great value, but it is what they symbolise that attracts me. The great skill and craftmanship that has gone into them is just as exquisite as any British masterpiece on canvas."

Mr Jacobs reverently put back the small netsuke and picked up another.

"This is made of walrus tooth," he handed Clara the netsuke which depicted a portly man pouring out wine or perhaps beer into a container.

"One of these was stolen?" Clara asked, handing back the small ornament.

"Yes," Mr Jacobs became downcast. "This one."

He pointed to an empty slot in the cabinet. It was at the top, in the middle of the row and it seemed to shriek out its emptiness to them.

"This item, as it may not surprise you, was one of my most cherished. It was made of green jade, a rare material for a netsuke, and was carved into the form of a royal dragon. The dragon is a great symbol of Japan and is deemed a bringer of good fortune, as well as a creature of potential destruction. The dragon was naturally valuable but it held further significance for me, for it was the start of my collection," Mr Jacobs quietly put down the lid of the cabinet and showed Clara back to the sofa. "My uncle Edmund was a great traveller during the last century. He particularly liked to travel to the far east. He always brought me back a gift. He was the one that sparked my interesting in Japanese antiquities and set me on the path I have pursued all my life.

"One summer he returned from a trip to Japan. It had been an exhausting trip for him, though he failed to explain why. I always suspected he had endured some misfortune during it. Anyway, he stayed at this very house on his return and he presented me with a gift – the green jade dragon. He explained what it was and its purpose. Then he asked me to keep it safe for him. I remember him placing it in the palm of my hand and folding my fingers around it, then winking at me.

Naturally I promised."

Mr Jacobs stared across the room at the raided table cabinet. His distress at failing his uncle, despite all the years that had passed since the promise was made, was palpable.

"A few weeks later my uncle died in a carriage accident in London. A terrible thing. He was crushed under the wheels," Mr Jacobs scowled at the memory. "I have kept the dragon safe for him ever since, and it was the spark for my future collecting. Now it is gone, and I want you to bring it back to me."

Clara nodded, completely understanding why the object was so precious and why its loss had come so hard to Mr Jacobs. Had it been merely valuable he might have been able to live with the notion that it would never be restored to him, but its emotional significance meant he could not resolved himself to its permanent absence.

"Can you tell me about the burglary?" Clara now asked. "When it occurred? And how they got in?"

"Yes," Mr Jacobs rose again. "This way."

He took her through a set of double doors at the back of the room and they found themselves in a dark hallway.

"This passage divides the sitting room from the dining room. I believe it was originally intended as a discreet passage for servants to use when attending to guests," Mr Jacobs pointed to his left. There was a window mounted in the wall. It was narrow and made narrower by a bar of stone that divided it in two. It was the only source of natural light in the passage and it was broken. "All my downstairs windows have shutters reinforced with steel, Miss Fitzgerald. I am well-aware of the many valuable things this house contains and I have made provisions to keep them safe. When I go away the shutters are drawn and locked across all the windows, all except this one which I always deemed too small for a person to enter by."

Clara stepped forward to look at the window which was high up in the wall. It was indeed narrow and would be difficult to slide through, yet someone clearly had. Perhaps a child?

"Once through this window, there was no obstacle for the thief left. The police believe he came through the doors behind us and went straight to the table cabinet. It does not have a lock, but even if it had I doubt it would have troubled the perpetrator for long," Mr Jacobs pulled a face at the broken window. The smashed glass had been cleared up and a wooden board placed over the hole.

"The house was completely empty when it happened?" Clara asked, having inspected the window to her satisfaction.

"Not entirely. My housekeeper remains on when I depart. She has a set of rooms in the attic and is meant to be another deterrent to thieves. Or so I thought. I don't like the idea of leaving the house absolutely empty. My butler, Mr Yaxley, comes with me when I travel."

"Your housekeeper heard nothing?" Clara asked.

"Apparently not. She did not become aware of the crime until the next morning. Unfortunately, at first she did not realise anything had been taken and assumed it was just an act of vandalism. She cleaned up the glass and blocked the window. Only when she was dusting later did she notice the jade dragon was missing."

Clara nodded, it would be natural enough to at first think the incident was just someone throwing stones when the rest of the house was seemingly untouched.

"And the police have been here?"

"For what good it did," Mr Jacobs shrugged his shoulders. "They looked around, complaining about the glass being removed. My housekeeper was most upset by their attitude. She has been sullen ever since. They wouldn't believe at first that someone could crawl through that window, even when it was pointed out about the missing item. They actually suggested I might have taken it myself without my housekeeper's knowledge when I went on my trip."

Mr Jacobs looked most indignant about the way his

staff and himself had been treated by the police. In the dark of the hall his face had taken on a haunted look as the shadows fell over it.

"Eventually they were persuaded I had not taken the dragon, when I came home the following evening and told them so," Mr Jacobs explained. "Even then, I suspect they think I did this as an insurance fraud. They are all fools, naturally I did not. But they look at all this with disbelieving eyes. Anyway, one of the more sympathetic constables took me aside and made it plain how difficult it is to retrieve stolen property. They don't hold out much hope of finding my dragon."

"They have not offered a suggestion of a suspect?"

"No, nothing," Mr Jacobs gave a gruff huff. "I gave them time to act, but whenever I pay a call on them to discover their progress I am given platitudes and sent on my way. Eventually I decided I needed an independent pair of eyes on the matter. Which is why I asked for you."

Mr Jacobs hesitated, a sudden pang of unease came over him.

"Can you help me?" he asked anxiously, perhaps fearing Clara would offer him the same sympathetic platitudes the police had done.

"I shall certainly endeavour," Clara replied, reassuring him with a smile. "I can make no promises, but there may be hope in the fact that the dragon was clearly targeted for a reason. Someone knew you had it and just where to look."

"Yes!" Mr Jacobs almost cried out with renewed hope. "Yes, that is quite right."

"Who would know about the jade dragon?" Clara asked. "Has it been shown to many people recently?"

Mr Jacobs' jubilant face now turned downwards into a parody of one of the tragedy masks seen at theatres. He motioned that Clara should follow him back into the sitting room. Opening a drawer, he pulled out a booklet and handed it to Clara. She instantly saw that it was a catalogue from a recent exhibition at the British Museum.

The catalogue proudly declared that the exhibition was of Japanese antiquities.

"Turn to page sixteen," Mr Jacobs said glumly.

Clara did as she was told and was greeted by a black and white photograph of a tiny carved netsuke. She could not tell from the photograph that the item was made of green jade, but she could see that it was shaped like a dragon curling around on itself. The text beneath the picture identified the item and also gave a polite credit to Mr Humphry Jacobs of Brighton for loaning the object from his private collection. Clara looked up and met Mr Jacobs' eyes.

"To answer your question," he said, "yes it has been shown to many people. I might offer a guess at thousands."

Clara sighed. That was an awful lot of suspects.

Chapter Three

Clara was introduced to Mrs Crocker, Mr Jacobs' housekeeper, in the kitchen. She was a woman who appeared to have been lumped together by an ungainly hand. She had an oval, nondescript body atop stubby legs, ornamented by two chubby arms and a head that merged alarmingly with her shoulders. She did not improve her appearance of being made from uncooked dough by the hearty scowl that seemed deeply ingrained on her face. Whereas some people have smile lines, she had scowl lines.

"Mrs Crocker, this is Miss Fitzgerald who will be investigating the disappearance of the dragon netsuke," Mr Jacobs introduced them.

The housekeeper said nothing, but her scowl seemed to deepen and Clara suspected her presence was resented. Perhaps Mrs Crocker was feeling guilt over her failure to realise sooner that the netsuke had been stolen.

"Miss Fitzgerald has a few questions for you, I am sure you will be accommodating," Mr Jacobs continued easily. "I shall not interfere. I shall return to my sitting room."

Mr Jacobs departed, leaving Clara alone with the unhappy housekeeper. Mrs Crocker had been in the process of ironing linen handkerchiefs when they had arrived in her domain. She quietly put the flat iron back on the stove.

"Perhaps you could tell me about the night someone broke in?" Clara asked her, smiling to try and ease the tension.

"What is there to tell?" Mrs Crocker shrugged her fat shoulders. "I was in bed."

"You have rooms up in the attic?" Clara asked.

"Yes. It's a long way from up there to down here," Mrs Crocker said pointedly. "I was asleep when it happened and heard nothing."

If Mrs Crocker was lying, she was certainly not going to admit it. Clara could see she was going to be belligerent over everything Clara asked her.

"When did you first notice there had been an incident?" she asked, still smiling and giving the appearance of not being fazed by the housekeeper's surliness.

"When I came downstairs," Mrs Crocker shrugged again, it was an abrupt, sharp action, almost as if the question was so foolish it was hardly worth her time to shrug at it.

"You came straight down into the hallway where the window was broken?" Clara queried with a pretence of innocence.

"No, of course not. I came down to the kitchen first. It was when I went about to do my dusting that I saw it," Mrs Crocker brindled at having to explain herself further. "I stood on the glass before I saw it."

"That hallway is quite dark, even with the window," Clara nodded, now trying the tactic of being sympathetic to the housekeeper.

Whether it was working was difficult to say. Mrs Crocker had sat herself at the kitchen table and folded her stout arms in front of her. Clara, in contrast, relaxed more in her own chair and tried to appear nonchalant.

"I never liked that hallway. Always thought it was a pointless piece of design. Idea seems to have been that it would prevent servants going through the sitting room to the dining room directly. It was a secret passage they could use to service each room without stumbling upon the household," this was the most Mrs Crocker had said, and it seemed Clara had touched on something that irritated her deeply. Mrs Crocker was the sort of servant who doesn't like to be reminded that that is exactly what they are. "It gathers spiders too. They like the dark and all the corners. I have to dust the ceiling for cobwebs at least twice a week."

"And you were doing that when you stood on the broken glass?"

"Well, I wasn't expecting to find that, was I?" Mrs Crocker tutted to herself. "The entire pane had been knocked out, not a fragment of glass left. When I stepped into the hallway, what with it being dark, I didn't realise there was no glass in the window until I heard it crunching under my feet."

Mrs Crocker's lips squirmed, it seemed a pang of conscience was coming over her. One large finger toyed with the cuff of the sleeve of her dress, teasing at a loose thread.

"It took me by surprise."

"There were no other obvious signs that someone had been in the house?"

"What do you want me to say? The police asked me exactly the same thing," Mrs Crocker glowered at the memory; the police had harassed her, made her feel she had something to hide when she did not. "It was not as though there were wet footprints on the carpet or something. There was just the broken glass. None of the doors were even open. I thought some kids had been playing silly beggars and thrown a stone at the window. So I swept up the glass and asked the gardener when he arrived to fix a board over the window."

"How long afterwards did you realise something was missing?" Clara asked steadily, gradually dragging the story from Mrs Crocker.

The woman gave another of her short, sharp shrugs.

"It was probably about an hour. I had to sweep up the glass and beat the rug from the hallway to make sure none remained. Then I spoke to Mr Hobbs the gardener. Finally I got back to my dusting," Mrs Crocker pulled in her lips, her face seeming to squeeze in on itself. "That was when I noticed the empty space in the netsuke cabinet. I dust that case every day and I know what should be in there. I realised the little green dragon was missing. That was when I knew it had not just been kids messing about."

"You rang the police?"

"Yes. For what good it did me," Mrs Crocker looked hurt. "At first they didn't believe me, said that maybe Mr Jacobs had taken the dragon with him. I said that was most unlikely, it was not the sort of thing you carry around in your pocket. Anyway, there was all that broken glass to think about. But they didn't take much heed of that either, because of the window being so small."

"They didn't think a person could squeeze through it?"

"No," Mrs Crocker stopped toying with her sleeve. "They made me feel like a silly old woman causing trouble for no reason. It was only when Mr Jacobs came home and he agreed that the dragon was missing that they took me seriously. Then I got it in the neck for clearing up the glass. They said if there had been fingerprints on it, I would now have destroyed them."

Mrs Crocker had clearly been rather offended by the attitude of the police. Clara began to see why she was so defensive towards her.

"I doubt there were fingerprints on the glass," Clara reassured her. "This sounds a professional job, and professionals know not to leave fingerprints."

"They said because I dusted and polished the netsuke cabinet they could get no prints off that, either."

"The thief would have worn gloves," Clara promised. "This is not some opportunist crime. Someone planned this."

Mrs Crocker wasn't listening, she was thinking about the accusations the police made towards her and dwelling on them. Clara decided that she had probably gained all she could from the woman.

"Thank you, Mrs Crocker," she rose to leave, neither expecting nor receiving a response from the housekeeper.

Clara returned to Mr Jacobs in the sitting room.

"Well?" he asked her.

"Mrs Crocker has confirmed what you first suggested, that the person behind this was a professional," Clara told him. "There is not a lot else to go on, but I will certainly endeavour to dig up the thief."

Mr Jacobs looked relieved as she said this. He had clearly thought she would tell him, much like the police had done, that there was no hope for resolving the matter.

"I imagine the dragon is very valuable?" Clara asked.

"Very," Mr Jacobs nodded. "In terms of its design, craftsmanship and quality it is virtually unique. I suspect it was made for someone very important, though, my uncle never offered me information on its provenance. Why would he? I was but a small boy and he died before I could ask questions."

"I shall see what I can do," Clara promised. That was the best she could offer.

Upon leaving Mr Jacobs' house she walked all the way to Brighton police station, to see if Inspector Park-Coombs was in and could offer her some insight. She first, however, had to negotiate her way past the station's desk sergeant who had little time for Clara and her investigating.

"Good evening," Clara nodded at him, it was now approaching seven o'clock and there was a fair chance the inspector had gone home but, then again, he might be working late.

"What do you want?" the desk sergeant responded in his usual tone of disapproval. Clara featured on his list of people he classified as nuisances and troublemakers.

"I would like to see Inspector Park-Coombs, if he is

about?"

"You can't just come waltzing in here demanding to see senior policemen," the desk sergeant barked. "You are just a civilian, I might remind you."

"I could remind you that, as a policeman, you are here to serve civilians," Clara pointed out, her indignation threatening to get the better of her self-control. She was trying not to lose her temper, but it was a perilously close thing. "Surely it is up to the Inspector whether he wants to see me or not?"

"This is the problem with modern women, they think the world owes them something," the desk sergeant puttered loudly, so others waiting in the police station could hear him. "The world owes you nothing Miss Fitzgerald."

Clara was becoming very annoyed. She gripped the edge of the counter with her fingers until her knuckles went white.

"Is Inspector Park-Coombs in the station or not?" she asked again.

"I couldn't say. I haven't seen him lately," the desk sergeant said priggishly. He turned back to the papers on his desk, filling in some form, probably about annoying women.

Clara closed her eyes for a second and tried to calm herself. Her working relationship with Inspector Park-Coombs had always been good and mutually respectful. They helped each other to solve crimes and avoided standing on each other's toes. But her relationship with the desk sergeant was fraught with trouble. He had never liked the idea of a woman having access to police business and he was always obstructive when Clara came into the station. Clara knew that belligerence was not going to get her any further. She stepped back from the front desk, letting the person waiting behind her take her place.

She could go home and try again tomorrow, but the same battle would ensue. The desk sergeant would be in no better mood after a night's rest, she knew that well enough. The question was whether she could be bothered to wait around and fight him when, for all she knew, the inspector could have already gone home. She wouldn't put it past the desk sergeant to torment her, keep her arguing, just to inform her the inspector had left over an hour ago. Clara was in two minds about it all when she heard the man who had been behind her in the queue speak.

"I would like to see Inspector Park-Coombs."

Clara turned sharply. She had not taken a good look at the man who had stood behind her, why would she? Now she noticed he was quite well-dressed in a navy suit, with an overcoat thrown over one arm and a suitcase held in his hand.

"So she has you working for her now, does she?" the desk sergeant said snidely. "Well, I'll tell you what I told her. It isn't for civilians to come in here barking orders about who they want to see. So you can clear off!"

Clara edged a little closer to the front desk. She had no idea who the man asking for the inspector was, but the look on his face suggested he was not going to take no for an answer. In fact, he looked rather alarmingly cross at the desk sergeant's scornful tone.

"You refuse to let me see him?" the man asked, the question very loaded to Clara's ears.

"Yes," the desk sergeant growled. "I've got better things to do than constantly put up with you lot. Hop off home!"

"I'm afraid I can't do that," the man at the desk pulled an identity card from his jacket pocket and handed it to the desk sergeant.

The sergeant's face had grown pale. He took the card in uncertain fingers and flipped it to read the name.

"Superintendent Foster," he read. "I do apologise, Sir."

"So you should. Your attitude both to myself and this young lady is unbecoming in a police officer. I shall be having words with the Inspector about your position, perhaps reassigning you to a patrol route would do you some good?"

"Oh no, Sir. I have bad feet," the desk sergeant cringed.

"You have a bad attitude as well. Watch your step," Superintendent Foster now glanced at Clara. "About time the Inspector was summoned, don't you think?"

The desk sergeant said no more. He picked up the telephone that connected internally and called Inspector Park-Coombs. He informed him that Superintendent Foster was downstairs, but omitted Clara's name. Even when cowed, he could not let go of his hate for her.

After a few moments the Inspector appeared. He glanced at Clara first, then turned to Foster.

"Superintendent," he held out his hand. "Pleasure to see you. I was expecting you first thing tomorrow."

"I caught an earlier train. I want to be back as soon as possible. I have a meeting late tomorrow. Now, if you can spare me a moment? Oh, and I think this lady wishes to see you too."

The superintendent motioned a hand to Clara, but she sensed there was something important going on and should not interfere.

"You are busy," she told Park-Coombs. "I'll come back tomorrow."

The inspector gave her a wry smile. She guessed he was not looking forward to his chat with the superintendent. She said goodbye to him and the superintendent and slipped away, wondering what was going on. Well, the desk sergeant had certainly suffered a scare by all accounts. Perhaps he would be more amenable to her in the future. Clara smiled to herself, doubting that hugely. Never mind, there was always time for another battle with him tomorrow.

Chapter Four

Clara returned to the police station bright and early the next morning. She was ready to joust with the desk sergeant, but that was to prove unnecessary. He wasn't there. Someone new had taken his place. For an instant Clara hesitated, then she walked over and asked to see Inspector Park-Coombs. Without a pause the new desk sergeant rang up for the inspector and asked if he was free to see Clara. A few moments later she was walking along the upstairs corridor towards Park-Coombs office.

"Morning Clara," the inspector greeted her as she entered his office.

"Morning. Thank you for seeing me," Clara cleared her throat. "I hope your meeting with the superintendent went well."

"Foster is a pain in the backside, but that is what superintendents are paid to be," Park-Coombs snorted, causing his moustache to jiggle. "He came to inform me of some new initiatives the higher ups are introducing and to inspect the station. Well, you saw what happened with the desk sergeant."

"Yes," Clara said, feeling a pang of guilt. Had she not been ahead of Superintendent Foster in the queue and stirred up the desk sergeant's ire, the man might not have been so awful to him. "Has he been replaced?"

"Temporarily," Park-Coombs reassured her. "I've got him on day patrols for a month, then maybe he will be more appreciative of his usual role and less obstructive. Superintendent Foster called him the worst excuse for a policeman he had ever come across. Which I find rather far-fetched. Do sit down Clara."

Clara took a seat opposite the inspector.

"I feel it was my fault he was so rude to the superintendent."

"He'll live," Park-Coombs shrugged. "Now, why did you want to see me?"

Clara roused herself from her guilt.

"I have been asked to investigate a case that was previously in the hands of the police."

"Ah, someone doesn't feel we are doing a sufficiently good job for them?" Park-Coombs raised an eyebrow, he was smart enough to know that people only hired private detectives when they had given up hope on the police solving a crime.

"To be fair to you, Inspector, there is so little to go on with this case I doubt you could solve it. I rather doubt I will be able to either, but I'll give it my best."

"Which case is it?"

"The burglary at Mr Jacobs' home."

Park-Coombs held up a finger indicating he wished her to pause while he consulted his files. He went over to his filing cabinet and trawled through the drawers for a moment or two before returning with a cardboard folder. Clara noted the name on the front of the folder was 'Jacobs'.

"We haven't closed the case," he said as he sat back down. "Else this would be in the archives. Let's see, ah, happened very recently. A window was broken to gain entry, but not much sign of anything else. And a small neft-u-ka..."

"Netsuke."

"Yes, a small one of them was lifted," the inspector

closed the folder. "No fingerprints, no witnesses, no suspects. Doesn't look hopeful."

"I feared as much," Clara admitted. "But I have been hired, so I will endeavour. I just felt I ought to let you know what I was up to, seeing how it is an active case."

"You are welcome to it. In truth, burglaries are a nightmare to resolve unless someone has a hunch who took the loot, or it turns up in a pawnshop. I don't think that is going to happen here."

"I agree," Clara nodded. "Oh well."

"Is that all you are up to?" Park-Coombs asked with a hint of something Clara could not place in his voice.

"How do you mean?" she asked.

"It's just that there have been rumours running about."

"Rumours?"

"About a new private detective doing the rounds. A woman."

Clara shuffled in her seat. She rather felt she had been the last to know about this Sarah Butler.

"I heard about her yesterday," Clara said. "There is no law against another person setting themselves up as a private detective."

"No, of course not," Park-Coombs gave her his knowing grin. "But it's the sort of thing that rankles. I could imagine how I would feel if another police station opened in Brighton."

"I am sure there is enough work for both of us," Clara didn't quite meet his eyes. "It is not as though I can do anything about her."

"What's her name?" Park-Coombs asked.

"Sarah Butler."

He shrugged.

"Name doesn't ring a bell," he said, "but I will keep my ears open for you."

Clara was beginning to feel that everyone was taking this new detective far too seriously. Surely they could see that she was not concerned?

"I'll let you get on," she said. "No doubt the

superintendent has lots for you to attend to."

"Too much," Park-Coombs groaned. "He has this idea that we need a female police constable."

"Not such a bad idea," Clara mused. "I could see the benefit."

"Yes, well, try explaining that to my existing constables. For that matter, where I am going to find a woman to take on the position?"

"Don't look at me, Inspector. I already have a career."

Park-Coombs managed a smile, then Clara sauntered out and went to her office.

She was just approaching the haberdashery shop above which she had her rooms, when she spotted Mr Stein who ran the shop waving at her from his doorway. As she approached Mr Stein hissed across to her in a stage whisper.

"That woman who is always calling is here."

Clara wasn't sure who he meant.

"Which woman?"

"The annoying one. Who brought the case about the dead canary."

"Oh, Mrs Wilton," Clara understood. The day Mrs Wilton had brought her the case of the 'murdered' canary, Clara had been out of her office and she had waited for her in the haberdashery shop. There she had told Mr Stein all about the case. He had found it as preposterous as Clara had when she returned. Canaries are rather prone to mysteriously dying, but Mrs Wilton saw conspiracy everywhere and was convinced the bird had been done in. It had taken several cups of tea and a lot of talk to persuade her not to pursue the matter.

"My wife made her tea," Mr Stein continued. "She seemed very agitated when she arrived, but she won't talk about it. That struck me as strange."

It struck Clara as strange too. Usually Mrs Wilton could not stop talking. She followed Stein into the shop and found Mrs Wilton out the back, sipping tea from a tiny porcelain cup. She almost dropped it in her excitement to see Clara.

"Clara! I must speak with you!"

"Why don't we go up to my office?" Clara suggested.

Mrs Wilton abandoned her tea, thanking Mrs Stein for it, and departed with Clara. Mr Stein managed to give Clara an amused look as she departed, and she responded by rolling her eyes. Up in her office she offered Mrs Wilton a chair and asked her what was the matter.

"I am most distressed, Clara. I really am. It is one thing to have this Butler woman setting herself up as a private detective, and quite another to have her deliberately mimicking you."

Clara was confused.

"What has happened, Mrs Wilton?"

"Do you take the Brighton Gazette?"

"Not regularly," Clara admitted. "Tommy sometimes buys a copy to read. But he is rather fond of the national papers."

"But you advertise in the Gazette?"

"I do," Clara answered. "It has always served me well."

"I imagine that is the reason Miss Butler has done this," Mrs Wilton produced a clipping from a newspaper from her handbag. It was an advertisement from the Gazette. For a moment Clara thought it was her own advertisement, until she read it.

"But... it is identical to my advertisement!" she said in horror.

The notice read – Female Private Detective. Available for cases both domestic and criminal. Reasonable rates, reliable service. Contact Miss S. Butler at 42 Abercrombie Street. The text was enclosed in a box made of one thick and one thin black line, each corner ornamented by a swirling leaf. Not only the design, but the text was the same as Clara's own advertisement, aside from the name and address.

Clara looked up at Mrs Wilton, her expression demonstrating how appalled she was.

"I spotted it this morning when I was looking through

the private ads for a local gardener. Mine has just retired, you know. And there was your advert, right in the centre of the page as I always see it, and slap bang next to it was this one," Mrs Wilton tapped her finger sharply on the clipped advertisement. "Disgraceful, I told myself, disgraceful. I can't believe it was allowed."

Clara couldn't believe it either, but the implication was plain enough. Miss Sarah Butler had deliberately copied Clara's advert to implicate that they were somehow connected, or perhaps to piggy-back on Clara's reputation. Anyone seeing Miss Butler's advert could not possibly fail to note the similarities. They might imagine that Clara endorsed Miss Butler, perhaps had even trained her up. They might think the two women were, in fact, in business together. Whichever way you looked at it, Clara's success and name was being used to promote her rival.

"I can't believe the woman would be so duplicitous!" Clara said in astonishment.

All the compassion she had felt for the woman, imagining her much in the same boat as herself and understanding what it was like to try and carve out a place for oneself in a male world, was gone. Whatever respect she had imagined for the woman was lost. Now she just felt cheated, as if the woman had somehow been in her office and stolen all her ideas and contacts.

"I'm afraid it gets worse," Mrs Wilton's tone had softened, she could see how shocked Clara was already. Dipping into her handbag again, she produced a small business card on cream stock. "I borrowed this from Mrs Butterworth."

As with the advertisement, at first Clara thought she was looking at one of her own business cards, but her recent surprise made her second guess that idea and, even before she had taken the card from Mrs Wilton, she knew what she would see. The card did not bear her name, but it did exactly mimic the design of her own cards, right down to the scales of justice symbol Clara had had placed in the bottom left corner. Clara closed her eyes and inwardly winced. The woman was trying to steal everything from her, even her business cards.

"Now do you agree we must take this seriously?" Mrs Wilton was looking worried, she could see how affected Clara was by this information and perhaps regretted bringing it up, but she knew she had to. "Whoever Miss Butler is, she has crossed a line, don't you agree?"

"This is serious," Clara said stiffly. "She is using my name and reputation, however obliquely, to attract clients. I cannot have that. I cannot have people thinking I am somehow connected to her. Not only might I lose business, but what if she proves a fraud or a bad detective? I could be tarred with the same brush!"

"Precisely! And now we must act!" Mrs Wilton sat up proudly in her chair. "You do not need to worry Clara, for I am on the case."

"You?" Clara asked, unable to mask her amazement.

"Yes, you are my friend and I will not see this woman ruin your livelihood. So I shall seek her out and put a stop to it."

"I am not sure that is such a good idea," Clara said, knowing Mrs Wilton's ability to cause chaos.

"I shall not be deterred. This woman is a menace. I told Mrs Butterworth as much, but she will not hear a word against her. Said the woman has been most reasonable with her charges, so far."

"Implying she is cheaper than me," Clara guessed.

"Cheap does not mean better, far from it. Why, do we not all know that for the saving of a few pence we are often supplied with inferior goods? Why should this be any different? She is a charlatan, I am sure of it, I feel it in my bones."

Mrs Wilton's reputation for sniffing out charlatans was not of the highest. She had, after all, been hooked in by a fake clairvoyant, but that was beside the point. Something certainly had to be done.

"First things first, I'll need to change all my

advertisements and cards," Clara winced at the time and expense that was going to cost her. "I will insist that my advertisement is unique and should not be printed next to that of Miss Butler. The cards are a real nuisance. I spent hours designing them."

"I am so angry on your behalf," Mrs Wilton bleated. "But together we shall put this scoundrel in her place."

Clara didn't like the 'together' part of that statement, but she suspected she had no choice. She took another long look at Miss Butler's advertisement.

"Who is she?" she asked rhetorically.

"Mrs Butterworth says she is in her thirties and a well-built lass with fiery red hair," Mrs Wilton answered. "She has a Scottish accent, Mrs Butterworth is most clear on that point. But she won't hear a word against her, says she is most diligent and reliable. Of course, when I asked if she had found Mr Butterworth yet I was treated to a cold stare. Too early, apparently."

Mrs Wilton suddenly brightened.

"You know, Clara, that's it!"

"I don't understand?" Clara asked, worried by Mrs Wilton's sudden animation.

"That is how you will prove yourself over her! You must find Mr Butterworth first!"

Clara didn't want a third case on her hands, what with the missing jade dragon and sorting out this matter with Miss Butler, chasing a missing husband was the last thing she needed.

"Yes, that is perfect!" persisted Mrs Wilton. "You will find Mr Butterworth first and demonstrate why you are Brighton's premier detective and this Miss Butler will be put soundly in her place."

"I am really not sure..."

"It's perfect. You must do this for the sake of your reputation!" Mrs Wilton insisted.

Clara closed her eyes and sighed.

"I don't intend to step on Miss Butler's toes, that is unprofessional."

"Nonsense! Besides, look how she has stepped on your toes!" Mrs Wilton tapped fiercely at the newspaper clipping again. "Time to stop being so nice, Clara!"

Clara didn't think she was being overly nice, just sensible. She didn't need to stir up extra trouble with this Butler woman.

"Of course, you will need to speak with Mrs Butterworth. I will arrange it."

"How?" Clara mouthed.

"Leave it to me, you worry about your advert and business cards. We'll have this woman bang to rights in no time!"

Mrs Wilton departed in good spirits, Clara was less convinced. She stared at the copied advert before her and sighed. When had life become so complicated?

Chapter Five

The Brighton Gazette operated out of an old building that looked from the front like a narrow chapel. Clara was not clear on what the property had originally been used for, but it was certainly one of the most awkward spaces within the confines of the high street to rent out. Clara could only conclude that the reason it had not yet been pulled down and replaced was because people thought it too quaint. Or perhaps it was very historic. Not that Clara had anything against awkwardly shaped, impractical buildings. She was just curious.

Inside the double-storeyed, open plan building was a narrow reception that had been divided from the main floor of the Gazette headquarters by a wood and glass partition. Beyond a door that was labelled as 'private' were the desks of the journalists, proof-readers and other personnel who compiled the material for the paper. Another partition at the back of the building created a space for the type-setters to work in, and also a private office where potential advertisers could discuss their requirements. On a mezzanine level above all this activity sat a solitary office with big glass windows from which the Brighton Gazette editor could look down upon his workers and contemplate his business.

Clara was so infuriated by the crass act of mimicry Miss Butler had performed with her advert that she had no time to dawdle with typesetters or advertising clerks. She wanted to see the editor of the Gazette and vent her fury. She wanted to know how the blatant copying of her advert had been allowed. She wanted to complain that her name had been printed side-by-side with that of Miss Butler's and with a clear implication that they were connected. In short, she was about to blow her top.

Standing in the reception of the Gazette she eyed up the receptionist who sat behind a compact wooden desk.

"I need to see the editor," she demanded.

"Do you have an appointment?" the girl asked blithely, rather used to irate people standing before her. The Gazette liked to print local gossip and that tended to bring in the people who were referred to in the gossip to complain. The reception girl, despite her youth, had dealt with a considerable number of people out for the editor's blood.

"No, I do not," Clara said plainly. "But I will see him all the same."

"He is a very busy man," the girl said politely. "I could arrange something…"

"Oh, for Heaven's sake," Clara turned and waltzed straight through the door that led into the main offices and was marked private. It was not locked. People came and went all the time, and no one had the energy to keep faffing with keys.

Clara stormed across the floor of the building, the reception girl tailing her. Clara dived between the tightly packed desks, made more impassable by heaps of paper that were stacked or piled beside each one. Some of the paper was fresh stock for the typewriters, a lot was scrap that had been thrown on the floor. Near the stairs that led up to the office of Mr Pontefract, Brighton Gazette editor, was the desk of Gilbert McMillan.

"Morning, Miss Fitzgerald," he called out as Clara marched past.

She gave him a fleeting smile of acknowledgement before clattering up the ironwork stairs.

"Please, miss!" the reception girl had stumbled over a pile of discarded copy and had fallen behind. "You can't just go up there!"

As she went to dart past Gilbert's desk to follow Clara, he shot out a hand and grabbed her arm.

"What's going on?" he asked.

The girl wrenched her arm from him forcibly.

"None of your business," she snapped, before chasing Clara again.

But the delay had cost her and Clara was already at the door of Mr Pontefract's office and striding inside. As the reception girl finally reached her, the damage was already done and Clara was stood before the editor glowering.

"Sorry Mr Pontefract!" the reception girl declared.

"Not her fault, the private door was unlocked," Clara said quickly. "And I need to talk to you Mr Pontefract, on a very serious matter."

Mr Pontefract had lived a life in journalism and had learned that what he considered serious was not necessarily the same as the rest of the world. So he did not rush himself or look unduly concerned at Clara's arrival. Instead he waved away the reception girl and politely asked Clara to sit, before offering her a drink. Clara refused, she was not here on a social visit.

"Mr Pontefract, have you seen the latest issue of the Gazette?"

"As editor it is my responsibility to have final say over the copy it contains," Mr Pontefract answered.

"Then you will already be aware of the mischief you have printed in the classifieds section?"

Mr Pontefract scratched his head thoughtfully.

"I rarely look at that. After all, that's what the proof-readers are for."

Clara glanced about the office and spotted a copy of the current issue of the Gazette resting on a side table.

She grabbed it and flipped the pages until she reached the classifieds. A fresh pang of anger went through her as she noted her advert sitting next to that of Miss Butler's, looking like two ink twins. She spread the newsprint before Mr Pontefract.

"This is my advertisement that I have been paying to be printed in your newspaper for the last two years," Clara pressed her finger into the centre of her advertisement. "This is what you printed last week."

Clara moved her finger over the rough paper and onto Miss Butler's advert.

"I am not affiliated with this woman, nor do I appreciate her copying my advert, or for you to allow it!"

Mr Pontefract adjusted his glasses and took a long look at the two adverts side-by-side.

"As I say, I don't personally deal with the advert copy," he said, his tone mild. He didn't entirely see the problem.

"However, you are the editor of this paper. You, ultimately, are where it all ends. I am very angry Mr Pontefract."

Mr Pontefract sat back in his chair and nodded. He did not consider the matter a big deal, but he was not going to lose a valued customer over it either.

"This is most unfortunate. An oversight in the advertising department."

"I thought my advert would remain unique," Clara pressed her finger into the paper repeatedly.

"I don't believe we say that in our advertising contract," Mr Pontefract said cautiously.

"But this is unspeakable!" Clara persisted. "The woman is effectively trading on my name. Look, people will see this and think we are associated! It must be changed at once."

Mr Pontefract held up his hands to calm Clara.

"I see the problem and we will resolve it. The woman is entitled to have whatever text she chooses, as long as she is not using someone else's trademark or slogan, but the design of the advert will be altered so it does not look like yours anymore."

"Thank you," Clara said, relaxing slightly. "And I want it put in writing that no one in the future can copy my advert's design."

Mr Pontefract opened his mouth to protest, but Clara held up a finger before him.

"I am a good customer Mr Pontefract. Not only do I advertise every week with you, but many of my cases provide your reporters with great stories to print. I have always been amenable to working with the Gazette and sharing information, but I could easily become uncooperative."

Mr Pontefract spread out his hands, palms up, in a placating fashion.

"There is no need to become agitated," he said. "I am sure I can arrange some sort of agreement that prevents your advert from being copied in the future."

"Write it out now," Clara demanded.

Mr Pontefract stared at her and briefly contemplated refusing, but he knew he would not budge her from his office until he agreed. With a light sigh he pulled forward his typewriter and began the process of creating the new agreement. It took half an hour for him to create something they could both agree upon. Then he signed it and Clara added her name.

Paper in hand, Clara went back down to the advertising office and confronted the head of the department. In truth he was the only person, aside from an apprentice, who worked in advertising. Mostly the same ads ran week after week and he just had to make sure they were all neatly arranged in the column space he was given. When Clara entered his little domain he looked up in surprise.

A similar conversation to the one she had just had with Mr Pontefract proceeded, only the advertising head was far more amenable and nodded sympathetically as Clara explained her concerns. Then he took Mr

Pontefract's new contract and filed it away safely. They spent another forty minutes reconfiguring Clara's own advert. She felt the old one was now spoilt by Miss Butler's copycat antics and she wanted something new to attract people's attention. She also insisted on having 'first' added to her title, now she was listed as Brighton's first female private detective. At the bottom of the advert she had a line that specified she worked alone and was in no way connected to other private detectives. Thus feeling some of the damage had been mitigated she agreed to the new advert and left the poor advertising head bemused and alone.

Clara took a deep breath as she stepped back onto the main floor of the Gazette's headquarters. Gilbert McMillan was eyeing her from his desk.

"Well? What's all this about?" he asked her.

Clara wasn't sure she wanted to explain to him, she felt tired by the whole affair.

"You need a cup of tea," Gilbert said brightly, knowing just how to draw conversation out of a reluctant person. "Sit down and I will make you one."

Clara obliged feeling that a cup of tea would restore her good humour. By the time Gilbert had procured a clean mug and made her a strong brew, they both knew she was going to tell him the whole story.

"This Miss Butler is trying to encroach on your business, then?" Gilbert said when Clara had finished her account.

"It would seem so," Clara replied.

"I think I saw her come in to place her ad," Gilbert mused. "Not everyone comes in, in person, and I am sat right near the advertising office. There was this woman last week, a broad sort of person, older than you and a bit taller. Looked like someone who had done a lot of physical labour, but she was dressed reasonable enough."

"Physical labour?" Clara was surprised.

"Her hands were rough and swollen, I could see that at a glance. Made me think she had done a lot of work involving water. Her hands were ruined, would always be that way. And she was very weathered about the face, been out in the elements. Though," Gilbert paused a moment, "it could have been because she had vivid auburn hair. People with hair that colour weather worse even in a little sun."

"Just who is this woman?" Clara said, mostly to herself. "No one seems to have heard of her before this last month or so. Where has she come from?"

"She rang no bells with me," Gilbert shrugged. "But then I don't know everyone. I would certainly poke about and find out more about her if I was you."

"Really?" Clara said, she was reluctant to start probing into this woman's life. It seemed underhanded.

"She is trying to steal away your business, or at least use your reputation to gain work herself. When someone acts like that, you can't waste time. You need to fight back, find out who she is, discover if she has any secrets."

"That sounds more like being a journalist," Clara countered.

"Being a journalist and being a detective are not so different. We are both rooting out the truth, bringing justice to ill-doers."

Clara thought that Gilbert was overrating his own work. Largely he rooted out any good gossip that would make an interesting story, and it was certainly not always to bring justice to anyone. Rather it was to sell papers.

"You can't let her get away with impersonating you," Gilbert insisted.

"Is that what she is doing?" Clara asked.

Gilbert gave her a despairing look.

"Isn't it obvious? The woman is trying to become Clara Fitzgerald. To take over your work, your life."

"Now you are being dramatic," Clara shook her head, not wanting to believe such a statement.

"It's true, look what she has done already," Gilbert folded his arms and sat back in his chair, looking amused. "You need to rattle out the truth of this affair."

He thought for a moment.

"Abercrombie Street," he said. "Why does that ring a bell?"

"Because several houses in that road were being let by Mr Dunholm, a rather unscrupulous little fellow who screwed every last penny out of his poor tenants, while failing to keep his properties in adequate condition," Clara explained. "You wrote an article about him, exposing his misdeeds."

"And you found out the rat in the first place. One of your charity cases," Gilbert was rapidly remembering.

"Mr Dunholm needed exposing. We both gave him quite a scare, even if we did not put him out of business. He still operates as a landlord, but now takes his responsibilities seriously."

"And he is renting a set of offices to Miss Butler? Well, two crooks in one place always excites me."

"I wouldn't go so far as to call Miss Butler a crook," Clara backtracked. "Misguided, perhaps."

Gilbert raised one eyebrow at her.

"Too generous as always Clara. Well, anyway, start with Abercrombie Street. Worry Mr Dunholm by asking questions. He is the sort of person who needs occasional worrying to keep him on the straight and narrow anyway," Gilbert thought he would rather like to be there when Mr Dunholm saw Clara on his doorstep again. "In the meantime, I'll dig around and see if I can find out any information on the elusive Miss Butler."

"Thanks Gilbert," Clara rose. "I am trying not to take this all too seriously. I have other business to attend to."

"A case?"

Clara smiled at his sudden eagerness.

"The burglary of Mr Jacobs' house. I am sure you have already written about it."

"Ah yes, the broken tiny window and the singular item stolen from his collection. The police refused to reveal what that item was," Gilbert looked to Clara hopefully.

"I would not wish to undermine the police," Clara said

with feigned horror at the very idea.

She left the Gazette offices smiling to herself.

"Spoilsport!" Gilbert called out with a grin as she departed.

Chapter Six

Clara was in two minds when she once again stood in the September sunshine. On the one hand she had a case to attend to, and on the other she had this matter with Miss Butler, which was getting under her skin and driving her insane. The woman was perfectly entitled to try her luck as a detective, but why try to steal Clara's reputation? Well, that was simply answered; she wanted Clara's business. Clara toyed with getting on with the Jacobs case, but she knew her irritation with Miss Butler was not going to allow it. She was too distracted to concentrate on a burglary. So she headed instead for Abercrombie Street.

The road where Miss Butler had her offices was a humble avenue of terrace houses, mostly the two-up, two-down variety. Families of ten or more crowded into this cramped accommodation, but despite the congestion, the residents of Abercrombie Street prided themselves on their respectability. They might be poor, but they were respectably poor. They kept their doorsteps washed, cleaned their windows, bleached their net curtains and made sure their privies never overflowed. And Mr Dunholm had abused that determined respectability, squeezing every last penny out of the poor souls who found themselves living in his houses.

Clara had first learned of the problem when she was investigating a case of minor fraud. The culprit was a resident of one of Mr Dunholm's houses who had resorted to crime to try and pay the rising rental costs. Clara had felt sorry for the man who was desperately trying to keep a roof over his family's heads. He was a low level clerk in a printing firm, a hardworking man who spent six days a week at his job without complaint. He had taken on extra work in the evenings to try and make ends meet, and his wife took in washing and sewing. Yet still they were constantly having to make a decision between eating that week or paying the rent.

When Clara investigated further, she was appalled at the liberties Mr Dunholm was taking. He was charging ridiculous levels of rent, often upping it on a monthly basis and threatening his tenants with eviction when they struggled to pay him. It was not a new story, and there was little in the way of laws to prevent it. But Clara wasn't going to allow Dunholm to get away with bullying his tenants.

She complained to a lot of people. She made a fuss, and when that failed to help, she passed the story to the Brighton Gazette and suddenly the world came crashing down on Mr Dunholm. The public were outraged, the story was even picked up by one of the national papers. Mr Dunholm was far from unusual, you could find examples of him in every town and city, but not every town and city had a Clara Fitzgerald.

When the full story broke, Mr Dunholm was hounded and vilified. Under the force of public pressure he lowered his rents back to a sensible level and new contracts were signed by his tenants with the stipulation that rent could only be increased once a year and only at a rate reasonable to inflation. Clara was the heroine of Abercrombie Street.

Now she stood in the road again and looked at number 42. As it turned out, No.42 had been converted into two small flats. The bottom two rooms were occupied by a widow, the upper two by Miss Butler.

The widow, Mrs Lowe, recognised Clara and was keen to talk to her. In fact she ushered her indoors and fed her tea and rock cakes. The woman had almost lost her home due to Mr Dunholm's greed, and she would always be grateful to Clara for helping her.

"It is so good to see you again," she smiled. "I am so much happier these days, you know. I feel a weight has lifted off me."

"I am glad you are doing well," Clara said, cosy in the warm front room with its neat little armchairs and numerous crocheted blankets. In pride of place on the mantelpiece sat a framed picture of Mr Lowe, a former train driver who sadly died in an accident.

"I am curious about your new upstairs neighbour," Clara continued, sipping her tea and trying to appear casual.

"Miss Butler?" Mrs Lowe said. She considered for a moment. "Can she be deemed a neighbour when she only uses the flat above for business?"

"What sort of business?" Clara feigned ignorance.

"Oh, I believe she is like you, dear. A detective," Mrs Lowe spoke innocently and clearly did not imagine this news would trouble Clara. "Women are getting so independent these days. I couldn't have imagined such a thing in my youth."

"Have you seen much of her?" Clara asked.

"Miss Butler? I see her coming and going. I can see the front door from my window. We share the front door, but she always goes up the staircase and doesn't bother me," Mrs Lowe fell quiet, as if she was rather disappointed at not being bothered by Miss Butler. "I did ask her in for tea once. I was curious about her. I do like to know the people living above me will not cause any problem."

"She was nice?" Clara asked, gently probing.

"She was very well-mannered, a little bit stern

though," Mrs Lowe's brows furrowed as she thought about her neighbour. "I found her reluctant to smile. She asked about Mr Lowe. I was pleased to tell her. She said her father had died in an accident too. I felt that still overshadowed her, as if it was not so long ago."

Clara glanced at the photograph of Mr Lowe in his train driver's uniform again.

"Is she a local?"

"No, I would say Scottish," Mrs Lowe explained. "Though I might be wrong. She didn't talk much, rather she listened to me rabbit on. She was very kind, but I sensed she found me tiresome. Eventually she made an excuse to leave and went upstairs."

Mrs Lowe sighed heavily to herself.

"Do you find me tiresome?"

"No, Mrs Lowe," Clara said honestly. She had always found the woman insightful, and she could understand loneliness. "I have always found our conversations very interesting."

Mrs Lowe smiled, her confidence renewed.

"You know, I really don't think Miss Butler will make as good a detective as you," she said. "She is just so difficult to speak with. A detective needs to be good with people. They need to be patient."

"Ever thought of taking it up?" Clara asked in jest.

Mrs Lowe laughed.

"What would my husband say? Oh dear, I am far too old for such mischief!"

Well stuffed with rock cakes and tea, Clara left Mrs Lowe and headed two roads away to the house of Mr Dunholm.

For a gentleman consumed by greed, who had drained his tenants dry with extortionate rents, Mr Dunholm was not a man who lived grandly, or even seemingly comfortably. His house was not vastly bigger than those his tenants rented and the outside was in a state of decay. The brickwork badly needed repointing where it had been blasted by the salty Brighton breeze, and the garden was an overgrown patch of weeds. Part of the garden wall had tumbled down, the old mortar dry as a bone and unable to support the bricks any longer. Clara knocked on the wooden door with its peeling paint. There was a great gap at the bottom which must have let in a terrible draught.

It was a long while before Mr Dunholm answered. The door was on a chain, ironic considering its flimsiness. The round, puffy face of Mr Dunholm was visible through the gap the chain allowed, one watery eye peered at Clara.

"You," he grumped.

"May I come in?" Clara asked politely. On their last encounter, she had informed Mr Dunholm that she would be returning in the future to ensure he was keeping to his new contracts. She doubted he was surprised to see her.

"Is anyone else out there?" Mr Dunholm's eye swivelled back and forth, trying to spy out the entire road.

Clara found herself looking behind her, his paranoia catching.

"Should there be?" she asked.

"I don't really want to talk to anyone," Mr Dunholm barked. "Especially not you."

"Tough," Clara informed him, her tone no longer polite but angry. "Open this door."

The one thing Clara had learned about Mr Dunholm during her investigations was that he was a cowardly bully, and anyone who stood up to him scared the life out of him. The chain rattled in its catch and the door opened to reveal the morally lacking landlord.

He was a man in his forties; shabby, plump and reeking of fried food and sweat. His clothes were probably not fresh, they were all grey, even the white shirt had taken on a soft grey hue. His waistcoat was unbuttoned, because the buttons were missing. The cuffs of his shirt sleeves and trouser legs were frayed. He was wearing old, worn carpet slippers.

"What do you want?" Mr Dunholm croaked. He

sounded as if he had not spoken to anyone in days and his voice had dried up.

"Information," Clara told him. "About one of your newest tenants."

Mr Dunholm grumbled to himself, but he let Clara into the damp, dark hallway, and through into his sitting room. The air smelt stale and there were hints of unpleasant odours. Clara would have loved to open a window and let in some fresh air. Instead she had to be satisfied with finding a reasonably clean place to sit. The sofa offered the best hope, even if there were dark greasy patches upon it where many backsides had sat over the course of time. There was no knowing how old the furniture in the house was. Mr Dunholm was a miser who had no interest in replacing perfectly serviceable, if somewhat unclean, furniture. The sofa could have lost all four of its wooden feet and he would still have kept it.

"I don't like talking to you," Mr Dunholm complained as he took a seat opposite Clara. He did, indeed, look on edge, perching at the very lip of the sofa cushion and clutching together his hands. He wouldn't look Clara in the eyes.

"I want to know about Miss Butler who you have rented 42 Abercrombie Street to," Clara said, getting right to business. There was no point dragging this out.

"I rented her a flat the other week," Dunholm shrugged. "What's there to say?"

"Come now, Mr Dunholm. One thing I know about you is that you are shrewd and you don't just rent properties to anybody. You like to know that your tenants won't skip out on you when the rent is due. You are the sort of landlord who insists on knowing his tenants' backgrounds and getting references."

"You give me too much credit," Dunholm muttered.

"You forget, I researched you. I dug into your history, into your business arrangements. I know the sort of man you are."

Mr Dunholm huffed and glared into the empty

fireplace.

"Let me make this easier for you," Clara said, relenting fractionally. After all, she wanted the man to help her, he was not the enemy on this occasion. "I would like to see the contract Miss Butler signed and the names of the people who gave her a reference."

"Those are private," Dunholm shuffled in his seat. "I can't just show them to you."

"I think you can, Mr Dunholm. You were never one for playing by the rules," Clara paused. "And the sooner you show me, the sooner I will be out of your hair. I know you detest my presence."

"Why do you want to know?" Dunholm suddenly found the spirit to counter her.

Clara smiled at him.

"Just because I do. Please can I see the contract and the references. I won't leave until I do."

Mr Dunholm muttered under his breath for a few moments. He didn't like people in his house, he liked being alone, and he really didn't like having Clara sitting opposite him. She troubled him deeply, in fact she scared him. After arguing with himself over the rights and wrongs of it all, he decided he really didn't care if someone saw Miss Butler's contract. He owed her nothing, and he wanted his empty house back. He got up without a word and departed the room. When he reappeared he was carrying a rectangular box.

Clara was surprised, considering the state of the rest of the house, at how new and clean the box was. It was a filing box, the sort businesses used and when Mr Dunholm opened it the papers within were alphabetically arranged. Clara had not expected such organisation within this disordered house.

Dunholm thumbed through the papers, his big thumb yellow with nicotine, and produced a two page contract. He passed it to Clara.

"The references are on the second page."

The contract was nothing extravagant. It asked for

Miss Butler's name, occupation, previous address and then outlined the terms of the contract. Miss Butler had listed her occupation as 'self-employed' and her previous address was in Scotland. Why she had upped sticks and moved all the way to Brighton was less explicable.

There was only one referee on the second page. Clara took note of the name and address of the person, who was fortunately resident in Brighton. Then she passed the contract back.

"Can you tell me anything about Miss Butler?" she pressed Dunholm.

"About a fortnight ago she came to me and asked if I had any small premises to rent. I had the flat," Mr Dunholm answered, with another shrug of his shoulders.

"The woman who wrote the reference for her, she says she has known Miss Butler for five years and that she is respectable and diligent."

Mr Dunholm flicked his shoulders in another shrug, still staring at the fireplace.

"That's good enough for me," he said. "And she paid the deposit in full and the first week's rent."

"Did she say how long she intended to stay?"

"No!" Dunholm growled. "Do you really think I ask all that stuff? I look at the references and if the person can pay the deposit up front, I am happy. What else matters?"

Clara knew they were at a dead end. She rose, thanked Mr Dunholm for his help, and left his home. She was very glad to get back out into the fresh air after the stifling stale atmosphere of the landlord's house. She was a fraction further forward, but only a fraction. The woman who had given Miss Butler the reference might be able to provide more insight. Clara's first question to her would be how had she known the woman for five years if she had only just come down from Scotland? And why had she come in the first place? Clara checked her watch. There was still plenty of time. She would follow up this matter and then return to the Jacobs case. Clara didn't like to admit to herself, as she headed off, that she was very worried. Miss Butler was causing her a great deal of unexpected anxiety.

Chapter Seven

The name on the reference had been Jocelyn Fawkes. Her address was several streets away from Mr Dunholm's residence, but Clara was used to walking. She found Mrs Fawkes in her back yard, hanging washing on a line.

"Good morning," Clara said over the wall.

Mrs Fawkes glanced up at her. She had two wooden clothes pegs stuffed in her mouth and, for the moment, could not speak. She was a middle-aged woman, thin as a rake and with the haggard lines of a hard life carved into her cheeks. She had grey eyes that narrowed suspiciously at the sight of Clara. She finished hanging a blanket on the line, removing the pegs from her mouth in the process.

"Who are you?" she asked, though keeping her head slightly turned away from Clara.

"I am with the Board of Trade," Clara lied, she had concocted a story for herself as she walked to see Mrs Fawkes. She didn't want to admit she was Clara Fitzgerald, but had to give some reason for probing into Miss Butler's affairs. "The Board has recently licensed several new business ventures and it is my responsibility to establish the backgrounds of the business owners. It is purely a perfunctory check. One of these new government schemes to try and prevent fraudulent businesses being established."

Clara rolled her eyes to imply that it was a nuisance to her as much as it was a nuisance to Mrs Fawkes.

"Now, you are Mrs Jocelyn Fawkes?" she asked.

"I am," Mrs Fawkes turned from her washing at last and gave Clara a good look.

"I have you down here as a referee for a Miss Sarah Butler who has recently opened a business in 42 Abercrombie Street."

"That's it," Mrs Fawkes nodded, though there was still an air of suspicion about her. Clara suspected the woman distrusted anyone who was in the slightest way attached to the authorities.

"Mr Dunholm, her new landlord, has been a concern to us of late, as you may be aware?"

"No," Mrs Fawkes frowned, now she looked less anxious and more interested. "Is he causing trouble?"

"Not currently," Clara brightened. "But a few months ago it was discovered he was raising his rents extortionately and harassing his tenants for extra money. We put a stop to all that, but we like to keep tabs on him. He is the sort of fellow who would slip back into his bad ways given the chance."

"Hmm," Mrs Fawkes pursed her lips, but added no more.

"Before I get onto the real matter I am here for, you couldn't say if Miss Butler has had cause for complaint about Mr Dunholm?"

"You would have to ask her yourself," Mrs Fawkes shrugged.

"I imagine I will at some point," Clara smiled. "If she does have any worries, do tell her to report them at once."

"Hmm," Mrs Fawkes repeated. It seemed she was a woman of limited words.

"Back to my original purpose," Clara said, pretending to read something off her notebook. "Firstly, could you advise me how long you have known Miss Butler?"

"Five years," Mrs Fawkes declared at once.

Clara pretended to write something down.

"How did you come to meet her?"

"Through work," Mrs Fawkes said firmly, offering no extra explanation for that statement.

"What sort of work?" Clara asked persistently.

"Does it matter?" Mrs Fawkes demanded in response. "I said she was a decent, respectable soul. Do you doubt my word?"

Mrs Fawkes had suddenly become defensive. Clara was not sure if this was her natural state of being, or whether there was something she was trying to hide. Could it be she did not want to say too much about her and Sarah Butler's past?

"We have to be thorough," Clara apologised with that same bright smile. "My superiors would be most displeased if I failed to ask appropriate questions. As I say, this government scheme…"

"The government is always interfering in the lives of ordinary folk," Mrs Fawkes interrupted angrily. "What does it matter to them how I know Sarah?"

"In recent years there have been scandals," Clara replied with a heft of her shoulders. "The government has been criticised for not properly overseeing things such as the licensing of businesses, or taking enough interest in the protection of workers. This is just one of a number of initiatives to try and remedy that. I know it is a nuisance and I do apologise…"

"Why are you apologising?" Mrs Fawkes snapped. "You are just doing as you are told. But I find it an invasion of privacy, that's what it is. Though what should I expect? No one gives a damn about the lives of people like me. They feel they can probe into them without a by-your-leave."

Mrs Fawkes tightened her lips into a righteous scowl.

"Any time a person tries to improve themselves some nosy official comes around and begins asking questions," she muttered. "No one wants the likes of me to improve our lot."

"Is that what Miss Butler is endeavouring to do? To improve her lot?" Clara asked, hoping her tone sounded suitably sympathetic.

"Sarah is a hard worker and she wants to make something of her life. Doesn't want to finish her days in a place like this," Mrs Fawkes looked up at her own home pointedly. It was a tidy terrace house, but small, much like those in Abercrombie Street. From the looks of Mrs Fawkes, she had to strain every week to make ends meet. Life was a continual struggle for money and there was always that nagging fear that one day there simply wouldn't be enough. The lines on Mrs Fawkes' face had been impressed upon her flesh by that constant anxiety. "Can you blame her?"

"No," Clara agreed, feeling a pang of guilt at how she was fudging around in Miss Butler's private life, trying to root her out like a snail from its shell. The only thing that mitigated that guilt was the knowledge that, either through intent or ignorance, Miss Butler had stamped about on Clara's territory first.

"I admire a woman who wants to make her own way in this world," Clara said honestly.

"Not everyone does. Some feel threatened," Mrs Fawkes gave another nod to her house. "Like him indoors. Can't abide the idea of women working in anything better than manual drudgery. He won't have Sarah in the house."

A sudden softening occurred within Mrs Fawkes' heart as she explained all this. Perhaps it was the kindly smile Clara still bore, or the way she was so apologetic. Or maybe it was just that it was nice to be able to talk about things such as women working without Mr Fawkes throwing a hissy fit. Mrs Fawkes found herself walking to the wall yard with the intention of speaking her mind.

"Sarah is a good woman. Reliable, strong, determined. All the things a person needs to be in this life to survive. She was never one for married life. The only man in her life was her father. She took care of the house for him, when she was home at least."

"She was often not at home?" Clara asked.

"Sarah started her working life like me, in the fish docks," Mrs Fawkes finally admitted. "But she never intended to stay there. She was just waiting for the right time, when she had enough money, to do something else. Something more."

"She was a fisher girl?" Clara elaborated, finding it a curious place for a private detective to start. "She would come down for the season to gut and pack fish?"

"Exactly," Mrs Fawkes nodded. "What other work will the men let women do on the docks?"

She huffed to herself with the unfairness of it all.

"My husband's a fisherman. More's the pity, I met him at the fish docks. I was a packer then. He had aspirations to become a skipper and have his own trawler. He never did, of course. But when you are young you believe people when they talk about such ideas," Mrs Fawkes snorted to herself. "He was always full of such rot."

"I have it in my notes that Miss Butler is originally from Scotland," Clara moved the subject along a little, Mrs Fawkes was becoming consumed in her own regrets a little too much.

"Yes, she comes from the south. Sarah has a lovely Scottish lilt to her voice. Different from some of the other girls who come down. Some of them speak the old tongue rather than English."

Clara pondered this piece of information. What other tongue was there in Scotland? Then it dawned on her.

"Gaelic?"

"Something like that," Mrs Fawkes shrugged. "All I know is you couldn't speak with 'em and they kept themselves to themselves. But Sarah spoke the King's English good enough, with just a little accent. And she is clever too. Too clever for gutting fish. I told her that once."

"That was why she decided to change direction," Clara

said in understanding. "I note she has listed her new occupation as private detective. Quite an ambitious move."

"She always wanted to use her mind and to be independent. Last thing any of us wants is to be stuck under the direction of men," Mrs Fawkes huffed. Her eyes flicked to her house and presumably to her husband sitting inside. "A lot of us fail in that, but not Sarah. She could have been a teacher, perhaps, or maybe a typist, but she would be most likely employed by a man. No, Sarah didn't want that, so she went out on her own."

"What about her father?" Clara remembered the previous mention that Sarah Butler had kept house for him.

"That was pretty awful," Mrs Fawkes shuffled her feet and cast down her eyes. "Sarah was close to her pa. He was a good soul who wanted her to do well for herself. Her mother died when she was five and she had looked out for her pa as soon as she was able. He made sure she had a decent education, nonetheless, and encouraged her to learn. But he was a humble trawlerman, so there was not much help he could give her with her ambitions beyond buying the odd book for the cottage."

"Something happened to him?" Clara guessed.

Mrs Fawkes gave a long groan, she seemed engulfed in grief herself, but probably it was just empathy for her friend.

"He was lost at sea. The trawler he was on simply vanished. It happens. I've expected it to occur to me many a night when Fred is out at sea in a storm," Mrs Fawkes' mood had mellowed and she now looked towards her house without the anger that had marred her earlier glances. "I would be lost without him."

"Men know how to break our hearts in so many ways," Clara mumbled.

Mrs Fawkes didn't seem to notice the sentiment.

"Anyway, the late Mr Butler had been sensible enough to insure his life with a fishermen's benevolent fund. The payment, along with the sale of the cottage, provided Sarah with enough to plan a new future for herself. She came to Brighton because she had me here and I promised to help in whatever way I could. And there are more opportunities here than in the Scottish village she was from."

"It was certainly a bold move," Clara was beginning to admire the guts of Sarah Butler, even if some of her tactics were underhand.

"Sarah had thought about it for a long time. She liked the idea of helping people and earning money at the same time. Also, well, I expect you know, there is already a private detective in Brighton and Sarah thought she could do a lot better than her," Mrs Fawkes was leaning forward conspiratorially.

"Oh really?" Clara said, her earlier admiration evaporating.

"Yes. I mean, you read about this woman in the papers all the time, but she mostly takes cases from important people. People with money. Sarah is going to help the little people, like you and me," Mrs Fawkes beamed proudly at the ideals of her friend. "She is going to help every poor soul, not just the rich ones. She already has a case on her hands."

"Jolly good," Clara said, her throat seeming to go tight over the words.

She was offended, there was no denying that. Clara helped everyone who came to her door, along with the charity cases she took on. But she had to be realistic; the 'little' people often could not afford a detective and Clara was not rich enough herself, or paid sufficiently by someone else like the police, to investigate without being paid for it. She would do free cases on the side that caught her attention and seemed deeply important, but on the whole she had to be practical and take on paying clients. If Sarah Butler wanted to make a living as a private detective, she would soon discover the same for herself.

Clara decided she had heard enough. She now knew a

little more about Miss Butler and her intentions, though she was unclear on just where the woman's feelings lay regarding Clara herself. From the way Mrs Fawkes spoke, it rather felt as if Miss Butler had an agenda, and at the top of it was giving Clara a run for her money.

"Thank you for your time, Mrs Fawkes," Clara said, detaching herself from the wall. "Everything seems in order. I won't disturb you any longer."

"I think you will find that Sarah will make an upstanding member of the business community here in Brighton," Mrs Fawkes said, lifting her chin into the air with an attitude of grandeur. "She has every intention of being a success and I don't doubt she will succeed."

Clara felt like adding that that was all well and good, as long as she stopped stealing other people's reputations and ideas, but that would have blown her cover, so she merely smiled.

"She sounds an amazing woman. One day I hope to meet Miss Butler in person."

"You will not be disappointed," Mrs Fawkes assured her.

Clara walked away muttering to herself. What did this Miss Butler know about her and her work? How dare she imply that Clara was somehow snobbish, only taking work from certain sections of society. Clara was surprised how that idea had hurt her. She had always considered herself egalitarian and certainly tried to do her bit for those worse off than herself. Mrs Fawkes' implications stung. But one thing she knew for sure; there was no way Miss Butler would be a better detective than Clara, she would not allow it.

Chapter Eight

Clara headed home with renewed determination to solve the mystery of the green jade dragon. Solving the crime and restoring the little netsuke to its owner now seemed the way to proving herself as a detective. She couldn't allow Miss Butler to get the better of her, and while she was dealing with a marital dispute, Clara would be working to solve a crime the police had given up on as hopeless. The only question that remained was how did she begin?

Clara mulled this over while she was eating her lunch. Her thoughtful mood, overshadowed by a frown of determination, had her brother and Captain O'Harris remaining silent while she ate. They sensed that something was brewing and now was not the right time for questions.

Clara had considered the problem from several angles. It seemed to her that to trace the dragon would involve a backwards, rather than a forwards journey. Beginning by asking herself who would want to steal it? Who had the resources to plan such a discreet burglary? And what did they intend to do with it, once they had it? That backwards journey would have to start by following the jade dragon's own footsteps. She would go to the British

Museum in London and talk to people there. Perhaps someone had been paying particular attention to the dragon while it was on display? In the meantime, she needed to try and track the person responsible for breaking into Mr Jacobs' house. With any luck, the culprit was a local lad who had been paid for the work. He might even be prepared to reveal his employers.

Finished with lunch and now resolved as to what she had to do, Clara set out to find an old friend. Bob Waters had been involved in a cold case Clara had found herself embroiled in the year before. The victim was small-time criminal Mervin Grimes and Bob Waters had been his childhood friend, a sort of punchbag for Mervin, as Bob was a quiet, inoffensive soul who tagged along behind the others. The only time Bob had stuck up for himself was when he insisted on having a respectable job and refused to go down the route of criminality that his friend had. Bob was a carpenter and an all-round nice guy. But he was also built of bricks, with fists the size of footballs and he did not like to see his friends hurt. He scared people a little, though not Clara who was rather fond of him.

After the Grimes case, Clara had stayed in touch with Bob, mainly so he would not be lonely. Bob had taken a fair few shocks during the case and had had his world rather shaken about him. Clara often asked Bob around for Sunday dinner; as Tommy pointed out once, Bob was yet another of Clara's waifs and strays. He had said it with an amused smile, for Tommy didn't mind Bob's company and he would be forever grateful to the man for protecting his sister when the Grimes case took a nasty turn.

Clara was aware that Bob was working on a new house down Queen's Drive and set off in that direction to find him. A light cloud was passing over the sun, and there were a few leaves tossing about in the road as if autumn was giving out hints about its future plans. It was still, however, a fine day to be out and Clara enjoyed the walk to the building site.

The house was going to be a villa style mansion for a wealthy businessman. It dominated a large plot between equally fine houses. The construction was in its early stages and the villa was no more than a wooden skeleton. Clara walked across the front lawn, there being no barrier around the work site. She saw several men carrying timbers or bearing hammers, but Bob was not among them. So she stopped a gentleman marking out planks to be cut and asked where he was.

Clara was directed to the far corner of the property and found Bob erecting the joists that would ultimately hold up a roof for a small garden room. It seemed the designer of the property intended for the property to be largely timber-framed. There was certainly a shortage of bricks about.

"Hello Clara," Bob grinned at her.

"I was hoping for a chat, but I can see you are busy," Clara paused beside him. "Have you hurt your thumb?"

Bob wriggled the digit which was wrapped in white bandages.

"Hit it with a hammer," he said in amusement. "Not the first time. I'm due a break shortly, if you could wait?"

Clara agreed she could and she wandered away to sit on the lawn and enjoy the sunshine while it lasted. Bob worked for another half an hour, fixing up the roof joists to his satisfaction. Then he turned and nodded to Clara. They walked away to a small hut that had been temporarily erected in the corner of the plot. Inside was a small oil stove and a teapot, and several unclean mugs.

"I'll forgo tea," Clara announced as soon as she saw the state of the tea-ware. "But you carry on, I don't want you to miss your break."

Bob started the process of brewing himself a mug of tea.

"What are you up to then Clara?" he asked.

Clara had found herself a stool to perch on. It wobbled if she moved too much, but was otherwise satisfactory.

"I am working on a case and could do with your help."

Bob raised his eyebrows.

"My help?"

"You still know a lot of people who are involved in the criminal side of Brighton?" Clara queried.

Bob blushed a little.

"You know I do. I can't go around cutting off my old friends."

Soft as butter, Clara thought to herself. Bob would always be friends with Brighton's criminal underworld because he had grown up with most of them as a lad and found it hard to understand why he should stop associating with them. It was not as if Bob ever did anything criminal himself.

"There was a burglary over a week ago. I have been asked to find the person responsible," Clara explained.

Bob frowned thoughtfully.

"I can't go around dropping my friends in the stew," he apologised to her. "They wouldn't ever talk to me again."

"I know, and I wouldn't ask you to do that," Clara reassured him. "I think the real person behind this robbery was someone who hired a thief to do the job for them. I want that person, not the actual burglar. In fact, my real concern is just the return of the stolen item. It's the police who can worry about catching the culprit."

Bob understood.

"You want me to ask around and see if anyone knows who committed the crime?"

"I do, Bob. And then I want to know who hired that person, but first things first. Do you think you can do it?"

"I don't see why not," Bob beamed his familiar good-natured smile. "Give me the details again?"

Clara went through what she knew about the case; the small window, the way the burglar knew exactly where to look and the stolen object itself, the green jade netsuke.

"I don't know anyone who sounds right for this," Bob scratched his head. "If the window is as small as you say, well, you would need a child or someone very thin to get through it."

Clara was disheartened to hear that. She had considered the possibility of a child being hired and that worried her, but she was also inclined to think that the crime was so professionally handled that it had to have been carried out by an experienced adult.

"Maybe the thief was not local," Bob mused to himself.

"That would be awkward," Clara sighed. "I won't be able to trace him so easily."

"Don't be so quick to fret," Bob winked. "The local lads are very particular about outsiders coming in and stealing their business. If they know a crime was committed and none of their friends did it, well, they will be making their own enquiries."

That possibility had not occurred to Clara. Of course, the criminal world was quite 'cliquey'. You were either in or you were out. And the local boys never liked when outside gangs, usually from London, stepped onto their turf. Perhaps, after all, Clara would get the information she needed.

"You haven't heard anything about the burglary?"

"Not so far, but I know something has gotten up the noses of the local boys. Wouldn't surprise me if it was this."

Now Clara was excited.

"As soon as you have anything, please tell me."

"Will do," Bob grinned. "Sure you won't have a mug of tea?"

~~~*~~~

Clara was looking forward to a quiet evening as she headed home. She needed time to think and muse over what she had been told. Certainly she needed to decide what next to do about Miss Butler. If only the woman had not gone about copying her advert and business cards then she could have ignored her. But that wasn't going to happen, so she had to figure something out. She wasn't against the woman being a private detective, she just didn't like the very personal attacks she felt were being directed at her. Surely there was room for the both of them in Brighton? Especially as Miss Butler had made it plain she was going to be helping a very different set of clients to Clara.

She arrived home and hung up her coat, thinking a slice of one of Annie's sumptuous cakes might be in order, when she noticed the second hat and coat hanging on the stand. She recognised them at once as Mrs Wilton's. Annie appeared in the hallway.

"She's in the parlour," she explained. "Be nice, she looks upset."

"I am always nice," Clara hissed under her breath.

Annie gave her a reproving look.

"Sometimes you are sharp," she said. "You know she annoys you."

Clara rubbed a hand over her tired eyes. The last thing she needed right then was a flapping Mrs Wilton to contend with. She took a deep breath, pulled herself back together, forced a smile onto her face and walked into the parlour.

Mrs Wilton was sitting by the empty fireplace, it was too warm as yet for the hearth to be lit. Despite the lack of logs and flames, Mrs Wilton was staring into the fireplace glumly.

"Mrs Wilton," Clara sat in the chair opposite and tried to sound enthusiastic.

Her first thought was that Mrs Wilton did indeed look glum and very deflated.

"Has something happened?" she asked, her own smile fading.

"I tried to persuade Mrs Butterworth to see you, but she point-blank refuses. She says she likes this Miss Butler person," Mrs Wilton almost spat out the name. "I am sorry Clara, I feel I have failed you."

"Nonsense," Clara assured her. "Mrs Butterworth is entitled to her opinion. Don't take it to heart."

"But how will you go about investigating her case if she won't talk to you? We agreed the best way to show up this Miss Butler is for you to solve the Butterworth case first."

Clara could not recall agreeing to that, but clearly that was the thought occupying Mrs Wilton's mind. Clara decided to be kind and offer her some consolation.

"Perhaps I don't need to see Mrs Butterworth?" she suggested. "After all, you, as her friend, must know a great deal about Mr Butterworth and his disappearance."

Mrs Wilton glanced up, a new brightness in her eyes.

"I do know a lot!" she agreed instantly.

"Then, you can give me the details of the case in place of Mrs Butterworth," Clara hinted.

Mrs Wilton sat upright in her chair, the slump of despondency that had come over her had completely disappeared.

"Why I can tell you everything!" she declared. "It happened the other Thursday. Mr Butterworth went to work as usual. Mrs Butterworth went to her painting class at two o'clock as she always does. Mr Butterworth must have slipped back then, for when she came home the cat was gone. Mrs Butterworth was very upset, she thought at first the cat had been accidentally allowed to slip outside. It never went outside normally. But then, as she was looking for the cat, a neighbour mentioned that Mr Butterworth had appeared home and then left again."

"And he never came home that evening?" Clara surmised.

"Precisely," Mrs Wilton nodded happily. "That was when Mrs Butterworth came to me. She was very angry, you know, not upset at all. Angry about the cat."

"The cat was more important than Mr Butterworth," Clara grasped. "The marriage sounds to have been in trouble before then?"

"Maybe," Mrs Wilton indicated she could not comment, that was one bit of gossip she did not have access to. "Our first thought was to seek Mr Butterworth out at his job, but it turns out he had been let go. The company was struggling financially. Mr Butterworth apparently declared it did not matter as he had found something else and was going to leave anyway. He left no indications of where he was going."

"He had planned this then," Clara leaned back in the armchair. "He won't want to be found easily."

"No and, as far as I can tell, Miss Butler has yet to come up with anything. Not that I am surprised," Mrs Wilton turned up her nose. "The woman is clearly an amateur."

Clara said nothing, though she laughed inwardly at Mrs Wilton's intense loyalty towards her. It made her feel better.

"Did Mrs Butterworth contact the police?"

"Oh yes, I suggested that at once. I mean, you should always contact the police first when a person goes missing," Mrs Wilton sounded very dutiful. "They said a grown man deciding to leave home was not really a police matter. The neighbours had seen him take a suitcase out of the house, you see, so it wasn't like he had vanished unintentionally. Mrs Butterworth was very unimpressed. That was when we discussed a private detective."

Mrs Wilton took on that haughty look again.

"Of course, if she had hired you in the first place the case would be solved by now."

"I think you give me too much credit," Clara smiled, "But I will take a look at things now."

"Thank goodness, Clara!" Mrs Wilton clapped her hands in delight. "Now we will show this upstart!"

Clara did not want to show up Miss Butler, but she did want to make a statement. The things she had heard today had convinced her that she could not just let affairs take their own course. Miss Butler had plans and they sounded decidedly unfriendly. As she showed Mrs Wilton out, she found herself considering things again. Perhaps it was time to take the fight directly to Miss Butler?

Chapter Nine

The next day Clara caught the train to London. Brighton and London had been connected by a railway line since the late nineteenth century, making a daytrip either way both simple and quick. Working class folk in London who had the odd day off would jump on the train to travel down and see the sea. While those in Brighton could easily travel to the capital to see the sights or even to work. More than one successful businessman had a property in Brighton and an office in London, offsetting the smoke and grime of the city, where money was to be made, with the clean air and good living of a house on the coast.

Clara did not often travel up to London, but on the occasions when it was necessary for a case, the convenience of the train was certainly appreciated.

London was cloudy that day. The September sun had disappeared behind thick white banks of cloud making it seem as if the world had suddenly acquired a blanketing ceiling. There seemed no end to the white and people were gloomy that this was perhaps a forewarning of the winter to come. It was a working day and people were bustling about with briefcases or bags of tools. Clara passed several building sites where workmen buzzed about like busy bees. London, she reflected, always seemed to be expanding or at least rebuilding itself.

When she reached the steps of the British Museum, she found that even here the builders were at work. One corner was encased in scaffolding and men clambered up and down. Clara glanced briefly up at them as she wandered through the museum's large front doors.

The museum was lively inside, a school party of girls in smart uniforms and straw boater hats was being herded through to one of the galleries, and there were several casual visitors loitering about. Clara went straight to the front desk where two women were on duty to direct visitors and take money for any purchases they made. Certainly there were plenty of books, exhibit catalogues and souvenirs dotted in displays about the front desk to tempt a person to part with their money. Clara gave the bric-a-brac a passing glance as she approached the nearest women at the front desk. She was an older lady, thin and wearing spectacles perched almost at the tip of her nose on a beaded chain. She observed Clara over the top of them which did not give her a pleasing countenance.

"May I help?"

"I would most like, if I could, to speak with Dr Vanderstom who recently organised the exhibition of Japanese artefacts?"

The woman peered over her glasses harder.

"Dr Vanderstom is the head of our Oriental department and does not usually speak with people without an appointment," she informed Clara haughtily.

"Oh dear," Clara said with a disappointed smile. "And I came all the way from Brighton. My employers will be most perturbed as they hoped Dr Vanderstom could answer some very urgent questions concerning the theft of an item that was recently in the exhibition."

The woman was not impressed by Clara's gentle bending of the truth.

"I doubt that has anything to do with us. If you wish

to consult Dr Vanderstom about a particular item then you must make an appointment. I believe he has a day free for such things next month."

"Far too long away," Clara shook her head, still with that gentle smile on her lips, like she was just debating on the price of soap. "You see, my employers are most concerned that the item in question was stolen because of the exhibition at the British Museum. They are debating the possibility of claiming some compensation from the museum for their oversight in security concerning the identification of items they were loaned for display."

"Employers?" the woman had looked a little uncertain when Clara had mentioned the words compensation and security.

"I work for an insurance firm in Brighton," Clara lied smoothly. "They insured the object that was stolen and have reason to believe that the thieves became aware of both the object, its value and its location through the exhibition here. If that is the case, it would be an awful lapse in common sense on the behalf of the museum. The object is extremely valuable and my employers would like to recoup some of the money they must pay out for it from someone."

Clara left the sentence hanging in the air. A man had drawn up beside her at the front desk, brandishing a book on Ancient Egypt he wanted to pay for. He had overheard the conversation and glanced at Clara, she met his eyes with a polite smile. The woman behind the front desk was now becoming agitated. The thought of the British Museum being sued for carelessness worried her greatly. The museum had a reputation, one she felt the need to defend. She had been working on the front desk for the last twenty years. She considered herself part and parcel of the museum, if someone was to criticise it, then they were criticising her. Like so many minor dictators who become intrinsically attached to the place they work in, she was always ready to defend the museum and would not hear a word said against it.

She was still bridling at the idea that someone might consider the museum negligent in its duty as she came to a decision.

"We can't have people spreading malicious stories about the museum," she said firmly. "Perhaps you ought to speak with Dr Vanderstom and iron out this matter. I am sure it was not anything the staff here did that resulted in the unfortunate theft. You might find Dr Vanderstom in the Japanese gallery, I believe he was attending to a display there today," the woman pushed her glasses further up her nose and gave Clara a hard stare. "I do not care for these insurance people."

Clara, resisting the urge to grin at her, thanked her for her time and then headed in the direction she had pointed. She found the Japanese Gallery after following a signboard nailed to the wall.

The gallery was, unsurprisingly, filled with objects that symbolised the culture and history of Japan. There were suits of ancient armour, intricate paintings, fans, statues, shoes and kimonos. Clara almost became side-tracked looking at the vast array of objects that were so very different from similar English items. She found the figures on the paintings peculiar to look at, often the men seemed to be grimacing, while the women turned away their heads sharply in efforts to look coy. Clara did not, however, immediately see any netsuke on display.

She moved about the glass cases, looking for someone who was not a visitor and might be Dr Vanderstom. She came around a large display containing an enormous suit of armour that seemed rather demonic to Clara's eyes and suddenly spied a man kneeling before a wall cabinet. He had opened the glass front of the cabinet and was very carefully removing a large vase to place in a wooden box lined with wood shavings. Clara wandered over.

"Would you be Dr Vanderstom?" she asked quietly; the museum inspired a hush rather like a library.

"I am," Dr Vanderstom said without looking up. "Would you excuse me a moment?"

He was wearing white cloth gloves as he lifted the vase and gingerly rested it down upon its new bed of wood shavings. Then he closed the cabinet and locked it once more. He rose from his knees and lifted the box with the vase up from the floor.

"It needs a little attention," he said to Clara. "We noticed a crack running down its length and fear it might break in two. Old porcelain can suddenly crack and disintegrate if you are not alert to the signs."

"That must be a worry," Clara replied, thinking about the number of porcelain objects the museum must contain.

"Oh, it doesn't happen often," Dr Vanderstom reassured her. "An object is usually already cracked to begin with and then something makes the crack worsen. I have a theory it is due to temperature changes and possibly moisture, or a lack of it, in the air. Last thing we need is to come in one morning and find the vase in two pieces on the display cabinet floor, so we are going to examine it now and hopefully prevent that happening. It's three hundred years old, you know."

"Gosh," Clara looked at the humble vase with its delicate decoration of flowers and birds. It did not look three hundred years old. "Would you have a moment to speak with me?"

"Who are you?" Dr Vanderstom asked.

"Clara Fitzgerald," Clara declared. "I am working for Mr Jacobs who you may recall loaned a netsuke to the museum for a recent exhibition?"

"Ah, yes, I remember," Dr Vanderstom nodded. "He loaned us a green jade dragon netsuke. A most exquisite item and quite rare to see in England. We placed it in a case all on its own. It seemed fitting, as it showcased the exquisite craftsmanship the Japanese could attain in the past."

"Sadly the dragon has been stolen," Clara continued. "I am trying to pursue its trail in the hope of restoring it to Mr Jacobs. I suspect there is a connection between the dragon being on display in the museum and its subsequent theft."

Dr Vanderstom became very serious, he recognised the implication.

"You think someone saw it here and then decided to steal it?"

"The burglary during which the item was stolen was very well organised and professional. The thieves knew exactly what they wanted. It seems rather coincidental that it was taken not long after it was put on public display for the very first time," Clara pulled the catalogue for the exhibition that Mr Jacobs had lent her out of her bag. "The description of the dragon in your guide not only included the name of the owner of the dragon, but also the town in which he resided. It would not have taken much detective work to locate Mr Jacobs' actual address."

Dr Vanderstom was silent a moment. He was clearly mulling over all these implications. To think that the museum had accidentally contributed to the theft of an object was most troubling.

"Why don't we talk in my office?" he suggested at last, and then he led Clara out of the gallery, through a warren of back passages and to a small room that served as his office.

There were more Asian objects in the office, not just Japanese items, but Chinese as well. Clara took one look at a set of disturbing masks glaring at her from a wall and decided she would stick with British art. Dr Vanderstom offered her a seat, while he put down the box with the vase.

"You must convey my sympathies to Mr Jacobs," he said once he was too sat down. "I am most distressed to hear about the burglary. He was very accommodating about the loan of the jade dragon."

"How did it come about the dragon was displayed here?" Clara asked.

"We plan exhibitions many months in advance, even

up to two years or more. We have to arrange so much, you see. Putting the items into the cases is purely the last stage. From time to time we place notices in suitable publications asking people for specific objects we might loan for exhibitions. For instance, we are soon to hold an exhibition of works by Dutch artists in the sixteenth and seventeenth centuries. Some of the finest examples of their work are held in private collections. So we apply to the owners and arrange to loan them, if we can," Dr Vanderstom frowned. "It would be most detrimental to future exhibitions if it was thought that thieves had somehow used the museum to window shop for items to steal."

"You might have to rethink your policy on crediting items in your catalogues," Clara agreed. "But how did you specifically get in touch with Mr Jacobs."

"When we were planning the Japanese exhibition, we placed notices in magazines and sent out notices to other museums, stating that we were looking for unusual items to display. Mr Jacobs saw one of these notices in a publication for antiques dealers and contacted us. He explained about his netsuke collection and suggested the green jade dragon might be of interest. Naturally it was," Dr Vanderstom met Clara's eyes. "We had nothing like that in the museum. Objects made of green jade are not easy to get hold of. Both the Japanese and Chinese nations highly value these items. The Chinese, in particular, once believed that jade could make a man immortal."

"Then the dragon is very valuable?"

"In more ways than one," Dr Vanderstom nodded. "I don't believe it has ever been valued, but since such an item is rare on the British antiques market I think it would be safe to say it would sell for hundreds of pounds, if not thousands. Something so rare would attract a lot of wealthy men. But, also, there are wealthy Japanese collectors who would like to acquire such an item."

Dr Vanderstom hesitated a moment. He glanced sideways at the ghastly masks on his wall.

"I will admit I had my concerns about the object. It was so unusual and Mr Jacobs could only give the most hazy account of how it made its way to England."

"His uncle brought it home last century," Clara said.

"Yes. But, such an item would be very treasured in Japan. I find it hard to imagine how it fell into the hands of an ordinary, albeit wealthy, English gentleman. Had the item been gifted to a member of the British Royal family I could understand it. But precious objects like that don't just land in the hands of ordinary people."

Clara was startled.

"Are you suggesting the dragon might have been stolen before it came into Mr Jacobs' collection?"

Dr Vanderstom shrugged.

"I just found it all very curious. Objects like that usually have a provenance. We have hundreds of netsuke in the museum, most are very ordinary, but a few items are special and all of these can be traced back to their origins. That the green jade dragon had so mysteriously arrived in England bothered me a little," Dr Vanderstom admitted all this slowly. "Look, might I pass you on to someone who could offer you a greater insight? I might be the head of the Oriental department, but my expertise tends to be on Chinese artefacts. I know someone who shared my views on the dragon and who would be better placed to advise you."

Dr Vanderstom took up a piece of paper and scribbled down a name and address.

"I could call him and see if he is available to speak with you today?"

"Please do," Clara answered as she took the slip of paper. "You have piqued my curiosity."

"Honestly?" Dr Vanderstom gave a wan smile. "My curiosity is piqued too. Not only that, but I feel my suspicions have been proved founded."

"Let's hope not," Clara countered. For Mr Jacobs' sake she really hoped she was not about to discover that his uncle had been a commonplace thief.

Chapter Ten

Dr Vanderstom's acquaintance was a Scotsman by the name of Gregory McFry. He had made a success of himself exporting canned meals to the various fringes of the empire, where beef stew was a luxury rather than a staple. McFry had spent some of the vast fortune he had amassed on a passion for all things Japanese. When Clara came upon him in his office, after Dr Vanderstom had kindly telephoned ahead, she found him surrounded by antiques, all of them Japanese. Mr McFry, himself, had abandoned his suit jacket for the afternoon and was wearing a Japanese blue silk robe. Other than the robe, there was nothing Japanese about him. He was well over six foot, a towering man with vast hands and muscles like those of a bullock, and he had the thickest Scottish accent Clara had come across in a while. When he spoke fast she had to listen very carefully to understand him.

"You must be the lass Dr Vanderstom was sending over?" McFry said, holding out one of those vast hands and shaking Clara's outstretched one. "He briefly explained you were investigating a stolen netsuke?"

"Yes. It was one loaned to the British Museum for their recent Japanese exhibition."

"Ah, now let me guess!" McFry held up a thick figure

to forestall her saying more. "The exhibition had a small display of very ordinary netsuke, not worth a lot but they attracted people for their novelty. But there was that very special one, a green jade dragon loaned by a gentleman. I remember looking at that one and thinking it was a very fine piece, very fine. Would that be the one that is missing?"

"You would be correct," Clara nodded. "The dragon netsuke belongs to Mr Jacobs of Brighton and just over a week ago it was stolen from his home. The robbery was very professional and seems to suggest the people involved knew what they were looking for."

McFry became sombre, which animated his broad face in a new fashion, reminding Clara of one of the scowling masks on Dr Vanderstom's office wall.

"I had my concerns about that piece," he said softly.

"Dr Vanderstom said as much. He outlined those concerns but said you would be able to explain them better."

"Aye, well maybe I can," McFry settled back in his chair, the springs creaking a fraction under his giant frame. He folded his hands across his chest. "You see, I have been a collector of all things Japanese since I was a mere lad. Back in Scotland, in the little town I grew up in, no one knew what a Japanese person was. Then one day there was this rare old shipwreck on the rocks. It was a terrible stormy night and this freighter ship, far off course from where it should have been, crashed upon the rocks and shook itself to pieces.

"All the lifeboatmen were roused from their beds and set out to sea in their cork life-vests and rubber boots. They rescued a fair few souls that night, others were dragged ashore by the women that went down to the beach and helped those nearest out of the waves. When dawn broke the rumour ran about the village that these rescued men were strange foreigners, with funny eyes and a peculiar tongue. Naturally, as a curious lad of twelve I went to look for myself.

"One of the rescued fellows spoke a little English, though not Scotch! You could see his eyes watering as he tried to understand the people about him, much like yours are right now!"

McFry roared with laughter. It was a generous, innocent laugh and Clara knew he meant no ill by it and, yes, she was working hard to keep up with his speech.

"I befriended this man, being curious and all," McFry continued when his amusement had subsided. "He told me he was Japanese and all about his homeland. He had worked on a lot of ships and travelled to both Britain and American, learning a number of tongues along the way. Not knowing where he had at first landed up, he thought we might be Russian when we opened our mouths to him. Poor soul only realised he was in Britain when he heard a word or two of English. He said he thought the Scottish were a peculiar folk."

McFry chuckled again.

"Anyhow, they were all stuck there until a ship was sent to rescue them or they had instructions to go someplace else. So I spent a lot of time with Hiro, learning all about Japan which sounded so very different to the town I had been born and bred in. When he finally left, he gave me a parting gift. I still carry it with me always."

McFry reached into his shirt and pulled out a leather cord, upon which hung a small piece of carved ivory.

"Is it a netsuke?" Clara asked.

"No, it's an ornament to be carried or worn. A lucky charm in the form of a toad," McFry removed the cord, lifting it over his head, and handing the lucky toad to Clara.

It reminded her of the netsukes in the way it was carved to favour the natural curves of the material it was made of. The artist had taken pains to ensure the grain flowed across the toad's body naturally, the whirls and knots being used to shape the form of the creature. Clara handed it back.

"And so a lifetime's passion was born?" she said.

"Not quite so simply," McFry shrugged. "It was years before I came across another Japanese object, when I was a grown man and in London promoting my business. Then I spotted a Japanese fan on a stall in Covent Garden. The seller only wanted a few pence for it, so I took it away and ended up at the British Museum asking about it. I found my way into the Japanese gallery and came home loaded with catalogues and books on Japanese art. That was when it truly began. I have specialised, honing my knowledge, to the point that occasionally Dr Vanderstom will even ask my opinion. Of course, there are experts in the British Museum, but sometimes they are blinkered by their university educations. I am a free-soul when it comes to learning. Dr Vanderstom calls me a breath of fresh air."

McFry winked at Clara. He was such an affable, agreeable man that just being in his company raised the spirits and Clara had almost forgotten why she was really there. Almost.

"Dr Vanderstom said he had concerns about the green jade dragon?" she said. "And that you shared them?"

"Green jade is a very precious thing, and very important to the Japanese. It is highly prized, the sort of thing only an emperor and his favourites should possess. Of course, the Imperial Court of Japan has softened over the years, like our own monarchy. Now especially wealthy Japanese men might own jade objects, but it is still very treasured and considered peculiarly Asian," McFry flicked his eyes about his office, glancing at his collection. "In all my years of collecting, owning a piece of green jade has proven to be most elusive. The items come onto the British market rarely and attract huge sums. The Japanese are very coy about letting significant objects leave their hands. I have seen a few jade netsuke for sale, but mostly modern pieces created in the last fifty years to sate the foreign market. Antique jade is almost unheard of."

"Which made Mr Jacobs' dragon special?"

"From the moment I saw it, and Dr Vanderstom was good enough to let me see it before the exhibition and inspect it closely, I could tell the dragon was not one of these modern pieces. The craftsmanship was exceptional, for a start, the details most intricate and not worked with modern tools," McFry agreed, getting into his stride again. "There were, on the dragon's leg, some very small characters. I studied them for nearly an hour, before I was confident enough to draw copies on a piece of paper. They were clearly the initials of the craftsman who had made the item and I proposed to Vanderstom that tracing the craftsman might offer us a clue to the object's origins.

"Many of the netsuke do not have such marks. But those crafted by a clever artisan sometimes do. It is like the signature on a painting. But not all these artisans are known to us. I had to refer to some Japanese guides I had imported to help me. I fortunately read Japanese, if not speak it."

McFry winked again, implying that to twist his big Scottish tongue around Japanese syllables was a challenge he had tried and failed.

"Anyhoo, I trawled through my guides and after many long hours by the reading lamp I found the name of the artisan who made the dragon listed. I was excited to find the man had lived during the sixteenth century, or rather our sixteenth century as the Japanese would have been using a different calendar system," McFry rocked his chair making it give out those complaining groans again. "More importantly, this craftsman was almost exclusively employed to work on objects for Japanese royalty, including the emperor himself. Now I was certain that Mr Jacobs' dragon had arrived in Britain by unusual means. It was not the sort of object the Japanese would relinquish easily, even if someone was prepared to pay a fortune for it."

Clara found herself returning to thoughts of Mr Jacobs' long dead uncle. How had he come across the object that he handed so freely to his nephew? Surely he had not stolen it himself?

"I am not implying that any of Mr Jacobs' kin knew it was stolen," McFry mistook Clara's silence for anger at his suggestion. "I would propose that someone removed the article from the Imperial Palace and sold it to Mr Jacobs' uncle. Such things do happen."

"They do," Clara agreed. "Sadly, the uncle died before he could explain to Mr Jacobs' the origins of the dragon."

"How did he die?" McFry asked curiously.

"I believe it was a coach accident," Clara answered. "Mr Jacobs did not know all the details himself."

McFry took his turn to be silent as he thought over this information. Clara read his mind.

"Perhaps it was not mere coincidence he died so soon after arriving home with the dragon?" she suggested.

"Oh, these things happen," McFry brushed off his concerns. "Some of these Imperial objects are said to have been cursed by their makers, to bring harm to any who gets hold of them illegally. I could as much argue the case for that, as to suggest the unfortunate uncle was the victim of someone trying to retrieve the dragon off him."

"Mr Jacobs has certainly not suffered from his ownership of the dragon," Clara concurred. "But, I can't help but think that someone realised its significance when they saw it in the case at the British Museum and opted to steal it."

McFry scratched at his chin. He had the stubble of a beard just growing there.

"One way or the other, the dragon is valuable enough to attract the attention of a thief. A collector would give their right arm for it," McFry produced a big grin. "I know I would."

"And that brings me back to my starting point," Clara sighed. "I still have no better idea of who the thief, or rather his employer, might be. I doubt the dragon is going to appear on the open market."

"No," McFry agreed. "And I have not heard about such

an object being offered for sale. Though I will keep my ears open. There is a part of me who feels it is such a shame Mr Jacobs offered the dragon for loan to the museum."

"I believe it was the first time the dragon has been on public display in Britain," Clara agreed. "I wonder how many people would have realised its true worth when they saw it. The museum catalogue did not suggest its value, but someone looked at that object, realised it was priceless and wanted it."

"Or they guessed it was an Imperial treasure long ago stolen," McFry pointed out.

"Without seeing the maker's marks?"

"You might not need to, if you happened to know that several decades ago a jade dragon was stolen, if it was stolen. We can only postulate on that."

"Indeed," Clara felt she had gained insight into the dragon's origins if nothing else, but she was no closer to pinpointing a suspect in its disappearance. "Do you know of anyone who would be as astute as you and Dr Vanderstom were to the dragon's significance?"

"There aren't that many British collectors with the depth of knowledge either I, or Vanderstom, have," McFry said, though it was an innocent remark, not meant to be immodest. "There are a handful of Japanese businessmen in the country, one or two of whom might have an interest in collecting antiquities from their homeland. I could find out their names for you?"

"I would very much appreciate that," Clara said gratefully. "And thank you for your time, I have certainly found our conversation enlightening."

McFry rose and showed Clara to the door of his office.

"It's strange, but the moment I set eyes on that dragon I felt something odd. A chill crept over me almost," McFry chuckled to himself, slightly embarrassed by his confession. "I am not particularly superstitious, but I concluded that the dragon was not something I would want in my possession. It had a bad feeling to it."

"The curse?" Clara teased him.

"Perhaps I am superstitious," McFry was amused with himself. "I did grown up among people who lived and breathed magic and folklore. My gran put out milk and bread for the fairies every night, though I remember my mother finding it rather foolish."

"Well, as long as the dragon realises I am only seeking the truth and pose it no threat," Clara smiled, shaking hands once again with the Scottish giant, "then I should be fine."

"As long as you bear all that in mind lassie," McFly tapped the side of his nose. "No knowing what lurks out there."

Clara went away from McFry most amused. The only things she feared lurking out there were the criminals who had robbed Mr Jacobs' house. Clara didn't believe in curses, that was for certain.

Chapter Eleven

Clara ran out of time to pursue anymore enquiries in London and was glad to get home. All the walking and travelling had exhausted her, but at least she now had a better idea of the circumstances surrounding the thief's first sighting of the green jade dragon. Whether the thief had chosen to steal it because of its value, or because they wanted to right the wrong of it being stolen in the first place was impossible to say for the moment, but it was curious, nonetheless.

Clara had just eased off her shoes and was sitting in her favourite armchair when there was a rap on the front door. Clara had her eyes shut, trying to ignore the twinge of a headache playing about her temples. She barely noticed the summons, and did not pay heed to Annie going to open the door. She was close to drifting into a happy doze when Annie appeared at the door of the parlour.

"Clara? Are you awake?"

Clara lifted up her head and murmured that she was – just.

"Bob is here, if you would care to see him?"

Clara almost groaned, but then she realised that Bob would not have called so late were it not important, and she had asked for his help. She opened her eyes and sat upright in the armchair.

"Send him in," she nodded.

A moment later Bob appeared in the parlour. He was still in his work overalls and there was the pleasant aroma of sawn wood about him.

"How is the house building going?" Clara asked, motioning for him to sit in the armchair opposite her.

Bob gave a grin.

"Seems ok," he shrugged. "I just do the wood."

Clara smiled with him, it was just the sort of light-hearted comment Bob would make.

"I have some news for you," Bob said. "I have been asking around, as you wanted."

"Anything good come up?" Clara leaned forward in her chair.

"Quite a bit, actually," Bob replied, his smile drifting away as he became more serious. "More than one fellow is rather unhappy about the burglary. Talk among them is it was done by an outsider."

That probably meant a Londoner, Clara mused.

"Anything else?"

"Lots of grumbling about why some rich fellow didn't hire a local lad for the job."

"They know who the employer of the thief was?"

"No," Bob shook his head. "But they all say that there was money behind the job. It wasn't some opportunist working alone. The thief was hired."

"I thought that might be the case," Clara sighed. "Makes it more complicated."

"And there were others," Bob continued.

"Others?"

"No one explained it specifically, but I gathered there were men watching the house and gathering information."

Clara nodded, that was logical enough. This had been very carefully planned out in advance.

"The local boys are really not pleased," Bob said.

"They feel offended, like they aren't good enough for such a job. And the way the fellow just walked into The Black Sheep all bold as brass has gotten right up their noses."

"Wait, Bob, which fellow?"

"The thief," Bob elaborated, looking surprised that Clara had not already guessed that. "He came into the pub for a drink. It's the Devil's armpit, that pub. Full of the worst sorts who all gather together to drink, fight and maybe arrange a bit of work."

"The criminal sort of work?"

"Exactly."

Clara mulled this over a while. Bob had certainly been busy, listening to the rumour train and talking with his friends, but Bob could not possibly know to ask all the questions that Clara had in her mind. After considering her options, Clara concluded that she would have to go to this 'Devil's armpit' of a place herself and find out as much as she could. Her weariness left her as she flicked her eyes back to meet Bob's.

"Take me to The Black Sheep," she said.

"Now?" Bob asked, starting to look worried. "It isn't a respectable place."

"That doesn't concern me," Clara shrugged. "I need to speak with those people who met the thief. I need to ask them questions."

"I'm not sure if I should take you," Bob dropped his head and concentrated heavily on his big hands, giving the impression of a schoolboy being asked to do something he disliked.

"I can always go by myself," Clara stated.

Bob's eyes flashed back up.

"You mustn't do that!" he almost cried out at her. "Bad people go there and the women are all… floozies."

"You know me, Bob, when I get a bee in my bonnet…"

Bob gave a miserable sigh. He shook his head like a big dog trying to shake a flea from its ear.

"I'll take you then, but the first sign of trouble we are leaving," Bob told her this very firmly and Clara guessed he would drag her out kicking and screaming if needs be.

Clara promised him, on her honour, that as soon as he said the word they would both leave. Then she went to fetch her coat and hat and apologise to Annie for having to nip out again. Annie gave her a scowl, her best 'what-are-you-up-to-now' scowl. Clara promised she would be back home before nine o'clock and would eat her dinner late, then she grabbed the reluctant Bob's arm and sauntered out into the night.

The Black Sheep was in Brighton's working class quarter. Brighton did not quite have the slums like London or other large cities did, but there were areas that came close. The Black Sheep was situated among such a collection of rundown houses and backstreets, where the commonest sounds were hacking coughs and curse words. The streets were narrow and the sky was barely visible above their heads. The pavements were largely non-existent, people making do with the hard packed ground instead. After the dry summer the dirt spooled into clouds of dust at the slightest step, hitting the back of the throat and making the eyes water. Clara tried to imagine what it must be like to wake up and go to bed in this same dusty, dirty world, with the rubbish piled just outside the doors and the pervasive smell of overflowing latrines drifting across the air.

The door to The Black Sheep was tucked down a side alley. This was not a pub with ornate front windows to advertise ale and stout, this place was secret, almost hidden away. The only window, fixed into the side of the building as it looked onto the street, was broken and boarded over. Looking at the grime gathered over the wooden boards, it seemed the glass had been smashed for a very long time. Bob turned them into the alley that ran alongside a pawnbroker's shop. Above them stretched a ceiling of brick, the original builders seeing no reason to not use the space above for extra accommodation. The result, on a rapidly darkening late summer's evening, was to walk into a gloomy tunnel with no knowing who was about in the shadows. Clara was glad she had Bob with her, she was sensible enough to know that coming here alone would not have been wise. She had just mentioned the possibility to encourage her escort. Now she looked into the dark, dim tunnel that hid the entrance to The Black Sheep and wondered how anyone could live in such a world. Of course, her mind provided the answer swiftly enough; this was not a place you lived by choice. A person lived here out of necessity.

Bob pushed open a warped wooden door set into the wall. It creaked on its hinges, but the second it opened there was a gush of light and sound. Clara followed Bob into a large, long room packed with rough wooden tables and stools. Opposite the door ran a bar, behind which were rows and rows of bottles, mainly beer and gin. The Black Sheep's landlord stood behind the bar, staring meanly at his customers as though he hated them all. The room was well lit by a combination of oil lamps and candles, making the pub one of the brightest places in this world of dark despair. The place was packed with drinkers, overwhelmingly male, though the odd woman sat among them. Several of the women were gaudily painted and had the appearance of prostitutes. Clara cast her eyes over this strange place, a complete novelty to her, and while she saw its many vices, and its many dangers, she also saw that this was the one ray of happiness in an otherwise bleak existence for many of the folks here.

"Over there is Charlie," Bob whispered to Clara, though it was quite a loud whisper because the noise in the room was overpowering. "He was the one telling me all about it."

Bob ushered Clara over to the aforementioned Charlie, who was sitting at a table with two other gentlemen. Charlie was a young fellow with sharp features and darting eyes. He had a tendency to open his mouth to reveal an overbite when he stared at people. The way he narrowed his ferrety eyes made Clara imagine he was in need of a good pair of glasses.

"Charlie, this is Miss Fitzgerald. She would like to speak with you," Bob said.

"Oho, Charlie!" the man on Charlie's right laughed. "You have a lady wanting to speak to you!"

"Shut up, Stan," Bob barked, his usually placid voice suddenly angry. It was when he spoke like that that people began to take note of his size and muscular build. It was enough to make anyone think twice, it certainly made Stan hesitate. "Show some respect!"

Stan fell silent, his amusement all gone. The drinker next to him, the third man at the table, made a point of keeping his eyes fixed on his pint mug.

"What do you want?" Charlie asked Clara, his voice openly hostile.

"I want to know about the man who robbed the Jacobs' house," Clara said calmly, trying to pretend she was not unnerved by her environment.

"What about him?"

"You tell me. I hear he was not local."

Charlie glanced at his drinking buddies. They did not attempt to help him.

"He was a Londoner."

"Are you sure?" Clara asked.

"I know a Cockney accent when I hear it," Charlie snapped. "I hear enough of that when those bastards come down in the summer to steal our work."

Clara was amused that Charlie would refer to his criminal activities as 'work', but said nothing.

"Does this man have a name?" she asked instead.

"None he gave us," Charlie snorted. "You should ask Tanner, the landlord. He spoke with him, not me."

At this, Charlie clammed up and refused to say anything else. Clara glanced at Bob, then nodded with her head to indicate they should speak to Tanner.

The landlord was cleaning a glass with an old rag, the habitual work that all keepers of bars seem to be unable to resist. He scowled at Bob and Clara, but then he seemed to scowl at everyone. Bob ordered a pint, Clara declined his offer to buy her a drink. She had seen the state of the rag the landlord was using to clean his glasses.

"I hear a Londoner swanned in here causing trouble recently," Clara mentioned casually as the pint was produced for Bob. "They are getting quite saucy. Bold as brass, these days."

The landlord grunted.

"Mind you, perhaps the fellow employing him could not find a local that suited his needs," Clara prodded him.

The landlord, as she suspected, was defensive about his clientele – loyalty comes in many forms.

"There was no call bringing in an outsider for that job," he snapped. "There are plenty of fellows here who could have done the work."

"How did you know the Londoner was here on a job?" Clara asked.

"Said as much," Tanner snorted. "Came up to my bar and leaned on it right where you are sat. Everyone knows everyone in here, so I knew he were a stranger. He asked for a pint, grinning all the time. Then the fellow asked if I knew the Jacobs' house."

"What did you say?" Clara asked as the landlord fell silent.

"I said I might," Tanner shrugged. "I didn't actually know the place, mind. But you don't say things like that to outsiders. And I am only saying them to you because you are with him."

The landlord pointed a grubby, grey finger first at Clara, then at Bob.

"Bob's a good lad," he said, mellowing a fraction. "Fixed up some of my tables after that brawl we had in here. And mended the rotten floorboards upstairs."

Bob grinned at the landlord, delighted to be praised.

"I respect him. One honest fellow among a bunch of rogues," the landlord spat violently onto the top of the bar, narrowly missing Clara's hand. "That's why I'll talk to his friends too."

"Thank you," Clara said. "I appreciate you speaking to me. I am trying to trace the thief, this cocky Londoner. Did he mention his name?"

"No," Tanner answered, the glass and the rag working round and round in his hand. "He didn't."

Clara was foiled. She paused a moment, trying to think.

"Is there anyone who might know who he was?"

"Why are you interested?" Tanner asked, "What is he to you?"

He was suspicious. Clara imagined that was rather a natural emotion for Tanner to feel, keeping the company he did.

"He stole something belonging to her," Bob interrupted before Clara could formulate her own answer. "When he was in the Jacobs' house."

"Go to the police," Tanner grumbled at Clara. "That's what your sort do."

Clara did not ask him to clarify what he meant by 'her sort', she could guess.

"And what good are the police?" Bob persisted. "They can't catch a professional thief, and we both know that. So I am helping her to find the thief for herself."

Bob lowered his tone and his eyes flashed darkly.

"Maybe I am also doing it to make a statement for Brighton. It's about time we stood up for ourselves."

The landlord became sympathetic again. Bob's words had struck a chord.

"Now you be careful, Bob. No call you getting yourself into trouble," he said. "But if you really want to track this fellow, well, I would talk to old Ezra next door. He knows more names of thieves than anyone else. Makes it his business to."

Bob smiled.

"Thanks Tanner, I shall ask him."

"I don't want to see you ending up in a prison cell," Tanner said before they could both leave. "Don't go making your poor late mother sad in her grave."

"I won't," Bob promised Tanner easily.

Then he escorted Clara out of the pub and across the road to the pawnbroker's.

Chapter Twelve

The sign above the door was almost falling off its metal hooks. It consisted of three gold painted balls, the standard sign of the pawnbroker, said to variously represent bags of gold or weights for a scale. The windows were filthy, so yellow with grime that it was almost impossible to see through them, though that had not stopped Ezra from putting items on display in his window. There was a full tray of rings, most looking like fairground prizes, and a tin bath next to a woman's dress hanging from a rail and looking like a particularly shabby ghost. There was no sign to indicate whether the premises were open or not for trade, but Bob did not hesitate to try the door. Old Ezra ran the sort of business that received a lot of trade after dark.

The shop was gloomy. A single oil lamp hung from the ceiling and barely touched the shadows. Clara felt, rather than saw, that she was surrounded by assorted belongings on shelves and stacked in heaps. Most would never be sold. They would sit in the shop for a few days, or perhaps a week, until their original owner returned with the money to claim them. Then, in a few more days, they would once again be pawned when the person ran out of money. In some ways, Ezra was a sort of lending library for household wares, only with money involved.

"Ezra?" Bob called out into the dark.

Clara could not see anybody about, but there was a dark set of shadows at the back of the room which suggested a doorway. Clara thought she saw movement there.

"Ezra Creek?" Bob called again.

"All right, all right," an old man emerged from the doorway Clara had glimpsed. "I was eating my supper!"

The man was grimy, like his shop. He gave the impression that he was filmed in grease, certainly his fingers and beard were stained by nicotine that gave them a yellow hue. He wore a smoking jacket or housecoat, a long threadbare thing that had once been a deep red, but which now looked more grey. It was very shiny at the elbows and cuffs, indicating years of use. Clara had the feeling that Ezra was only wearing trousers beneath it, not a shirt. There was a hint of bare flesh as he moved and the coat briefly opened for a second or two. She tried not to cringe at the thought of the unclean old man's white flesh being flashed before her eyes.

Ezra bore a full set of sideburns to accompany his long white hair. His locks were just as greasy as the rest of him and fell to his shoulders. He was not very tall, shorter than Clara, and had a very lined face with a bulbous, pockmarked nose that dominated his features. He scowled at the pair of them through a pair of tiny round glasses that constantly slipped from behind his ears. He was still carrying a boiled egg in his hand which apparently formed part of his supper.

"Well? What do you want to pawn?" he demanded.

"Nothing," Bob started to say, instantly rousing the man's anger.

"Then why are you bothering me?" he croaked. "Leave me alone!"

He stormed back towards the doorway.

"Wait!" Clara called out. "I have some questions about a recent burglary, and I think you might be able to answer them!"

"Are you the police?" Ezra snorted. "Only the police get to waste my time asking questions."

"I'll buy something," Clara quickly added. "If you will talk to me."

Ezra stopped just inside the doorway. Clara had calculated right when she imagined the man was dominated by money and the making of it. Any opportunity to line his pockets enticed him.

"What sort of thing will you buy?" he asked.

Clara quickly glanced around the shop. Most of the items were worthless, she would pay pennies for them if that. Then she spied something tucked behind an old trunk and a pile of clothes; it was an old-fashioned jardinière. The sort of thing people years ago kept goldfish in, and which the Victorians liked to use for plants. Bob helped Clara pull it out from among the clutter. It was very pretty and Clara guessed quite old. She took one look at it and knew it would suit Captain O'Harris' house perfectly.

"This. I'll buy this."

Ezra looked delighted. There was a price tag of five shillings on the ceramic pot. Clara gave him six to make him amenable to chatting.

"Now, about the man who burgled the Jacobs house?"

Ezra cocked his head on one side. He was a canny old bird and now his curiosity was piqued. He folded the coins into his hot palm.

"You are interested in that?"

"I am," Clara said. "I was told you could provide me with some information on the subject?"

"Yes I can," Ezra grinned. "The fellow who burgled that place came to see me. Stood in this shop and yarned with me."

"Why did he do that?" Bob asked, suspicion in his eyes.

"He had time to waste," Ezra shrugged. "He was waiting for dark, and the pub had proved a little too hostile for his liking. They don't take kindly to strangers there."

"And what did you talk about?" Clara asked.

"All sorts," Ezra gestured with his hands that this statement included a vast number of topics. "He was a chatty sort."

"What was his name?" Clara insisted.

Ezra now frowned.

"He did not give it. Not many of my customers do. But later some other fellows came in here, locals who do a little extra work on the side," Ezra drew a smile with his lips that showed small, brown teeth. "They were moaning about the fellow and trying to guess who he was. I heard them mention a few names, but they never settled on one for him."

"Which names?" Clara pulled out her notebook ready to write them down.

Ezra glanced at the pad of paper. Clara was suspicious he was stringing her and Bob along, but she remained silent and waited.

"There were three possible names. One of the fellows had followed this thief all the way to the Jacobs house. He was describing him to his companions and they were suggesting names of thieves they had heard of that matched the description," Ezra was being very accommodating now he had money in his hand. "I believe the names were, Stumpy Pete, John Knacker and Ugly Dickson."

Clara took down these names, disappointed that two appeared to be aliases. Tracing them would be tricky.

"How would you describe the man who came in here?" she asked.

Ezra considered this for a while. He had forgotten the boiled egg in his hand and it was slowly disintegrating under the pressure of his fingers.

"Not so tall. Not tall at all. Barely above five foot, if I had to guess," Ezra's eyes wandered to the ceiling as he trawled through his memory. "He would have been in his thirties. Not bad looking, despite being short. Dark hair, dark eyes. A lop-sided smile. But what struck me the most was his slender build. He was so thin it almost beggared belief. He was like a moving skeleton, yet he did not look to be starved or anything of the sort. He was just extremely lean."

"Did he mention anything about why he was in Brighton?" Clara asked as she made notes.

"No more than to say he was on a job. I guessed what that meant."

Ezra's limited store of knowledge had been exhausted. Clara concluded the interview, feeling rather disheartened. Would it be possible to trace these men with strange names? Well, at least she had names.

Bob was good enough to carry the jardinière home for her. He left her on her doorstep with a farewell after insisting she promise not to return to The Black Sheep without him. Clara could readily assure him of that. She had felt deeply uncomfortable in the place and would not like to be there alone. She dragged the ceramic pot into the front hall and gladly collapsed back into her armchair.

~~~*~~~

The next morning she wound her way to the police station. The desk sergeant was still absent, replaced by an earnestly helpful constable who allowed Clara through to the station archives as soon as she showed him her official card – the one Inspector Park-Coombs had arranged for her.

Clara was hoping the archives might hold a file or two on the names she had been given by Ezra. If the Brighton criminal fraternity had heard of them, it was probable they had been in the town at some point. Most of the Brighton crew did not travel far abroad (other than when forced to by the interference of law and order) so they would be unlikely to have associated intimately with thieves outside the town. Of course, they could have just been repeating gossip, but Clara had to hope.

She was trawling through the shelves marked S, looking for Stumpy Pete, when footsteps behind her alerted her to someone else being present. She glanced over her shoulder and saw the inspector.

"The constable at the desk informed me you were here," he said. "I wanted a word. I've had a complaint from a Miss Sarah Butler."

Clara stepped back from the shelves and faced the inspector, she was curious now.

"She came in to report that someone was poking about in her private affairs. Said a person claiming to be from the council had been enquiring about her through her friends. I rather had a hunch who that might have been."

Clara had the decency to blush.

"Inspector, you must think me awful. I would not be investigating the woman if it was not for the fact she has made it her business to worm her way into my life," Clara briefly explained about the newspaper advertisement and the business cards. "I admit, I was probably prying where I should not have been, but I was hurt and felt the need to defend myself."

"I see your point," the inspector nodded. "But don't keep at it."

"Easier said than done," Clara sighed. "She has been hired to locate a missing husband, one Mr Butterworth who has absconded with a cat. Mrs Wilton is insisting on hiring me to resolve the same case."

"Surely it is not Mrs Wilton's concern?" Park-Coombs queried.

"Mrs Wilton makes everything her concern," Clara sighed. "I will attempt to keep my distance, but the woman is making that difficult."

Inspector Park-Coombs seemed amused.

"Perhaps it would reassure Mrs Wilton to know that the absconding husband is perfectly safe and living at a certain address in Hove."

"You traced him?" Clara was surprised.

"Mrs Butterworth came to us first, claiming her

husband was missing and had taken their cat with him. We had to investigate, but it did not take us long to locate him. Mr Butterworth made it plain that he does not want to be found by his wife."

"What about the cat?"

"That was somewhat of a grey area," Park-Coombs admitted. "The beast belonged to both of them, so we could not accuse Mr Butterworth of stealing it. In the end, we concluded that the affair was not a police matter and left it at that."

Clara relaxed.

"At least I can inform Mrs Wilton that I know where the husband is," she said. "She will be delighted."

"Now, what are you doing down here?" the inspector glanced about at the shelves. "What are you looking for."

"A needle in a haystack, it feels like," Clara sighed. "I have three names, one of which might be the correct name for the thief who stole from Mr Jacobs. But the names are all I have. I was hopeful there might be files on them here."

"Can I see the names?"

Clara handed over her notebook gladly enough. Park-Coombs read from it with a frown.

"They don't ring a bell, though Ugly Dickson might be a fellow I arrested a few years back for housebreaking. They aren't locals."

"No. Londoners," Clara agreed. "I am slightly stuck."

The inspector stared at the names a while longer.

"I could ask my colleagues at Scotland Yard for some help," he said at last. "No need to say it was for a private case, I could mention these lads have been named in connection with a burglary and I want to know more about them."

Clara became excited.

"That would help enormously."

"I'll need a favour in return," the inspector quashed her enthusiasm before it grew too much. "I have the superintendent breathing down my neck about employing a woman police constable. I don't have the foggiest how to go about it. Usually, when I need an extra constable, I have names on my books of lads interested in becoming policemen and just looking for the chance. But I don't have any women."

"You want me to find you a woman?" Clara grinned, enjoying the pun of the statement.

"Something like that," Park-Coombs returned the smile, but more coyly. "A suitable woman will be efficient, respectable and of good character. And preferably tall."

"That rules out Annie," Clara teased.

"I am sure you will think of someone, or rather, I hope you will!" Inspector Park-Coombs chuckled to himself. "You don't want to join the force?"

"I value my independence," Clara winked. "But I am sure there is some suitable girl out there."

"I'll listen out for any information on Miss Butler too," the inspector reassured her. "Though I can't say I have heard her name mentioned much. I did do a little digging after our last conversation, but I found nothing. As far as I could tell, Miss Butler had never existed in Brighton until a few weeks ago."

"Really?" Clara was interested. "Yet the woman who gave her a reference said she had known her for five years, and implied that she had worked, albeit seasonally, in the town during that time."

"People slip through the net of officialdom," Park-Coombs was unperturbed. "She might never have been of interest to the police or anyone else for that matter. But I will keep looking, mainly so you don't have to."

He gave Clara a sly smile, which she opted to ignore.

"Thank you for your help Inspector, I ought to be on my way again."

"I'll drag out those names for you, if I can," the inspector promised.

Clara headed back for the street outside. She felt a walk was in order, a chance to clear her mind and mull over the information she had so far received. Not just about the jade dragon either, but about Miss Butler too. That woman was causing far too much consternation for Clara's liking. Just who was she and what was she about?

Chapter Thirteen

There was no getting away from it; Clara felt guilty. She felt she had thudded into Miss Butler's case and interfered in a fashion she would normally associate with Mrs Wilton. And that was the worst of it, feeling she had behaved like Mrs Wilton and had gone completely against all her charitable words about people being entitled to start up businesses, even if it was the same business as her. The more she thought about it, the more she felt Miss Butler had a right to feel annoyed by Clara's prodding around in her past.

Yes, there had been that debacle with the advert and the business cards, but perhaps it had been a careless mistake? A moment of naivety on Miss Butler's behalf? Even if Clara was not so generous and imagined the woman had deliberately copied her, had that really necessitated Clara sticking her nose into the woman's private affairs?

The more Clara dwelled, the more she felt she had behaved badly. She had felt threatened by the woman, that was the truth of it all. From the moment she had heard that someone else was running a detective business – another woman, at that – a knot of anxiety had settled in her belly and, like it or not, she had allowed that anxiety to fuel her behaviour. She could only imagine what Miss Butler must think of her. Here was the great detective seemingly going out of her way to unearth some dirt on her rival. How would Clara feel if the roles were reversed? She didn't like that idea at all.

And what made things worse was that Clara had solved Miss Butler's case for her, just as Mrs Wilton had demanded she do and in a way that Miss Butler could not hope to emulate. Miss Butler did not have the working relationship with Inspector Park-Coombs that Clara did. She could not ask him for help as Clara had loosely done. Yet again Clara had stomped in and shown up her rival in an awful fashion. Clara felt a bully, even if she had acted out of fear for herself, it certainly did not look like that now.

What was Clara to do? She had information that rightly belonged to Miss Butler, information that resolved her case. But Mr Butterworth had asked the police not to let his wife know where he was. If she told Miss Butler his location, was she wronging him?

Clara asked herself what she would do if it was her case. First, and foremost, she would do what she was hired to do. She would locate Mr Butterworth and ease his wife's mind about his whereabouts. Then she would go see him and talk with him, perhaps arrange for him to write to his wife and assure her he was well. The cat was an extra complication, but Mrs Butterworth did deserve to have her concerns alleviated. Clara thought it would be awful to have someone missing and not to know if they were safe and well. You could imagine all sorts of things, horrific accidents, sudden illness, even murder. Without knowing the people directly in question, Clara could not say for certain what was best to do, but perhaps Miss Butler could. After all, it was up to her discretion to decide how to resolve this affair smoothly.

Clara had a choice; she could give Miss Butler the information she learned from the police, or she could say nothing and allow Miss Butler to continue her enquiries.

The odds were, if she was any sort of detective, that Miss Butler would locate Mr Butterworth eventually. He was not precisely in hiding, the police had clearly found him very easily. The problem that pestered Clara's thoughts was whether she was being pig-headed by withholding what she knew from Miss Butler. It would hardly look good if it was later discovered that Clara had known all along where Mr Butterworth was and had kept it from people. She could, of course, tell Mrs Butterworth directly, but that would once more be going behind Miss Butler's back and she did not want to stir up the woman's ire further.

In the meantime, while Clara dithered and said nothing, Miss Butler was racking up the hours she had worked for her client, costing Mrs Butterworth money, which as a now abandoned wife it was difficult to say she could afford. And here was Clara with that priceless information at her fingertips, keeping her mouth shut.

There was no way to resolve the crisis fairly. She was damned whichever choice she made. More than ever Clara wished she had never heard of Miss Butler and certainly that she had not embroiled herself in the woman's case. There had been no call for it and now Clara had to make a difficult decision.

Before she had finalised her thoughts aloud, Clara knew in her heart which direction she was going to go. It was time to hold out an olive branch of peace to Miss Butler and hope the woman could forgive her. It would certainly be better than turning her into a stalwart enemy.

With this in mind, Clara headed for Miss Butler's office address. She was relieved, as she came into the street, to see someone standing in the upstairs window of the property. She was hopeful this was Miss Butler herself, and not a client she was seeing. Clara wanted to speak to her alone, without anyone knowing she had paid a call on her rival. That strange, fearful jealousy was still coursing through Clara's veins.

She opened the front door of the house and climbed the stairs to the door of Miss Butler's rooms. There she knocked and waited. A broad shouldered woman with fiery red hair opened the door and scowled at the sight of Clara. Clara guessed this was Miss Butler.

"Sarah Butler?" she asked, her voice noticeably uneasy.

"Miss Fitzgerald," Sarah Butler crossed her arms over her ample chest. She was a woman of fine proportions, but that did not make her ugly or ungainly. She carried her weight elegantly and her face was pretty, if no longer in the first flushes of youth. She was older than Clara, probably by a decade or so, and had been outdoors a lot. There was an earthy tone to her skin that was not gained from sitting before the living room fire. Her hair was her crowning glory. A rich auburn, that sparkled with hints of gold in the sun, it was an untameable mass of curls that felt about her face in tumbling waves.

She was a handsome woman, the sort a Victorian painter would have liked to have used as a model for painting an avenging Valkyrie. She gave the impression of a person capable of defending herself and her people should the need arise. Clara felt rather deflated before her. She did not have that sort of presence, nor the fiery hair. Clara was traditionally pretty, but considered herself largely unremarkable in appearance. Once again that pang of jealousy came over Clara; she could never hope to give off the aura of confidence and command that Miss Butler did.

"Could we talk?" Clara asked, her voice still alarmingly squeaky.

Miss Butler surveyed her with hard, green eyes.

"Aye, let's talk," she said at last, though the edge to her voice rather made Clara feel as if she was about to face an inquisition.

Clara was allowed into Miss Butler's spartanly furnished rooms. Rather like Clara's office, there was a front and back room, the front overlooking the street and with the biggest window which made it the natural space for Miss Butler's office. There was a small fireplace, unlit as the day was still warm, and a solitary desk with a chair either side. The room was otherwise barren, no paintings to alleviate the cold pale yellow of the walls, no rug on the floor, no ornaments of any description. The room felt unlived in, as if someone had hired it that very morning to use and had not bothered to add their own personal touch to it.

"You can sit," Miss Butler commanded, like a prison wardress accosting her charge.

Clara took a seat.

"Well, why have you come to disturb my peace?" Miss Butler asked, sitting in her own chair.

"Firstly, to apologise," Clara said quickly, before she baulked at the woman's tone and became defensive again. "I have been poking about in your private life."

"You have," Miss Butler agreed coldly. "Going to see my friends, interfering in my business."

Clara's patience was beginning to falter. She was aiming to make amends with the woman, but the woman's tone was causing the devil inside her to start making her wanting to snap back. She drew in a discreet breath of air.

"Perhaps you will give me the chance to explain myself? I will admit it unsettled me to realise there was another female private detective in town, but I was not moved to do anything until I saw your advertisement in the Brighton Gazette and someone handed me one of your business cards," Clara paused, waiting to see the response this statement received.

Miss Butler flicked her head a fraction to the side, her eyes didn't quite meet Clara's.

"What about them?" she said, though her pretence of innocence was not entirely convincing.

Clara now knew the duplication of her advert and cards had been deliberate. Miss Butler was clever enough to know what she was doing. This was not a woman who could be called naïve.

"You copied my own advertisement and business cards

virtually word for word and even used the same design," Clara said, her tone becoming sharp. She had been prepared to forgive naivety, but not this clear calculation. "I was shocked. Perhaps one could say, offended. It made me angry and that anger clouded my judgement."

"There was no harm meant," Miss Butler deferred, though the anxiety on her face said otherwise.

"I think you hoped to tap into my reputation," Clara said coolly. "Or to imply we were somehow connected. But I am prepared to forgive all that, if you are prepared to forgive the snooping I conducted after I discovered the duplication."

Miss Butler laid her hands flat on her desk and considered everything for a moment or two. Slowly she raised her eyes.

"Neither of us has perhaps gotten off to a good start," she said, she had lost the hardness in her tone now she saw that she too had caused offence. "Perhaps I had thought the adverts would encourage people to imagine I had some of your reputation, Miss Fitzgerald. You are, after all, quite renowned in Brighton. When I contemplated starting up my own business I feared I could not compete with you. I therefore tried to use deceit to achieve what I feared my own abilities could not. It was a careless thing to do, and I did not consider it as rationally as I should have done."

"Much the same could be said about my attempts to learn about you," Clara replied, the tension in the air lifting. "When I saw you had copied my advertisements I felt threatened. I created this idea in my head that you were endeavouring to steal all my business. I turned you into some deadly rival in my anxiety and the only way to alleviate my fears was to find out who you were and what you were about. I do regret my antics."

"I do not want to drive you out of business," Miss Butler said gently. "My only desire is to earn a living doing something where I am my own boss. I want to be independent. I suppose I have envied you from afar.

Admired the way you have taken your own life in your hands and made it something that no one else can dent. I don't want to be governed by others, and certainly not men."

"Then we have a lot more in common than we first imagined," Clara now smiled. "We should learn to work together and help each other, rather than try to fight each other. I rather feel we are much more similar than we might have first imagined."

"You could be right," Miss Butler returned the smile. It was hesitant at first, but then she relaxed a little and the grin broadened. "I have wanted to meet you for so long, Miss Fitzgerald."

"Please call me Clara, all my friends do," Clara was suddenly feeling very amenable.

"Then you must call me Sarah," Sarah Butler replied. "And can we agree that there is room for both of us in Brighton?"

"I believe we can," Clara said. "I would much prefer to have you as a friend than an enemy. After all, us independent girls need to stick together. There aren't that many of us and fighting between ourselves would only be counterproductive."

Sarah seemed to expel the tension that had been hanging over her. Her shoulders went down and she no longer had that hard scowl on her face.

"Can I offer you tea?" she said.

"I would like that," Clara nodded. "And then I must discuss the other reason I came here."

"Another reason?" Sarah was surprised.

"I have some information that will be useful to you," Clara explained. "I have my own case to work on, but while I was doing so I came across a snippet of news that would benefit you. I will admit it took me a while to decide whether I should tell you or not."

Sarah looked uncertain again, she seemed to hesitate to get up and fetch the tea. Her trust was easily broken.

"I have no intention of interfering in your case," Clara

promptly said. "But it seemed churlish to withhold this information from you. I won't even advise you what to do with it. I shall purely impart it."

"Now I am curious," Sarah said, rising to deal with the kettle and start the process of making tea. "I only have one case at the moment, that of the missing Mr Butterworth. I imagine you have information concerning him?"

"I do," Clara admitted.

"I am trying to decide if I want to hear it," Sarah Butler fussed with the teapot. "I can't make my mind up if letting you tell me something is not somehow cheating."

"No different to asking a witness for information," Clara pointed out. "I always take my information where I can get it. I can assure you this information came to me quite by chance."

Sarah Butler had that look on her face, the one that meant she was thinking hard and close to refusing Clara's offer of help simply because she felt it rejected her own independence.

"You should never refuse an offer of information," Clara reminded her. "No matter the source. What you do with it afterwards is your own decision."

"All right," Sarah said carefully. "I'll hear you out, but let's go into the back room where it is more comfortable. And it is my decision how I use the information."

"Absolutely," Clara promised. "Independence is assured."

Sarah gave one final nod, then she filled the teapot and showed Clara through to the back room.

Chapter Fourteen

The back room was furnished with a small old sofa. It had the time-worn look of most of the furniture Mr Dunholm put in his properties. There was a hint of mouse about it. Sarah Butler had draped a woollen rug over it to mask most of its failings. Clara and she sat side-by-side on the threadbare seat.

"Now, what have you to tell me?" Sarah asked, offering tea to Clara.

"I know where Mr Butterworth is, unless he has moved again," Clara said, deciding not to beat about the bush. "I was in the police station archives, researching my own case, when Inspector Park-Coombs came to have a word with me about the complaint you had made against me."

"Oh," Sarah Butler said, though she did not apologise for her actions.

"I briefly filled in the inspector on the circumstances surrounding my unfortunate probing into your affairs. In the process I mentioned Mrs Butterworth. You see, that is how I learned of your name in the first place. He was somewhat amused by it all," Clara sighed. "I imagine he thinks I have been terribly silly."

"You should not worry what a man thinks," Sarah

declared stoutly. "They like to make us feel silly."

Clara was not sure if that had been the inspector's intention, but she did not counter her new friend.

"Anyway, I think he was partly amused because, for him, the Butterworth case was done and dusted. Mrs Butterworth reported her husband missing to the police first and they not only followed up the mystery but solved it, at least to their satisfaction," Clara slipped her hand into her bag and pulled out a piece of paper. "The inspector gave me Mr Butterworth's new address. The police have been to see him and report that he does not want to see his wife anymore and, for them, that is that. They have no interest in pursuing the matter further."

Clara gave Sarah the address.

"The police don't like domestic affairs like this," she said, feeling the need to defend the inspector's indifference. "They are more interested in actual crimes."

Sarah took the piece of paper and read the address.

"Thank you," she said cautiously.

"I leave it up to you to decide what best to do with it," Clara told her. "I know nothing about the Butterworth situation, except for a few things I have been told by a certain person who thought they were being helpful towards me."

Sarah stared at the writing on the paper for several moments.

"I feel I have misjudged you Clara," she said thoughtfully. "I imagined you arrogant and someone who would do all they could to hurt a rival. I suppose that was why I mimicked your advertisement. Going on the attack, rather than waiting for you to strike."

"I misjudged you too," Clara answered. "I hope we can move past this now?"

"I believe so," Sarah stood and tucked the piece of paper under a small tin on the mantelpiece. "There are enough cases in town to keep us both busy, and I am not so attracted to the publicity that accompanies some of them. I prefer to keep my name and face out of the papers, other than for my advertisement."

"That is how I began," Clara smiled. "Somehow I found myself solving a murder and everything changed. Though I can't say I court publicity, I much prefer to just get on with my work."

"Why did you decide to become a detective?" Sarah suddenly asked.

Clara almost laughed. The decision seemed a lifetime ago, almost as if it was made by a different person. She had learned a lot along the way, changed a lot, but the reason she became a detective still remained vividly in her mind.

"I lost both parents in the war, and my brother was badly injured. He could not possibly work to provide for us when he came home and my father's investments only covered the bare basics of life. I wanted to employ a nurse for my brother, so I started to cast around for ideas for making money. I didn't want to work away from the house all day, because I had to keep an eye on Tommy. He was quite shaken when he first came home."

"I am sorry to hear that," Sarah sympathised.

"I rather fell into detective work. Someone was missing a cat and there was a reward for finding the creature. I rather fancied I could find it, and I did, though it took some effort. The person was so delighted they doubled the reward. The next thing I knew someone heard of what I had done and asked if I could find their missing pet tortoise. After that I realised I was rather good at solving little mysteries and thought I could make a living by it," Clara laughed to herself, it seemed such a minor thing now. She had never envisioned at the time that she would be solving murders and high stakes robberies. "Now it is your turn. What made you decide to pursue this detective lark?"

Sarah Butler was still standing by the fireplace. She was looking at the small tin box on the mantelpiece. It was the only thing in the room that hinted at personalisation. Clara guessed the box meant something to her.

"It is not easy to hide that I am Scottish," she remarked. "I was born and raised a fisherman's daughter in Aberdeen. My mother died when I was a wee girl and I felt it necessary to look after my father. His grief at her loss near enough destroyed him. I took charge of him, dropped out of school, cleaned the house, cooked his meals and worked when I could at the fishmarket. When I grew older I would travel on a train along the coast with other girls, we would follow the fishing fleets and gut the herring that they would catch. Sometimes I would come to Brighton. I liked the town, it felt homely, but I never gave it much more thought than that.

"I was not inclined to be married. I had offers when I was younger, but I always said I had to look after father. In any case, I did not want to be a fisherman's wife. It was hard enough being a fisherman's daughter. Fishermen go to sea and you have no knowing if they will come back. I know girls widowed before they are twenty-five, with three or four bairns to raise up alone. That sort of life terrified me. I didn't want to be trapped like that."

"I can understand," Clara nodded along. She could well imagine the hardship Sarah was referring to.

"So I carried on as I was," Sarah shrugged. "Some people thought it was sad, that I was trapped with my father and had no future. As if the only future a woman can have is to be a wife and mother. I always had plans, even then. I might have left school, but I kept up my learning. I read books from the library, not novels, but educational books. I had a friend who was a schoolteacher and would give me exercises in maths and English to practice. I didn't know what I was going to do with it all, but I knew I would do something.

"And then father..."

Sarah stopped talking. She picked up the little tin box and cradled it in her hand. It was a tobacco tin, battered about the edges, the image on the lid half worn off. She clutched it tight.

"The thing that everyone related to a fisherman dreads happened," Sarah said softly. "Father went to sea and didn't come back. None of the men on his trawler did. All at once I was truly alone and I had to make a decision as to what I would do with my life.

"Father had paid into a benevolent fund all his years and they provided me with some compensation when he died. I gave up the cottage and I took out all my savings. I couldn't stay in Aberdeen, too many things reminded me of my father. So I moved to the place I had always been enamoured with – Brighton. I thought I would get some shop work at first, but I didn't like the idea of being beholden to anyone. While I was wondering what to do I picked up the newspaper and read about a case you had just solved. And I sat there, thinking to myself 'I could do that.' And that was when I decided to give it a go."

Sarah came to a halt again. She walked across the room and handed the worn tin to Clara.

"Father's tobacco tin," she said. "There wasn't much in way of mementoes to keep of him. I have a picture in my lodging rooms. But I like to keep him close."

Clara turned the tin carefully in her hands and smiled.

"I have a painting of my father in my office," she said. "I like to look up at him and think about what he would do in my situation."

Sarah was amused.

"You were right, we are very similar."

The box was restored to its place on the mantelpiece and the women finished their tea.

"There is a rumour going about that you are investigating a burglary," Sarah said when they were done and she was gathering up their empty teacups.

"That is true," Clara replied. "And it is taking me into some difficult territory."

"Difficult?"

"Dangerous might be the better word," Clara grimaced. "I need to investigate some London criminals. Whether I can get the thing back they stole is another matter."

Sarah frowned.

"I think I will stick with missing husbands," she concluded.

"I would," Clara agreed. "Though even then you never know what trouble you will find yourself in."

Clara made her farewells to Sarah Butler and headed for home, her heart lightened and a weight off her conscience. Clara was glad she had made the trip, she actually rather liked Sarah. She was barely back in her own front door when Annie accosted her.

"The inspector rang, said he had been talking with his colleague in London and had a list of names and addresses for you," Annie was pulling a face that suggested she was not best pleased at having to impart this news. "He says he can't guarantee the men are still at these addresses, but they are the last known locations for them. I don't like the look of this list Clara, the names are dubious to say the least."

"I thought Ugly Dickson a rather amusing nickname," Clara replied lightly. "As long as one has a good sense of humour, that is."

"These are all criminals, aren't they?" Annie demanded.

Clara noted that Tommy and Captain O'Harris were hovering just inside the dining room door and listening to every word.

"I believe they are," Clara said. "Their names have been given as potential suspects in the burglary of Mr Jacobs' house."

"And you intend to go and interview them?" Annie persisted.

Clara gave a small groan and hung up her coat.

"What else am I supposed to do? I have been hired to restore the green jade dragon to its rightful owner and these men are my best lead."

"It was bad enough you going to that awful pub last night," Annie was looking quite worried now. Clara had accidentally let slip where she had been the night before within Annie's hearing range. "I don't like you doing these things Clara. These people are dangerous."

Clara put aside her casual comments to take her friend's concerns seriously. Annie might be the Fitzgeralds' housekeeper, but she was far more than just that. She was the best friend Clara had, the one who would see her through whatever mischief she got herself into. The one who worried when Clara was late home or went off on one of her wild adventures. Clara stepped towards her and put a consoling arm around Annie's shoulder.

"I am going to be sensible," she promised. "I will be taking Bob with me."

"You'll be taking us too," Tommy appeared from the doorway of the dining room, looking sheepish for having been caught eavesdropping. "We are both agreed that we shall accompany you and keep you safe."

Clara managed not to sigh at this new complication. While she appreciated Tommy and O'Harris' honourable intentions, it would be more troublesome to travel about London with three men in tow, rather than just Bob. Clara was well aware that it would be foolish to go alone, but she was satisfied that between her and Bob, they could keep themselves safe.

"We both agreed," Captain O'Harris appeared by Tommy. "That we would insist on joining you."

"To interview three thieves?" Clara appealed to them.

"You will be wandering into dangerous territory. Criminal districts. We insist," Tommy crossed his arms and looked immoveable.

"Well, there you have it Annie. I am in perfectly safe hands," Clara said with amusement.

Annie gave a wan smile. There was the hint of a tear in her eye. She had churned herself up over the thought of Clara deliberately putting herself into such danger.

"You mustn't worry about me so," Clara whispered in her ear. "I am not such a big fool as to run into danger.

Besides, I am handy enough with a poker if I am in trouble."

Annie properly smiled this time as Clara reminded her of an incident from the previous year when she had had to defend herself against a dangerous criminal. She had clobbered him over the head with a fireplace poker and scared him so badly that he had demanded that the police be called to arrest her. Annie looked relieved.

"Now, I suppose I ought to make the arrangements for another trip to London," Clara looked at them all. "Poor Bob will wonder why he ever agreed to help me. He only gets one day off a week and I insist on dragging him to London during it. Oh well, perhaps I ought to bake him a cake as a thank you?"

"I'll bake him a cake," Annie said firmly. "We don't want to kill him off."

Clara pretended to be offended, though her cookery skills were not to be remarked upon. She was just glad to see the smile restored to her friend's face. They agreed not to talk about London criminals anymore and to enjoy dinner when they were, for once, all together. Restoring the green jade dragon to its rightful owner could wait for a little while longer as yet.

Chapter Fifteen

The following Saturday Clara, along with her three protectors, clambered aboard the train from Brighton to London. It was, unsurprisingly, quite crowded, with a lot of people intending to spend their day off in the capital. Clara squeezed between neatly dressed mothers and their overexcited offspring. The odd businessman looked appalled at being forced into the stuffy compartments with day visitors and clearly regretted going to work on a Saturday. Clara was lucky enough to find a compartment where there was room for them all to sit. Captain O'Harris opened a window at once, the autumnal sun making the small space feel like the hot public baths.

"We have names and addresses," Clara addressed her little party, the only other person in the carriage was a gentleman hidden behind a newspaper who was clearly endeavouring to ignore them. Clara still picked her words carefully. "I brought a map and marked the streets we need to go to. I think we should get to them all within the day."

"And when we find the right man?" Tommy asked, looking dubious about the whole affair.

"We ask politely what happened to the dragon," Clara answered, the cynicism in her voice overriding the word 'politely'. They would find their man and extract an answer, one way or another.

The train chugged into London. The sun made the city look more amenable; the grime less grimy, the dust less dusty, the smoke less smoky. They had to catch an omnibus to take them to their first location – walking would simply take too long. They bundled onto the first 'bus they came across and asked how close it would take them to their destination. Clara was delighted to find the omnibus route took them nearly all the way.

The omnibus deposited them in a road crowded with mean terrace houses, the sort where two or three families shared space to try and save money. Clara could imagine Mr Dunholm owning places like these and squeezing every penny he could from the occupants. They walked along the road, avoiding heaps of rags and broken belongings piled in the gutter. A man with one leg and one eye sat huddled on the pavement, rocking himself back and forth. Tommy grimaced to see the man's war medals pinned proudly to his chest. He dug into his pocket and produced a shilling, but when he tried to give it to the man he seemed not to be aware of their presence. He just continued to rock himself back and forth. Tommy slipped the shilling into the man's jacket pocket and hoped he would notice it later.

They carried on down the road, turning into an even narrower street where young children danced in the dirt, the toddlers among them almost naked, and the older ones barefoot. They glanced up at Clara's party with strangely old faces.

"This is the address," Clara paused before a small, black building. A worn door bore no number, but Clara had been given a description of the place. A rat sat on the doorstep and glared at them boldly, before they got too close and it scurried away. Captain O'Harris gave a low sigh, somewhere between disgust and despair.

Clara knocked on the door. Bob positioned himself right behind her, looking big and mean to confront whoever came to the door. As it happened it was a child of about ten. Clara stared down into a skinny little face with a suspicious pair of dark eyes that seemed unnatural on one so young.

"I've come to see Frank Dickson," Clara explained to the little girl.

"Can't," the girl answered, drawing a long sniff through her nose. "Ain't here."

"What a shame," Clara said, feigning disappointment. "And just when I was prepared to pay him a bob or two for his services. We shall have to find someone else for the job. Where does that gentleman Knacker live that you mentioned Bob?"

The hint of money, and the possibility of it going to a rival thief, spurred on the girl. Her eyes widened with excitement, though for the most part she kept her emotions controlled. She turned her head and bellowed into the house;

"Ma! Someone to see Uncle Frank!"

A woman appeared in the small hallway of the property. She shoved the girl back from the door roughly and glowered at her visitors.

"What do you want?"

"To speak with Frank Dickson, Ugly Dickson as he is called. About a job in Brighton," Clara explained quickly. "There is money in it for him."

"Well you won't find him here," snapped the woman.

"Where might I find him?" Clara said, starting to lose her patient with the tight-lipped residents of the property.

"Manchester nick," the woman snorted.

Clara was thrown for just a moment.

"He is inside?" she said, her hopes of finding her thief this early on diminishing.

"That's right," the woman answered. "Got himself caught trying to rob a house up there with his mates. He got five years, stupid fool."

"How long has he been inside?" Bob asked in his gravelly voice.

The woman glanced up at him and her stance changed. Bob was rather like a big bear standing beside Clara, there was an air of menace about him. You had the impression that, if he wanted to, Bob could be very mean.

"Six months," the woman told him, some of her surliness gone.

"Then he can't be the one," Clara crossed Frank Dickson's name off her list.

She thanked the woman and passed her a shilling for her trouble. The woman almost spat at her, but Bob's presence kept her at bay.

The next address on Clara's list was only a few roads over. They walked along streets that all started to look the same. Captain O'Harris seemed to be finding it quite revelatory. He had lived a privileged life, even if his younger days had been overshadowed by the fear of poverty caused by his father marrying an actress and being disinherited. But the wealthy rarely reach the level of poverty that the truly poor do and the O'Harrises had always kept a smart house, even if their façade of respectability masked the crippling debt of their real circumstances. O'Harris looked about him with an expression of perpetual mild shock on his face. Clara wondered if it was perhaps helping to put his own issues into perspective. Sometimes it took seeing the strife others were in to realise that your own life was not so rotten.

They came to the property of John Knacker, aka Knacker's Yard, aka Scrawny Jim, and Clara knocked on another well-worn door. This time an elderly gentleman answered. He walked with a stick, or perhaps it would be better to say that he shuffled. He gazed at them with an anxious expression, he was almost bent in two by a chronically bad back and the necessity of hobbling with a too short stick.

"Yes?"

"I was hoping to see John Knacker," Clara said gently, feeling the man needed a kind hand to remove some of the fear in his eyes.

The old man jammed his lips together in a thin line.

"Will you be wanting me to take you to him?" he asked.

"If you wouldn't mind," Clara said.

The old man nodded, and asked them to wait while he fetched his hat and coat. He didn't, however, change out of his carpet slippers. He eased himself out of his front door, every step painful and with the risk of him falling into a heap on the ground. O'Harris politely offer him his arm, but the man refused. Hunched up and with great difficulty he led the party down the road. Clara was beginning to feel bad for asking him to take them to the man.

"If you want to just give us directions..." she suggested.

"I'll take you," the old man insisted. "I haven't seen John today anyway. I pay him a visit every day, usually."

For every few shuffling steps the old man took, the others took one. Slowly but surely, watched by curious children and the odd cat, they made it to the bottom of the road and turned right, finally coming to a churchyard on the opposite side. The old man hobbled through the gate.

"Getting there," he told his followers, his breath coming in short rasps. "What was it you wanted to see John about anyway?"

"I was hoping he could help me find something," Clara said cryptically.

"I'm afraid, he probably won't be able to help much," the old man had walked up the path of the churchyard and then moved onto the verge, pausing before a gravestone that had been recently erected. There he stood and waited for the others.

Bob was bemused, he wondered why they had stopped, but Clara understood. She came beside the old man and looked at the headstone simply marked 'John Knacker, beloved son, 1889 – 1921.'

"How did it happen, Mr Knacker?" Clara asked the old man quietly.

"Fell from a roof. He was trying to break in a window, only someone spotted him and pushed him," Mr Knacker stared at his son's headstone and grimaced. "Sorry I deceived you, but I don't like coming up here alone. I'm alone a lot these days."

Clara laid a hand on his shoulder, trying to comfort him.

"I'm very sorry, Mr Knacker."

"Why couldn't he get a respectable job, huh?" the old man let a tear slip down his cheek. "He had an education, after all."

Clara could not offer him an explanation. She just stood with him while he mourned.

"Two down, one to go," Tommy remarked after they had returned Mr Knacker to his house. "Lucky last?"

"Let's hope," Clara replied. She had taken out her map and was referring to it as they made their way to the last of their potential candidates for dragon theft.

Stumpy Pete, real name Petroski Lenikof, lived on the top floor of a tenement building. When Clara asked for him at the door, his landlady pointed up the stairs without saying a word. It seemed she did not speak much English. The little group wandered upstairs and found Petroski's door open. He spotted them on the landing from where he was lounging on an old sofa.

"What you want?" he demanded nervously.

"Nothing sinister, just information," Clara assured him, stepping inside the room which smelt of onions and body sweat. "I am trying to find the man responsible for the burglary of a property in Brighton last week. I don't mean him any trouble, I just want to ask who employed him."

"Well, you look in wrong place," Petroski declared, then he rolled up his trouser leg to reveal a heavily bandaged ankle.

"I fall down stairs," he added in way of explanation. "I

fracture it. Is just out of plaster."

Clara now noticed the crutch by the sofa. Mr Lenikof had not been climbing through any windows recently. Clara thanked him for his time and began to leave.

"I give you information!" Petroski said swiftly.

Clara turned back to him.

"For money," he added.

"All right," Clara agreed, guessing the man was down on his luck and perilously close to being thrown out of his room by the landlady for not paying his rent. He would do anything for a little bit of money. "As long as it is honest information."

Bob lumbered through the doorway to back up her caveat with the mild threat of his presence. Petroski's eyes wandered to the man automatically.

"I give you good information," he promised.

"Have you heard about someone from London going to Brighton to commit a burglary?" Clara asked.

Petroski nodded.

"Is small world," he said. "Thief steals jade dragon to order."

Clara felt a pang of hope. If Petroski knew that much, then perhaps he knew who was behind the burglary.

"Go on," she said.

"Thief working for important man," Petroski nodded solemnly. "Man ask for me first, but…"

Petroski glowered at his damaged ankle.

"Would have been good money," he muttered. "I am best thief in London. I climb through narrow, narrow spaces."

Petroski raised his hands and used them to indicate the small spaces he could squeeze through.

"I am best," Petroski insisted. "I train in Polish circus. I am acrobat. But I can't help man, so he goes for second best."

Petroski was clearly bitter about this and felt he had been unfairly bypassed.

"Who is the second best?" Clara asked diplomatically.

The man's pride was clearly ruffled.

"Second best is Englishman," Petroski sneered. "Not circus trained. Just amateur. Simon Clark."

Petroski expelled the name from his mouth as if it tasted bad.

"Where can I find him?" Clara asked, ignoring his expression.

"In Chinese district. He poppy lover," Petroski mimed the act of someone smoking a pipe.

"Opium?" Clara said.

"When not working, he smoke," Petroski agreed. "All his money go on poppy. My money I send back to family in Poland."

Petroski looked proud of this statement, overlooking the fact that his money was earned through criminal activities.

"I am professional," he reiterated. "Simon Clark just a fool!"

Professional pride and a desire for money had made Petroski talk freely and for that Clara was grateful. She politely asked how far he was behind in his rent and how much it was. Then she gave him three bob, enough to cover his debts and tide him over for another month or so. Petroski beamed at her and called her a very kind lady, and insisted that, should she ever have call for a nimble, slender thief, she must come to him at once. Clara agreed she would, actually taking a shine to the Polish criminal with his deep-set professional pride.

The group headed back downstairs and outside. Clara glanced at her watch. It was only just noon.

"I suggest we eat some lunch and then head for the Chinese district of London. I didn't even know London had such a thing," she said.

"Lots of Chinese immigrants in London," Bob explained. "They like to live together, so eventually you get areas where all the residents are Chinese."

"And the Chinese run the best opium dens," Captain O'Harris said darkly. When everyone looked at him he clarified his statement. "Before I went off to war, I went with several other of my fellow pilots to ease our nerves at an opium den. Never again. I felt out of my head for days after."

"Well, that is where we are headed next. But lunch first, agreed?"

Everyone agreed to that, so they carried on with Clara's map guiding their path, keeping their eyes open for a suitable venue to pause for some dinner.

Chapter Sixteen

The Chinese district of London was certainly an eye-opener. It didn't look like London for a start. All the shops had Chinese characters over their doors and were painted in shades of red, green and gold. Strange oriental arches seemed to come out of nowhere and shadow the street, and everyone was wearing robes of exotic colours. There was the odd Englishman or woman wandering about, buying unusual goods from the open market or popping into the shops, but mostly this area had the feel of another land. Clara was flummoxed, especially as neither she nor any of her companions spoke Chinese.

"How do we find Simon Clark?" she said to them, looking around the market where chickens squawked from cages and peculiar fruits and vegetables sat in crates waiting to be bought.

"Someone will soon point us in the direction of an opium den," Captain O'Harris said knowledgeably. "Finding the right opium den is another matter."

"There is more than one?" Clara said, not sure whether to be appalled or dismayed.

"And finding an Englishman in them is rather like finding tea leaves in a teapot," O'Harris admitted. "The Chinese cater as much for the English as they do their own people. We might need a guide."

That was all well and good to say, but finding a guide in the packed streets was not so simple. Most of the residents seemed to want to avoid the lost little group of English folk, who gave the impression of souls on a Sunday outing. Clara had the feeling they were being laughed at for their hopeless ignorance behind their backs. They exited the market and drifted down a side street that offered some respite from the hustle and bustle and noise of the main roads. There was something unsettling about being bombarded by loud voices speaking a language you could not understand.

The side street was virtually empty except for an old woman sitting on a doorstep. She was smoking a clay pipe while peeling potatoes, depositing the skinned vegetables into a large wicker basket. Clara went over to her, ever hopeful.

"Excuse me, could you direct me to the nearest opium den?" she asked, cringing at how silly her words sounded. No wonder people were laughing at her when she sounded so very much like a lost tourist.

The old woman made no response, did not even look up at Clara.

"Opium den?" Clara said, a bit louder thinking the woman might be deaf. With the level of noise she lived in, it would not surprise Clara if her hearing had been battered badly by it all. "You know, poppies?"

The woman smoked and peeled potatoes. She had a faint smile on her face.

"She won't answer you."

Clara glanced to her left at the new voice. A girl, late teens, leaned against a wall. She had just appeared from the doorway of a house. She was Chinese and very pretty, wearing a blue robe with wide sleeves, and her dark hair plaited down her back.

"She has lost her marbles," the girl tapped the side of her head. "But as long as she has potatoes to peel she is no bother."

"You speak good English," Clara complimented her.

"I am English," the girl shrugged. "So far as this country is concerned. My parents and I were born here. I went to an ordinary school and spoke English for my lessons. I speak Chinese as well, naturally."

The girl was confident, bordering on arrogance. She had a poise to her that was both becoming and disturbing, for it spoke of a mind much older than its years.

"Why do you want an opium den?" the girl asked. "Don't you know those places are the Devil's work."

Now that sounded very English, straight out of some Bible class. Clara smiled at the girl.

"I don't want to visit an opium den, as such. I am looking for someone and I was told the best place to find him was in an opium den."

"Ah," the girl seemed to understand. "Do you know which one?"

Clara shook her head.

"There are a dozen in this area," the girl clucked her tongue. "You are going to have a long search. Who are you looking for?"

"An Englishman called Simon Clark," Clara explained, seeing no reason to hide the name.

The girl pricked up her ears.

"I know who that is. Simon Clark spends a lot of time in the Chinese district," the girl nodded. "Every Chinese person knows Clark. He is a common sight going about. I also know which dens are his favourite. Shall I show you?"

"If you wouldn't mind," Clara said, relieved to have a guide who seemed to know what she was doing.

The Chinese girl led them along the road and through several tight passageways, talking all the time.

"Is Clark in trouble?"

"Not exactly," Clara answered. "I just need information from him."

"I don't much care if he is in trouble, anyway," the girl assured her. "Clark owes my father a lot of money and won't pay it. He threatened my father when he asked for the money. I don't like Clark."

Clara was sensing she may have just made an unexpected ally.

"My name is Jasmine," the girl continued. "It's a compromise. Sounds English, but with an oriental slant."

"I am Clara, this is Bob, my brother Tommy and Captain O'Harris," Clara responded.

"Captain of a ship?" Jasmine asked curiously.

"No, I was in the air service during the war," O'Harris explained. "What they now are calling the RAF."

Jasmine took on board this information but did not make further comment.

"This is a den," she announced as they came to a door down a side alley.

Jasmine didn't bother to knock, she just opened the door and escorted them in. Clara was struck at first by the fragrant smoke that hung about the entire room almost like a fog. She found herself anxious not to breath it in, lest she find herself out of her head as Captain O'Harris had described. There were couches and piles of cushions strewn all about the room. Reclining on them were a range of gentlemen, some Chinese, others English. Most seemed lost in a daze, their jaws slack, their eyes gazing into the opium mist as if they were seeing some magnificent vision. Perhaps they were. Clara wondered how people could just abandon themselves to such lethargy. For the perpetually busy Clara, such inactivity was anathema and made her twitch just looking at it.

Jasmine had gone straight over to an old Chinese woman and was saying something in her sharp native tongue. Clara had no hope of following the conversation, not with the clipped syllables and strange elongations the two women were making of their words. Jasmine finally returned.

"Not here, he owes them too much money," she said, a grin lighting up her eyes. "They won't let him in through the door."

Jasmine escorted them from the first den to another, and then another after that. At each she asked her question and was greeted by a shake of the head, or sometimes by an irate rant from the owner of the den. Simon Clark appeared to accrue a lot of debts, certainly he was rather unpopular among the opium dealers.

"I have an idea," Jasmine said as they departed from the fourth such den and Clara uneasily looked at the time on her watch. "There is a den recently opened. Let's try there, maybe they haven't worked out Clark is a bad payer yet."

Jasmine took them on another circuitous route through the back streets. Clara was beginning to wonder how the girl knew so much about the opium dens, but was not in the mood to ask. It wouldn't be much longer before they would need to catch the last train back to Brighton. Time was running out and Clara did not want to leave London without something to show for her day's excursion.

They came to a building much like all the rest and once again Jasmine marched in without a hint of trepidation. Clara briskly followed. By now she was growing used to the opium smoke and, while she did feel a little light-headed, she could not say that it was affecting her dangerously. Clara waited impatiently while Jasmine went to talk to the owner of the place.

"Wild goose chase, springs to mind," Tommy puttered. He had done a lot of walking that day and his legs, still suffering from his war wounds, were complaining.

Clara wished she could counter his statement, but she was feeling the same way. Maybe Simon Clark was in his lodgings or, worse, stuck in a prison cell. This might, after all, be another red herring.

Clara was about to suggest they give up when Jasmine ran up to them looking excited.

"He's here," she said. "In a side room. I told you they don't know he is a bad payer yet."

Clara breathed out a sigh of relief. Now all they had to do was drag the man out of here and ask him some questions.

"Show us, Jasmine."

Jasmine showed Clara to the side room, which was really just a partitioned section of the main room with curtains draped over the front to afford privacy. The owner of the opium den followed them, complaining about something. Jasmine shot a few words at her, but the woman lingered nearby, watching their every move.

Pulling back the heavy curtain, Jasmine revealed a man lying on a pile of cushions. He looked like someone had just dropped him there. His arms sprawled out either side of him, one still clutching the mouthpiece of the opium pipe, which was a largish device somewhat like an Arab hookah. The man's head was thrown back, falling off the cushions. His mouth gagged open and his eyes were rolled up in his skull.

"Is he dead?" Clara asked in astonishment.

"Probably not," Jasmine clambered over the cushions and slapped the back of her hand on the man's cheeks.

The opium den's owner began to putter again. Clara shut her up by handing her some money.

"We'll have to sober him up before he can talk," O'Harris observed grimly.

"First things first, we get him out of here," Clara strode into the room and bent down by Simon Clark. She felt his cheek first and was reassured by its warmth. "He's breathing. Though if he stays like this for long he might not be. He could easily choke to death in that position."

O'Harris joined Clara and Jasmine as they heaved Simon Clark upwards. He was a dead weight and Bob wandered in to help. Eventually the unconscious man was slung between the shoulders of O'Harris and Bob. They dragged him from the room and negotiated around recumbent figures until they found the door and made their way outside. The den owner, Clara's money safely in her hand, did nothing to try and stop them.

"What now?" O'Harris asked, readjusting the weight of Clark on his shoulder. "We'll need to take him somewhere."

Clara found herself hesitating; where could they take him? Perhaps there was a hotel or lodging house where they might rent a room for a short time, but she didn't like the idea of too many people seeing her consorting with Clark and reporting her 'interview' to those who had commissioned the robbery. She knew she was dealing with powerful people, the sort of people who had money and no qualms about hiring a thief to steal someone else's property. Clara didn't want her name getting back to them too soon. Not until she was ready to confront them, at least. Dragging the unconscious Clark into a hotel would make her activities all too obvious.

Jasmine was looking at them curiously, assessing them and their dilemma. She was also eyeing up Simon Clark, who was standing before her (if you could call it standing) completely helpless. She had not forgotten how he had threatened her father, nor how frightened her father had been. Jasmine, on the contrary, did not frighten easily and had been looking for a way to revenge the wrong Clark had done her family for some time.

"Bring him to my rooms," she said. "Father works in the shop until late. No one will be there apart from us."

Clara hesitated. It was a way out for her, but she was concerned about putting the girl into danger. Simon Clark, from what she had gathered, was not a nice piece of work.

"I don't know…" she started, but Jasmine interrupted her.

"Where else will you take him?" she asked. "He'll need tea and probably something to eat to rouse him enough to talk to you. I don't see you have a choice but to accept my help."

Clara suspected she was right.

"Could we make a decision?" O'Harris moaned. "This man is surprisingly heavy and he smells like a wet dog."

133

Bob turned his head and sniffed Clark to confirm what O'Harris had said.

"He's right," he agreed.

"All right, we'll take him to Jasmine's rooms," Clara conceded reluctantly.

Jasmine seemed delighted by this pronouncement, but Clara shared an anxious look with Tommy. He shrugged his shoulders, they were running out of options.

It seemed a long walk back to where they had first been introduced to Jasmine. O'Harris grumbled every time Clark's dragging feet hooked on a loose stone or scrap of rubbish. Bob didn't seem to notice the burden. Clara suspected he could carry the recumbent man all by himself if he wished, but did not want to offend O'Harris' pride by doing so. Everyone was filmed in a layer of sweat by the time they reached the side road where the old Chinese lady was quietly peeling her potatoes.

"I think he is waking up!" O'Harris announced sharply.

Jasmine hurried to open the door to her lodgings and directed the party up the stairs with eager flicks of her hand. They clunked Clark up the steps, his feet catching on every single one. Jasmine slipped past them and hurried forward to open a door. By now O'Harris was weary and even Bob looked tired. As they negotiated their load through the doorway, they clipped Clark's head on the doorpost. He opened his eyes, gave a delayed cry of pain and started to take in his surroundings.

"Quick, tie him to this chair!" Jasmine pulled a wooden chair into the middle of the room and Clark was dropped onto it.

He was beginning to take an interest in what was going on as they hurried to use some washing line to fasten his hands to the back of the chair, and then his ankles to the chair legs. Simon Clark was coming alert fast. He pulled at his tied wrists and scowled around at them.

"Hey! What's going on?" he demanded.

Clara placed herself before him.

"Mr Clark. Nice to meet you. I have a few questions I would like you to answer for me."

Chapter Seventeen

Simon Clark was everything you might expect from a professional criminal and opium addict. He was scrawny, the sort of scrawny that looks close to being considered emaciated. The opium no doubt kept hunger at bay, with the result that he was skin and bones. But Simon did not mind that because he had made a career for himself specialising in getting into places that other people could not. Eating was a professional hazard, so he didn't touch food unless absolutely necessary. There was not an ounce of fat on the man and that was just the way Simon liked it.

He was not overly tall, which was another benefit for his thievery. His face mimicked his body, being merely a layer of skin over the bone of his skull. He had unpleasantly defined cheekbones and a slight overbite which, with his taut skin, meant his front teeth were prone to protruding from his mouth even when it was closed. He had cut his hair close to the scalp and could have passed easily for a victim of starvation, had he wished.

Simon's outer appearance did not inspire friendliness and his personality didn't help. Mean, selfish and bitter towards the world, Simon saw everything in terms of how it benefited him. He cared little for people, they were just a means to earning money. He ran up debt because often he was skint and his opium addiction cost the earth. But he hardly cared. When he had used up all the credit he was allowed at one place, he simply moved on to the next. There was always someone gullible enough to accept his promises to pay later. And when he did do a job and had some ready money, he would pay off some of his debts and restore himself in the eyes of those he had previously bled dry. Simon was good at persuading people that this time he would pay them promptly.

He took a good look at Clara as he sat in the chair, hands tied behind his back. He was angry already and the woman before him was only making things worse by the way she glared at him. He was not impressed and not inclined to talk.

"Let me go!" he demanded.

"I have it on good authority that you burgled a house in Brighton the other week," Clara ignored his demand.

Simon Clark wriggled in his chair.

"What is this? You want money?" Simon glowered at the men around him, then his eyes settled on Jasmine. "Is this your father's doing? Where is the squinty-eyed runt!"

"This has everything to do with me," Clara stepped right in front of him and spoke. "Look at me when I am speaking to you."

Simon Clark looked squarely into Clara's face, then he spat at her. In truth, she had been half expecting such a response and did not satisfy him by flinching in surprise. However, he did earn the indignation of Bob, who rested one large meat-slab of a hand on his shoulder. Bob rather looked like he could eat Simon Clark and still have room for pudding. Just the weight of his hand on Simon's shoulder made the thief reconsider his antagonism.

Clara wiped her face with a handkerchief.

"And all I wanted was a nice little chat," she grumbled in mock disappointment. "Bob was hoping you could give me all the answers I wanted."

Bob squeezed Simon's shoulder a little too hard,

making the bony man wince. That was the problem with a lack of fat, each touch went straight to the bone. Tommy and O'Harris moved to stand behind Clara and they too had a mean look in their eyes. They had both been on the verge of reacting to Simon's disrespect of Clara, but Bob had beaten them to it, and Bob was an expert at silent intimidation.

"He's like a puppet," Bob remarked, his large fingers further squeezing into Simon's shoulder. "Like a wooden puppet. No flesh on him at all. How does he not break anything when he moves about?"

Clara could see Bob's face, and knew the question had been purely innocent, a casual remark that didn't imply anything. But Simon took it as a threat, a hint that if he didn't behave bones might get broken. In the world Simon lived in, that was a very real possible ending to a conversation. Some of his defiance evaporated.

"Shall we try again?" Clara asked him sweetly. "The other week you committed a burglary in Brighton, yes?"

"What of it?" Simon growled, deciding that she already knew he was responsible and he had nothing to lose by admitting to it. "You aren't the police, why do you want to know?"

"Correct, I am not the police. The police have lost interest, just another burglary with no clues left behind. They don't have the time to dabble around in these affairs like I do," Clara smiled. "I am looking for the green jade dragon. I am going to restore it to its rightful owner. You are going to help me, because it is in your best interest to do so."

Simon cast a sideways look at Bob. The man seemed built of bricks.

"I might have been in Brighton," he said, reluctantly.

"Please don't play games," Clara gave a bored sigh. "I know you robbed the house, now all I want to know is who employed you to do so?"

"I was working off me own back," Simon said quickly, too quickly.

Clara narrowed her eyes at him, though Simon was keeping a close watch on Bob and did not notice.

"You travelled all the way to Brighton on the off-chance you would find a house to burgle?" she said, incredulously.

"No, I had heard of the place," Simon answered. "Heard it had nice stuff in it."

"And you went to all that effort," Clara countered, "to steal just one small object? You could have filled a bag with dozens of things from that house, enough to keep you in opium for years. And you just stole one thing?"

Simon Clark realised how ridiculous he sounded, but he insisted on playing along.

"Yeah," he said.

"Pretty rubbish thief then, aren't you?" Clara scowled at him. "You had an opportunity to make a small fortune and instead you stole one object. The one object in the house, in fact, that was the rarest and therefore potentially the easiest to trace by someone looking for it, should it happen to come up on the open market."

Clara paused for a second to let this information sink in.

"Who did you pawn it to?" she asked.

"No one."

"Then who did you fence it to?" Clara rephrased her question, in case Simon was trying to be clever by being pedantic.

"I didn't fence it," Simon barked back.

"So you still have it?" Clara queried. "Where is it? Hidden in your lodgings? You can take us to it."

"No, look, I don't have it!" Simon squirmed in his bonds, playing coy was only buying him so much time and he had yet to figure out how to escape. His hands he might be able to work free, his legs were another matter and the second he tried anything the three men in the room would be all over him like dogs on a fox. He could see that all very well. Simon thought it might be time to offer them something, to start to negotiate. "I sold it."

"Who to?" Clara asked.

"A man," Simon shrugged as well as his bonds would allow. "I didn't get his name."

Bob's meaty hand clenched on his shoulder.

"I was hoping to be home for my supper," he said in a sad little voice, loud enough they could all hear. "I don't like missing my supper. I don't like it when people make me miss my supper."

Simon felt his chest tighten in anxiety, he took a breath through clenched teeth.

"You need to start being more specific. You really ought to remember who you sold the dragon to," Clara said patiently. "Unless you did not sell it. Perhaps you gave it to the person who hired you?"

"I worked alone," Simon hissed, but he was no longer sounding convincing.

"Can I hit him," Bob said with a forlorn sigh. "He isn't going to say anything until I hit him, and I am getting fed up."

"So am I," remarked O'Harris. "The fellow is a little weasel and he will lie through his teeth to you unless you start getting mean."

"I was hoping this would not come down to violence," Clara told them both. "I thought Mr Clark would have the sense to talk."

"Clearly not," O'Harris snorted. "I don't usually hold with torture, but this little man has rather gotten under my skin."

"If you won't hit him, I will!" Jasmine appeared at the side of the group holding a metal ladle. "I've been wanting to hit him since he threatened my father."

The ladle was of the stout iron kind, it was probably decades old. The sort of household item that is so robust that it is inherited by generation after generation with barely a notch or a scratch on it. Simon's eyes widened as he looked at the culinary weapon that Jasmine waggled dangerously.

"For the moment, no one is hitting anyone," Clara put

out her hands to calm her friends. "Mr Clark will clearly have enough sense, given time, to realise it is best to speak honestly with us. The sooner he does so, the sooner he can go back to his opium with all his fingers and toes intact."

Simon turned his full attention on her, a nasty snarl forming on his lips.

"Supposing I did work for someone else?" he said. "What do you think they will do to me if they find out I told you?"

"I don't know," Clara shrugged honestly. "But first they have to find out and catch you. In contrast, we already have you. The question you have to ask yourself is whether the danger you imagine happening is more frightening than the very real danger you are currently in."

Clara allowed this to sink in to her captive, who looked around at all the faces maliciously scowling at him. Except for Bob. Bob seemed bored and gave Simon a smile and a friendly squeeze of the shoulder which threatened to break bones.

"Nothing personal, on my part," Bob explained. "I'm just helping."

Simon felt that somehow made things worse.

"I've had enough," Jasmine declared and she swung the ladle and would have very nearly smashed in Simon's nose had Tommy not guessed what was to occur and grabbed her arm at the last minute. The ladle swung barely an inch from Simon's face, and he could feel the whistle of air as it went past. The thought of that heavy iron spoon cracking into his face, breaking bone and teeth was enough to make him reconsider his silence.

"I was hired by Mr Earling!" he said swiftly. "He acts like an agent for thieves and other criminals. Who employed him I don't know, but he hired me!"

Jasmine pulled herself out of Tommy's arms with a huff of affront, but she winked at Clara. Clara managed not to grimace. The girl was a little too wild.

"What did he say when he hired you?" Clara turned to Simon instead.

"He gave me an address, said the only way to get in was this small window, hence why I was hired. People had been watching the house for days."

"People hired by Mr Earling?"

"No," Simon shook his head. "Mr Earling only hired me. The rest was done by the people who worked for the guy who employed Mr Earling. Whoever this guy was, he had his finger on every action, from the guys scoping out the place, to learning the routine of the victim and his staff. Only thing he didn't have was someone who could climb through a window like me."

"How do I find Mr Earling?" Clara asked next.

"I don't know," Simon shrugged. "You don't find Mr Earling, he finds you. Look, he said there was a job that would suit me. It would pay me well, only I had to swear I would not steal anything but the item I was told to. They didn't want anyone to realise the place had been burgled too quick. I promised and Mr Earling was satisfied I was trustworthy. He gets me a lot of work, and if I had broke my word he would never have hired me again."

Simon shuffled in his chair, trying in vain to move away from Bob.

"I knew something was up with it all. There was too much money involved," he moaned to himself.

"You know nothing else?" Clara persisted, hoping to wring out one last drop of information from Simon.

But Simon Clark had told him what little he knew. Mr Earling never gave out more information to his hirelings than was necessary.

"I was told to sneak in and steal this green dragon. I was told where the window was and shown a map of the place. I knew exactly which door to go through and where the display case was," Simon shrugged helplessly. "I had exact instructions. I was to leave everything as I found it. The only thing I could not help was the glass from the smashed window."

Clara could see that the burglary had been extremely well planned, and Simon Clark was merely the helper in this affair. He was of no further use to her.

"All right, I'm satisfied," Clara informed her friends. "We can let him go."

Bob started to untie Simon's bindings.

"Now you are a wealthy man, Clark," Jasmine loomed over the figure in the chair with her ladle, "you might think about paying my father what you owe him?"

"I don't see…" Clark began, but he had no time to finish that statement because Jasmine clobbered him over the head with the ladle so hard his ears rang. "All right! You damn bitch! Take the money from my pocket!"

Jasmine did exactly that. She had taken the exact money her father was owed just as Bob finished with the rope and Simon leapt to his feet and fled out the door. Clara let out a whistle of breath. She glanced at Jasmine who was smiling at the money in her hand.

"Did you have to hit him?" Clara asked.

Jasmine grinned at her.

"What next Clara?" O'Harris asked, unperturbed by the girl's actions. "Find this Mr Earling?"

Clara looked at her watch.

"We are out of time. Besides, finding this Mr Earling might be tricky. We should head back to Brighton and plan our next move."

They thanked Jasmine for her help and the use of her lodgings, then hastened out to find an omnibus and get back to the train station.

"Interesting girl," Tommy remarked to them all as they hurried.

"Violent!" Clara replied sharply.

"I bet she makes a good soup with that ladle!" Tommy laughed.

They put aside thoughts of Jasmine and her wild antics as they rushed away, perilously close to missing their train. Clara tried not to think too much as she moved. There was still a lot to do in London and it felt wrong to be leaving so soon, but she had no other choice. She would come back, and on her next visit she would be paying a call on this Mr Earling, to discover just who was behind the disappearance of the green jade dragon.

Chapter Eighteen

Clara slept a little on the train ride home. Her dreams were dark; slender men roamed through darkened houses and strangely formed dragons loomed around corners. She woke herself with a start just as they were pulling into Brighton's train station.

After all he had done to help them, it was natural to invite Bob home to supper. Bob lived alone, so the invitation was warmly received. Clara popped into the station office and asked to use their telephone. After some wrangling over the cost, she was allowed to make a brief call home to inform Annie they were on their way and were all sound and hearty. Annie sounded most relieved.

The day had turned wet and rain fell down as they hurried the last few steps to Clara's house. Tommy was stiff from all the walking he had done, but tried not to complain. Clara gave him a sympathetic smile and locked her arm through his. O'Harris seemed quiet too. Clara watched as he walked ahead of them, seeming lost in his own thoughts. She worried about him after his nervous breakdown. She hoped the visit to London had not shaken him.

Annie greeted them on the doorstep with the sort of smile usually reserved for travellers who have been away for months, not hours. But then Annie hated people straying too far from home.

"I have made a steak and kidney pudding," she informed them as they appeared. "With lots of potatoes, fresh peas and extra gravy. And there is a blancmange for dessert."

She shuffled them inside, took coats and hats without allowing arguments and herded her little company into the dining room.

"I cooked some fresh bread rolls, as well," Annie pointed to a basket of rolls on the table and the butter dish all waiting for them.

"You have been busy," Tommy grinned settling himself gratefully into a chair. There was a joyous yelp and Bramble, the Fitzgeralds' small poodle, dived into his lap and smothered him with canine affection.

"That dog has pined all day!" Annie declared. "He hates everyone being out."

Clara thought, but did not say, that Bramble and Annie had an awful lot in common.

Dinner was served and everyone ate hungrily. Annie made sure Bob had extra helpings, as she worried he did not get enough home cooked meals. Considering the size of the fellow, Clara did not think she need fear. But Bob hardly argued as Annie thrust more pudding and potatoes onto his plate. Clara was relieved to see that O'Harris ate well too. Whatever thoughts had been swirling in his mind as they left the station no longer seemed to disturb him.

They were just consuming the blancmange when there was a loud rapping on the door. Annie put down her spoon crossly.

"Who calls at this hour? Surely everyone is eating their dinner?" she complained.

"Don't answer it," Clara suggested promptly, thinking that for once they were entitled to some peace.

But the person on the doorstep hammered on the wood again, bouncing the door knocker so fiercely against the wood Clara envisioned scars forming in the paint. Annie could not ignore such a summons. She rose from her chair and went to see who it was. Clara took another spoonful of blancmange, one ear open for voices. More often than not, an urgent rapping on the door meant someone wanted her. The voices from the hallway were muffled, but there was an agitation to one of them that implied to Clara that someone was not happy. Annie reappeared in the dining room.

"There is a man on the doorstep demanding to see you, Clara. His name is Mr Butterworth."

Clara put down her spoon, undecided for a moment whether to interrupt her dinner, but she supposed she ought to.

"He sounds upset." Clara mused to Annie.

"He is. I can send him away?"

"No, send him through to the parlour."

Clara excused herself from the table. She waited until Annie returned to the dining room before heading to the parlour herself. She closed the door behind her as she entered, guessing that Mr Butterworth would appreciate the privacy.

Mr Butterworth was a man in his middle years; a little bald, a little plump and a little short. He was the sort of nondescript person who, a few seconds after meeting them, you promptly forget. He was trying to coax a moustache to grow on his upper lip, but it didn't appear to be working.

"Mr Butterworth," Clara held out her hand to shake.

Mr Butterworth was too agitated to respond, he was pacing back and forth before her fireplace.

"How could you do it?" he demanded of her, waving his arms up and down. "What business was it of yours?"

"I'm sorry, but I don't quite know what you are referring to?" Clara said, though she had a hunch.

"You told my wife where I was living!" Mr Butterworth pointed a finger at her. "Isn't a man entitled to his privacy?"

"Mr Butterworth, I did nothing of the sort," Clara assured him.

Mr Butterworth continued to pace.

"She said she hired a detective to find me. Her very own words! That's how I know it was you!"

Clara was beginning to realise that here was a perfect example of the extra complication having two detectives in Brighton could cause.

"She did not hire me, Mr Butterworth," Clara persisted. "You can ask her that yourself. I am not working for your wife."

"But..."

"There is another private detective in Brighton. She recently set herself up in business," Clara grabbed the newspaper from the table. It happened to be the latest edition of the Brighton Gazette, containing Clara's new advert along with the one placed by Miss Butler. Clara opened it to the classifieds section and showed it to Mr Butterworth. "See? Your wife has hired this woman. I know this because a friend of mine informed me."

Mr Butterworth stared at the paper and slowly his fury dissipated. He was not a man who became angry easily, nor one who maintained that rage for long. He was deflated and embarrassed.

"I apologise, Miss Fitzgerald," he said sheepishly.

"That's quite all right," Clara made him sit down in an armchair. "I can understand you're upset. I take it your wife came to visit you?"

"She did," Mr Butterworth said glumly. "She took the cat. Agamemnon was all I had of worth from that wretched marriage, and she insisted on taking him too."

"Who owns the cat?" Clara asked.

"That's the problem, no one can say," Mr Butterworth shrugged. "We bought the cat after we were married so technically, I am told, he is marital property, much like the house or the furniture in it. We both own him and neither of us have a greater right to him. But, even so, she could have let me have him."

Mr Butterworth slumped into his chair. He looked utterly downcast. Clara felt sorry for the poor man.

"Would you like some blancmange, Mr Butterworth? We were just having dessert?"

Mr Butterworth admitted that he was rather fond of blancmange and Clara ran across to the dining room to fetch him a bowl. He seemed to brighten at the sight of the pale pink pudding wobbling in its bowl.

"Now," Clara said once he had eaten it up. "Why don't you explain all this to me?"

"I left my wife," Mr Butterworth said, as if it was that simple.

"There must have been a reason for that?" Clara nudged him gently.

"Oh, I don't know," Mr Butterworth sighed deeply and his head fell down to his chest until his chin seemed to vanish into his collar. "I suppose, once, we were happy. But things had changed. She is such a demanding person and I felt... stifled. Some days I felt more attached to the cat than I did to her. Which was when it occurred to me that I might just leave her.

"I had to be sensible about it. I didn't want to go and then have to come crawling back. Money was, of course, the biggest concern. My wife inherited money from her father and it was arranged into trusts that I could never touch, so I knew she would be fine without me. I wouldn't leave her in the lurch, not after all these years. My situation was more complicated."

Mr Butterworth tapped his spoon in the empty dessert bowl.

"I have had to work all my life to supply myself with an income. Not that I begrudged the fact. Instead of relying on my wife's trust investments I paid for everything. The trusts were going to be for our old age together. But then I started to see how things would be once I did not bring in any money. Once it was all about my wife's money, then... well, she would control me completely. Any time I wanted to buy the littlest of things I would have to ask her. My freedom would be gone completely."

Clara imagined that was the way many wives felt about their marriages, but did not bother to protest. It was the way things were supposed to be for women. Not that she didn't feel for Mr Butterworth, she would feel for anyone in his position.

"Is that what decided you?"

"That and a lot of other little things," Mr Butterworth explained. "Too many to list. Niggles that built up over the years until they formed this huge pile of complaints and with very little in the way of kindnesses to offset it all. I had to wait until the time was right. The company I worked for as a clerk was closing down. I didn't tell my wife, but I knew I would be offered a small sum of money in return for my years of service. When the time came, I took the money and then pretended to still go to work every day. In the meantime, I was looking for another job.

"I found it and straight away I arranged for new lodgings in Hove. I gave the job my new address and suddenly I was free. She couldn't find me easily. That afternoon I went home while she was at one of her painting classes. I collected Agamemnon, my lone friend through the final years of my marriage, and I walked out. That night I slept the best sleep I have had in years."

Mr Butterworth let out a long, peaceful sigh as he recalled the moment he realised he was released from his shackles.

"She reported you missing to the police," Clara interrupted his thoughts.

"I know. They found me. I suppose for them it wasn't so hard. I explained the situation, told them I didn't want to see my wife and they left it at that. They had better things to do."

"If only you hadn't taken the cat with you, you would probably still be living in peace," Clara pointed out.

"Agamemnon was worth the risk," Mr Butterworth gave a little sniff and his thin moustache twitched. "How can I get him back?"

"I couldn't say. Perhaps you ought to hire a solicitor?" Clara thought for a moment. "If you could arrange a divorce, then it could be ironed out that way."

"My wife won't agree to a divorce," Mr Butterworth shook his head. "I know that well enough. She will keep her fingers hooked into me as best she can. But I will hire a solicitor, see if I can get Agamemnon back. In the meanwhile, I suppose I shall be moving lodgings again."

"I'm sorry," Clara said quietly.

"Not your fault, Miss Fitzgerald. It's the fault of this other woman. I shall have to go see her instead."

Clara knew that was not quite true. She had been the one who had told Sarah Butler, in good faith, where Mr Butterworth was living. She had trusted to the woman's judgement and discretion, now Clara could see she had been mistaken. Where Clara would have tried to gently mediate between the unhappy couple, Sarah Butler had just passed on the information directly with no real thought or consideration as to the consequences. Clara guessed that Miss Butler was not a great diplomat or very tactful and that could cause a lot of difficulties in the business she was now running.

"It's just so unfortunate," Clara added. "But a solicitor would be your best port of call."

"I apologise for disturbing your dinner and accusing you," Mr Butterworth replied, now standing to leave. "I made my own assumptions that were very clearly wrong."

"No matter," Clara shrugged, eager to accept his apology as it somewhat assuaged her own guilt.

She showed him to the door.

"Maybe I need to accept things for what they are," Mr Butterworth said as he turned to take his leave. "Get another cat."

"Maybe," Clara said.

"Then again, I really am rather fond of Agamemnon. Oh well, goodbye Miss Fitzgerald."

"Goodbye."

Clara closed the door and stood silently in the hallway. What a mess. She should have been angry, after all, it was all Sarah Butler's fault that Clara had been accosted in her home. She had an awful vision of this happening more frequently as Sarah continued her business. Was Clara now going to have to spend her evenings explaining to irate people that she was not responsible for their misfortune but that it was the other female detective in town. Oh dear, that did not sound appealing.

If only Clara had not allowed her guilt to sway her into revealing the information she had on Mr Butterworth to Sarah. Now she felt a whole new form of guilt. Maybe she should have a word with Sarah about professional discretion... No, she had already interfered too much and made a mess of things. She would just have to keep Sarah Butler at arms' length and hope no one else came calling to complain about her. It was a nuisance, but one she could overcome and with time people would realise there were two private detectives in Brighton and would not immediately assume she was working on any given case.

At least.... That was what she hoped...

Chapter Nineteen

The burglary had been carefully planned. Clara was clear on that. Which also meant that it was possible someone had seen something important without realising it. People watching a house for days, or even weeks, do get noticed, even if it is just by the busybody across the road. Then there was the knowledge that Simon Clark had seen a map of the house, and had clear instructions of exactly where to go when inside. Someone had to secure that information for him. Someone involved in the planning of the burglary had been inside Mr Jacobs' house and had made a careful study of it.

Clara was not ruling out the possibility that the staff were involved. The butler, Mr Yaxley, had been away at the time of the intrusion and seemed likely out of the picture. But Mrs Crocker had been present and she had not heard a thing, nor had she reacted very swiftly to the discovery of the break-in. It might be true that she thought it was purely an act of vandalism, then again, she might have removed the glass and delayed calling the police to buy her accomplices time. Had she deliberately swept up a clue to who was behind the theft?

The next morning, having risen a little later than usual, Clara set out to see Mr Jacobs and to have a word with his employees. She hoped she was not about to discover that he had been betrayed by the people he needed to trust the most.

Mr Jacobs was at home, or so Mr Yaxley informed Clara as she stood on the doorstep. Behind the stern looking butler a party of workmen in blue overalls were milling around. A distinctive wire was hanging down from the centre of the hall ceiling and the workmen appeared to be arguing about the best way to attach a large chandelier to it.

"Having the house wired for electricity?" Clara observed.

"Indeed," Mr Yaxley said in his brusque fashion. "Mr Jacobs has given instructions that should you call you are to be shown to him at once. Please follow me."

With that Yaxley led Clara through the hall and into the sitting room where Clara had first met her client. The room looked a little disordered today, with dust sheets draped over the furniture and the netsuke display case. Mr Jacobs was browsing through an auction catalogue while sitting on a sheet covered sofa.

"Miss Fitzgerald, Sir," Yaxley introduced Clara and then departed in the discreet manner that is perfected by butlers.

"Hello Miss Fitzgerald," Mr Jacobs looked up from his catalogue. "Excuse the mess, we have workmen in."

"Fitting electricity," Clara nodded.

"Ah, I see you spotted the chandelier installation. Yes, I heard them clattering about and thought they must be on to that. Electricity is the way forward," Mr Jacobs became enthusiastic. "My neighbours tell me electricity is so clean compared to candles, and much brighter than gas. And none of them have experienced any mishaps with it. Yaxley was convinced that we would all be electrocuted within the week should I go ahead with my plan. Well, I suppose we still have to wait and see on that!"

Jacobs laughed.

"I might be a collector of antiquities," he continued. "But I don't hang about in the dark ages. I like the modern world. I bought a new chandelier specifically designed for electricity, I didn't want to just convert the old gas one. And let me show you this."

Mr Jacobs rose and motioned for Clara to follow him. He went to the tower alcove where his armchair stood with a pile of books awaiting his attention on a table nearby.

"This is a standing lamp," he indicated a tall lamp, around four or five feet tall with a shade hiding its bulb. "It plugs into the wall here, and I can move it about as I please. Instead of those frustrating gas fittings attached to the wall. No more reading by lamplight for me!"

Jacobs was very pleased with his modern innovation.

"It is certainly convenient," Clara agreed.

"Now I have rambled on about my renovations like the gauche rich man I am, I should ask why you have come to see me," Jacobs brightened. "Might there be news?"

"In a way," Clara compromised with the truth. She followed him back to the sofa where they both sat. Jacobs insisted on ringing for tea before she continued. "I have found the man responsible for the burglary, in the sense that he climbed through your window and stole the dragon. However, he was employed by someone else. This someone spent a great deal of time planning this crime and watching your house."

"Oh," Mr Jacobs' face had fallen, he looked a little stunned by the revelation. Clara guessed he had not given a thought to the crime being expertly planned.

"The thief was supplied with a map of your home, Mr Jacobs. And precise instructions on where to find the green jade dragon."

Mr Jacobs looked even more shocked. He started to say something, but the words died in his throat.

"Have you noticed anybody suspicious watching the house?" Clara asked.

"I can't say I have," Mr Jacobs admitted. "I spend most

of my time in this room and, as you can see, the view of the street outside is obscured from the windows."

Clara looked over her shoulder to the main window of the room, which faced the front garden. The garden was enclosed by a tall brick wall, with iron gates mounted in the middle. It would be difficult to see the street from the window, other than a small glimpse through the gates.

"What about unusual visitors to the house?" Clara suggested. "Have you had an unexpected guest? Someone who might have wanted to look over the entire house?"

Mr Jacobs considered this for a while.

"Most of the people I have to the house I know well," he said slowly. "I tend to visit other people more than I have guests. I am usually the stranger in the house, going to peoples' homes and examining some precious object they own. Of course, there have been all the workmen in the house."

"When did they begin wiring the house?"

"Last month," Jacobs explained. "I only have them in the house while I am at home, so Yaxley can keep an eye on them. There are three men working on the project and Yaxley lets them in and out of the house. They are all local men. Mr Thomas and his son are builders who specialise in the wiring of houses for electricity and also gas piping. They employ one man. I don't see any of them being particularly nefarious. In any case, only Mr Thomas saw the entire house when he first came to offer me a quote for the work. And even then he only briefly went about counting rooms, and was more interested in the under stairs cupboard where he intends to fit the fuse box."

"And they haven't begun work on this room yet," Clara noted, pointing up at the gas fitting still hanging from the ceiling of the room.

"No, they hope to start today after the chandelier is installed."

As Jacobs spoke there was a loud cry from the hall and the sound of crystal cut glass jangling. Clara had to concede the workmen seemed unlikely culprits for scoping out the house. In any case, Simon Clark had stated that all the men, apart from himself, were individuals who already worked for the man behind the theft. It was improbable that he had hired Brighton workmen to do his dirty work. He would not want to risk them saying too much. This was all too professional to allow for such carelessness.

"Has anyone else visited the house?" Clara asked again. "Anyone at all? Maybe not someone coming to look at your collection."

Mr Jacobs paused for a moment and contemplated this. His eyes wandered up to the gas fitting soon destined for the rubbish heap. His face lightened, an idea had occurred to him.

"Now I think on it, there was a man here. Let me see, it was three weeks ago, roughly. The workmen had just started the preliminary chore of cutting channels in my walls for the wiring. This man appeared on a Sunday. He was in a suit and had a clipboard. He said he was from the electricity board and had come to inspect the work being done and to ensure it met with their regulations," Mr Jacobs looked excited as he explained this to Clara. "Yaxley had no reason to doubt him. It seemed a perfectly logical explanation. He was shown over the entire house and made notes on his clipboard. I briefly glimpsed it as he came into this room. He was drawing a rough map of the ground floor. I assumed this was so he could make a note of where the wiring was being placed."

"This fellow sounds suspicion," Clara prompted him. "I don't recall anyone else I know who has had electricity installed being visited by the electricity board. Especially on a Sunday."

"Yaxley did think that odd," Mr Jacobs said. "But the man stated he had a large backlog of inspections to conduct and so was having to work unusual hours. He apologised profusely for the inconvenience."

"It was useful for him to not arrive on a day when the

workmen would have been about and might have failed to recognise him from the electricity board," Clara nodded. "Did he state his name?"

"Not to me, maybe to Yaxley. Yaxley showed him round. You ought to speak to him, he could describe him as well."

"I will," Clara said, having every intention of grilling the two servants once she had finished speaking with Mr Jacobs. "There is one other thing I must ask you, and it is a somewhat delicate matter."

"Oh?" Mr Jacobs had become enthused in his excitement about remembering the strange electricity board man, but now he became sombre. He sensed from Clara's tone that the next question she asked might cause him consternation.

"It is about the jade dragon, itself," Clara explained gently. "From the experts I have spoken with, including those at the British Museum, it would seem it is a very unusual item to be found in a British gentleman's collection. You don't happen to know how your uncle came across it?"

"He never really explained," Mr Jacobs said. "I was merely a boy. I remember him handing me the dragon, and telling me it was very special. 'Keep it safe, Humphry' he said 'it will bring you luck'. That was the last time he spoke to me before he was killed."

"He was involved in a carriage accident?"

"Yes. My uncle lived in London when he was not travelling," Jacobs elaborated. "He was an adventurer, he liked going to far flung places. He had traversed deserts and had even been on an expedition to the Arctic, though that did not end well. We all imagined he would perish one day on one of these grand adventures. My mother was convinced he would fall down some mountain, or crash through the ice of a frozen lake. My father tried not to think too hard about it.

"We were all shocked when we learned he had died in such a very mundane sort of way. People are having carriage accidents all the time, especially in London. I think there must be at least one death a week in the capital because of some collision on the roads, if not more. It seemed a very absurd way for my uncle to die."

"There was an inquest, I suppose?" Clara asked.

"Yes. I don't really remember the details. I was too young. When I was older I did ask about it and my father said that he had walked out in front of a coal cart and been crushed," Jacobs grimaced. "Such a pathetic way for a man like him to go."

"And this was shortly after he brought the jade dragon home?" Clara pressed.

Mr Jacobs now looked at her hard.

"Yes, are you implying a connection?"

Clara hesitated, knowing what she must say next was indelicate to say the least.

"Some of the people I have spoken with," she hedged, "have implied that the jade dragon could not have been removed from Japan, at the time your uncle was there, without some slightly dubious circumstances being involved. That is not to say your uncle did anything wrong. Rather, it might be that he was sold stolen goods."

Mr Jacobs was clearly surprised by this statement. Presumably, despite all his expertise, he had never contemplated how unusual it was for an Englishman to possess an ancient jade dragon made for the imperial court. He let the information sink in before he could respond.

"Are you saying my uncle was killed for the dragon?"

"I don't know," Clara shrugged. "Maybe it was all just a coincidence. But I can't help wondering if this burglary was motivated by something other than a desire to own a rare object or financial gain."

"My uncle would have bought the dragon in good faith," Mr Jacobs assured Clara. "If someone sold him a stolen object, it was not his fault. He was a stranger with a lot of money, prepared to buy all manner of oddities and antiques. He came home once with a small mummified crocodile from Egypt, I remember that vividly as my mother would not let him bring it into the house to show me. Someone may have supposed he was a good way to rid themselves of a forbidden item."

"Unfortunately, without your uncle to ask, we shall never probably know," Clara smiled. "He may have been given it as a gift by someone from the imperial court, someone important enough to own the dragon in the first place."

"Precisely!" Jacobs said, relieved to be given this alternative explanation. "He was a very good diplomat in his own way. He befriended people easily."

"What a shame he did not leave some note about the dragon to explain its origins. What stories that little carving could tell," Clara was aiming to reassure Mr Jacobs now, she didn't want to leave him to dwell on notions that he was the owner of a stolen item.

"Yes, indeed. Mind you, he did leave diaries," Jacobs brightened. "I have never read them, but they are safe in the attic. I shall get his one from Japan down and go through it, perhaps it shall offer an explanation."

"Perhaps," Clara said, trying not to raise his hopes too high. "Now, I have disturbed you long enough. Might I speak with your servants?"

"Of course, my dear, if you think they may have witnessed something."

Clara was concerned that one of them might have done more than just witness something, but she didn't say so. She thanked Mr Jacobs for his time and went in search of Yaxley.

Chapter Twenty

The chandelier was fixed to the ceiling and the workmen were testing the wiring to see if it was working as Clara returned to the main hall. Yaxley, as she had expected, was stood in a corner watching the proceedings with the intensity and concentration of a rather maniacal hawk.

"Might we have a word?" Clara asked him.

Yaxley scowled at her, his expression, if not his tongue, demanded to know if she could not see how busy he was? But he merely sighed and nodded to a doorway next to them. Watching the men all the time, Yaxley escorted Clara into a vast dining room. A long table, suitable to seat twelve, dominated the centre while an extravagant fireplace topped by a gilt mirror ornamented the far wall. A sideboard ran nearly the length of the room and was topped with a huge range of decanters. Clara perceived that, among other things, Mr Jacobs was a connoisseur of spirits. She glimpsed silver tags on the decanters that revealed their contents to be various types of whisky and port.

"Why did you wish to see me?" Yaxley distracted her from her inspection. He had taken up a space near the fire, with one eye on the now closed door. He didn't want to be away from his scrutiny of the workmen for long.

"I just wanted to elaborate a few points," Clara explained. "I have some new information about the burglary."

Yaxley appeared unmoved by this information.

"You recall a man coming to the house on a Sunday claiming to be an inspector for the electricity board?"

"Of course!" Yaxley said with annoyance.

"I am now wondering if that man was not really who he claimed to be, but rather was working for those behind this burglary. His inspection of the house would have been an excuse to draw a map of the property and learn where the netsuke collection was kept."

This revelation struck Yaxley hard. Something, or rather someone, had slipped under his eagle vision. However, the only indication of his affront was the slight twitch of an eyebrow. Yaxley was too well controlled to allow anymore.

"I thought the man had an odd air," he said after a moment. "And to visit on a Sunday was most inconvenient. My instinct was to send him away, but one does not just send electricity board inspectors away."

"Did he show you any identification?" Clara asked.

"A little card, bearing his name and role. I had no reason to doubt it. The thing seemed battered as if he was accustomed to carrying it around, and he seemed knowledgeable on electricity. He made a number of appropriate comments on the work," Yaxley was trying hard to explain away his failure to catch the spy in their midst. "He seemed purely interested in the wiring of the house."

"What was his name?" Clara queried.

"According to the card he was Douglas Jones," Yaxley said. "He seemed quite respectable."

"Might you describe him?"

"Around forty in age, shorter than me. Dark hair, slicked back, and a small black moustache. He had a round face with a rather pointy chin."

This description was so vague as to be almost

worthless, though Clara noted it down just the same.

"There was one other thing," Yaxley interrupted, making Clara glance up at him. "I thought it rather odd in an inspector, but these days the world is not quite how it used to be."

"What was it?" Clara asked eagerly.

"Briefly his right sleeve rode up as he was writing on the clipboard and for a moment I had a clear view of a tattoo on his wrist," Yaxley pressed two fingers to his wrist to indicate the location of the tattoo. "I am a very alert man, Miss Fitzgerald, and though Mr Jones rapidly pulled down his sleeve I was left with a vivid impression of the tattoo. It was of a sea serpent, I would estimate the tattoo ran along the top of the man's entire forearm, and along its side were some Japanese characters. I recognised them because of Mr Jacobs' collection."

Now Clara was really excited. This information indicated that the man who had come to the house knew about Japanese culture and suggested he might have links to someone willing to pay well for the return of a lost Japanese treasure.

"What did the characters spell?" Clara asked.

"I couldn't say, I do not read Japanese," Yaxley told her coldly, as if she should have known better than to ask such a thing. "I could, however, draw them for you."

Clara handed him her notebook without hesitation and Mr Yaxley was silent a few moments as he sketched the symbols on the paper.

"Was there anything else?" he demanded once he had handed back the notebook.

"Have you seen anyone loitering about the house? Perhaps someone appearing to watch the property?"

Yaxley gave the question the decency of lengthy consideration before answering;

"No."

That was disappointing. Clara had hoped the astute butler might have seen something. Perhaps his keen eyes were a little too fixated on the internal affairs of the house?

"You were away with Mr Jacobs at the time of the burglary?" Clara unnecessarily checked.

"Indeed."

"But Mrs Crocker was here?" Clara decided to try one last ploy to break through the man's cool façade. She knew there could be intense rivalry between servants and Mr Yaxley did not strike her as the sort of man who liked spending time with others, especially other servants. "Did you wonder at her not hearing anything the night of the burglary? The glass smashing would have made a distinctive noise."

Yaxley narrowed his dark brows.

"Mrs Crocker is rather deaf. I did not consider it strange she heard nothing."

"Had you been in the house, would you have so quickly written off the broken window as a boy's prank?" Clara pressed, playing on the man's ego.

"No," Yaxley could make that one word sound uncommonly condescending. "I would have summoned the police at once, and I would not have removed the glass."

"What do you make of the fact that Mrs Crocker did?" Clara persisted.

"She is a woman of mean intelligence," Yaxley stated coldly. "It does not surprise me that she would fail to see the importance of leaving the evidence untouched. If you wish to imply that she may have been connected with the crime, perhaps bribed to not notice anything, I could not comment. The woman was hired by Mr Jacobs and I have not known her a sufficient time to fully assess her character."

"She has been here a few years?" Clara pointed out.

"As I say, I have not known her for a sufficient time," Yaxley repeated himself, clearly annoyed by Clara's statement. "She seems honest enough, for the work she is given. If you think she might be involved in the crime, I would suggest you speak to her."

That was exactly what Clara intended to do. She thanked Mr Yaxley and left him to resume his post observing every move the workmen made. She did not envy Mr Thomas and his men working under such an intense gaze. It was enough to make anyone suddenly clumsy and self-conscious.

Clara made her way to the kitchen where she found Mrs Crocker up to her elbows in soap suds. She was washing out glass jars, the sort used for storing pickles and jams. She gave Clara no more warm a welcome than Mr Yaxley had. Clara wondered if it was a particular requirement of Mr Jacobs' servants to be so unusually unfriendly.

"Good morning," Clara greeted her brightly, refusing to be intimidated by the woman's glaring eyes. "Might I ask you a few questions again?"

Clara sat herself at the kitchen table and laid out her notebook, making it plain that she was not really asking permission.

"You can," Mrs Crocker said gruffly. "But I'll keep on with my work while you do."

Clara did not complain.

"I have located the man who broke into the house," she informed Mrs Crocker, waiting to see if the woman flinched or looked concerned. She did not. "He was working for someone else, and I now know that the house was being watched for a considerable period of time."

"Doesn't surprise me," Mrs Crocker sniffed. "Thieves are always eyeing up places like this."

"Because they assume they contain many things of value?"

"Precisely."

Clara paused, then she said;

"Only, the thieves observing this house already knew of the one item inside that they wanted. They were not opportunists casing a house that appeared full of valuable things. They knew where the dragon was."

Mrs Crocker was unmoved. She rubbed a cloth in a

glass jar until it squeaked. Clara was reminded of Annie's vigorous cleaning of their own windows.

"Have you noticed anyone suspicious about the house?" she changed tactic.

"Don't know," Mrs Crocker shrugged. "I don't know everyone here. And mostly I am in this kitchen."

Mrs Crocker paused in her cleaning to cast a disgruntled look about the room. She was not a person content with her allotted place in the world.

"Do you remember an inspector from the electricity board?"

"No. He came around on my day for visiting my sister," Mrs Crocker shrugged. "Mr Yaxley mentioned him later. Wanted me to go through the house and check he had not left any mess behind him. Yaxley can't abide footprints on the carpets."

"Had the man left any trace of himself?"

"Not as far as I could see."

Clara felt she was not getting very far. If Mrs Crocker was involved, she was hardly about to admit it, and her caution made it very hard to trick her into revealing herself.

"You've worked here a while?" Clara asked, mainly to buy herself some thinking time.

"Since the last housekeeper died, God rest her soul. I imagine that Yaxley worked her to death."

"You don't like him?"

"More like, he doesn't like me," Mrs Crocker huffed to herself. "He considers me common because I don't speak nice like him and I don't go about in a fancy uniform."

Mrs Crocker's irritation as she thought of Yaxley was taken out on the glass jar, which squeaked in protest as the cleaning cloth was fiercely rubbed against it.

"Does he think I had something to do with this?" she asked suddenly.

Clara saw an opportunity.

"He just remarked that he would not have swept up the broken glass," she said casually.

Mrs Crocker turned from her sink of soapy water, a flush of anger had risen up her neck and across her face.

"He would!" she snapped. "The man is always criticising my work. I stick by my actions. I had no reason to think the house had been burgled, so I cleaned up the mess."

"Why were you so sure boys might have broken the window?" Clara asked. "After all, the glass was smashed at the side of the house. It would not be possible to do that from the street."

"I never thought it was street boys," Mrs Crocker snorted, as if she was finding Clara unbelievably stupid. "The family next door has three sons. Rogues the lot of them. I have caught them climbing over the wall into Mr Jacobs' garden before now. When I chased them off they threw stones at me. Then, another time, they threw stones when I was hanging out the washing. I would complain, but the father is an important barrister who would not take kindly to the likes of me criticising his offspring."

"Ah, so you assumed they had been up to their antics again?"

"Exactly," Mrs Crocker agreed. "There were no stones about on the floor, that I will admit. But I just thought they had smashed the window with a brick, or something. Hammered at it rather than throwing things at it. Those three will grow up to be horrible young men."

Clara was beginning to understand why the housekeeper had been so blithe about the smashed glass, and why she had failed to see its real purpose.

"I think, given the circumstances, I might have been inclined to think the same as you did," Clara told her. "And I imagine I would have acted accordingly."

Mrs Crocker, finding someone prepared to defend her actions, mellowed.

"I am not as big a fool as Yaxley likes to make out. Had doors been open I would have realised there had been a burglary. As it was, I saw nothing to concern me until later," Mrs Crocker paused. "Now you mention it, something springs to my mind. I noticed a fellow on the corner of the road a few times when I went to do my shopping. He was there at the same time every day for around a week and I never could fathom what he was about. Then he was gone again."

"He may have been one of the men sent to watch the house," Clara told her. "They would have been paying attention to the times when Mr Jacobs left the house and for how long he was away."

"I still get the shivers thinking how I was upstairs alone with a man prowling about down here," Mrs Crocker visibly trembled at the memory. "I have no hearing in my right ear due to a childhood illness. When I lay in my bed upstairs, I tend to turn in my sleep onto my left side, so I cannot hear a thing. It distresses me to imagine I was up there, vulnerable, and unable to hear anything."

"At least now the remaining window is secured," Clara pointed out.

"Mr Jacobs has always been conscious of the security of this place. He knows he has many valuable items here. He insists on the shutters being drawn at night, even when everyone is home. I always felt safe here," Mrs Crocker looked around her kitchen, a sadness coming over her. "Now I don't. I'm not sure I can continue here. It is bad enough feeling Mr Yaxley's suspicious eyes on me, but to not feel safe in my own bed as well? Maybe I will have to change positions."

"It is still early days," Clara told her reassuringly. "The shock is still fresh. Give it time. Any house can be burgled, but at least now Mr Jacobs knows where his house is vulnerable."

Mrs Crocker seemed unconvinced. She went back to her sink and her glass jars. Clara left her in peace. She had come for information and she was now satisfied that Mrs Crocker was not involved in the burglary. Nor, for that matter, did she think Mr Yaxley involved. But this mysterious inspector was another matter. First she would need to discover if there really was a Douglas Jones at the electricity board and, if not, then she would need to see if she could learn who he really was. Things were definitely hotting up.

Chapter Twenty-one

Brighton's Electricity Board was rather a humble affair; three men, one secretary and a small office in the town hall. When Clara visited them and asked if they had sent an inspector to the Jacobs' house one Sunday, they laughed. They were far too busy, she was informed, to send people out to private homes. They had enough trouble keeping the main system operating and ensuring places such as Brighton's hospital were kept functioning. There was no time for random inspections. Nor was there any sign of a man named Douglas Jones. Clara had expected as much.

Her next port of call was the police station, to see if Inspector Park-Coombs was free to talk to her. She rather fancied that if anyone knew how to track a mysterious man with a sea serpent tattoo it would be a policeman.

The atmosphere in the station was tense. Clara nodded to the constable on the front desk. He was young and very green. He was looking anxious and his eyes kept flicking unconsciously to the stairs that led up to the inspector's office.

"What's going on?" Clara asked conspiratorially.

The young constable started to open his mouth, and then hesitated.

"Can't say, miss," he mumbled.

"Oh dear," Clara smiled at him. "Well, is Inspector Park-Coombs around?"

The constable's eyes swivelled to the stairs again.

"Can't say, miss," he repeated, looking embarrassed by his failure.

Clara wondered what was going on. She almost wished the old desk sergeant was back so she could have an argument with him. He usually gave something away when he became cross. The young constable, instead, was playing dumb.

She was about to ask another question when footsteps came thumping down the stairs.

"It won't do, Park-Coombs. I told you to start the process and yet you have done nothing," Superintendent Foster appeared in the police station foyer.

Inspector Park-Coombs was trailing him.

"Hardly nothing, sir," he protested, looking very hang-dog about the whole affair.

"It is not a difficult thing, inspector," Foster persisted. "I expect progress and I expect it soon."

Superintendent Foster donned his hat and marched out of the station without a word of goodbye. Park-Coombs stood on the bottom step of the staircase and grumbled to himself. Clara watched on, partly bemused, partly upset on the inspector's behalf. The lack of respect the superintendent had shown him was most pointed and rude.

"Is everything all right?" she moved next to Park-Coombs.

The inspector gave a start. He had not noticed her.

"Clara," he sighed. "No, everything is not all right. But never mind."

"It's lunchtime," Clara pointed out. "Would you like to grab a bite to eat and a cup of tea? You look in need of some fresh air?"

The considerate invitation eased some of the tension in the inspector's shoulders. He glanced at Clara.

"Why not?" he said. "I could do with a change of scenery."

They strolled to a nearby tearooms which offered light lunches along with big pots of tea. They were soon settled at a table by a window, waiting for cheese sandwiches and fresh scones.

"So," Clara asked after their order was placed, "what has caused the superintendent such consternation that he can't even remember to say goodbye?"

Park-Coombs gave a long sigh.

"It's this female police constable business. Apparently, I am not moving fast enough on the matter for his liking."

"Have you anyone in mind for the role?"

"Not really," Park-Coombs rested his arms on the table. "It's not the sort of thing you advertise in the paper either. I don't want all and sundry turning up to give it a go."

Clara doubted there would be that many women in Brighton prepared to try their hand at police work, but she grasped the inspector's point.

"I'll keep my ears open, if I hear of someone suitable I'll let you know."

Park-Coombs thanked her as their food and tea arrived.

"Now, why were you in the station?" he asked.

"Curiosity, as always," Clara smiled. "I have a couple of leads on the Jacobs' case. I wanted to run them past you."

"Go ahead," Park-Coombs mumbled through cheese crumbs. "The case has come to a dead end for us, but it still sits on my desk taunting me and adding to my 'unsolved crimes' statistics. Which, by the way, is another reason for the superintendent's consternation. The police force as a whole is failing to solve too many crimes. Naturally, informing him that half the problem is a lack of resources and funding would not go down well."

"Naturally," Clara replied, sipping tea. "I have two potential leads in the Jacobs case. I managed to track down the thief who broke into the property, but as far as he goes he is meaningless, merely a tool in someone else's schemes."

"So you are pursuing the theory that this was a professional job? Someone carefully planned it and hired the thief?"

"Exactly. Suggesting this was a mere opportunist at work defies belief. The person responsible knew precisely what they wanted. I now know that the thief was hired by a gentleman called Mr Earling. Earling works as a criminal agent. He knows who is best for a given job and supplies them. I suppose he gets a good commission from it."

"He is not a man who has come to my attention," Park-Coombs said apologetically. "But I know his type. Never one to get their hands dirty, but always somewhere behind a crime."

"I would like to trace him. To ask who he was acting for."

"That would be very dangerous," Park-Coombs' dark brows folded together in a look of intense seriousness. "Men like this Mr Earling are nasty and they have important friends. He won't tell you a thing, you can trust me on that. And he might just decide you need taking care of if you keep asking questions."

Clara was no fool. She had imagined as much, but hearing it from the inspector made her own concerns seem less silly.

"I do have another lead," she said.

"A safer one?" Park-Coombs asked.

"Well, it depends," Clara smiled. "The thief who robbed Mr Jacobs was supplied with a detailed plan of his house. Someone had to have been inside the property to be able to draw it. I have ruled out the servants and the workmen at the house, however, a man called upon Mr Jacobs one Sunday before the burglary. He said he was an inspector from the electricity board, but the board have never heard of him."

"Did he give a name?" Park-Coombs wondered.

"Douglas Jones. An alias, I would imagine."

"It doesn't ring a bell," Park-Coombs shook his head before starting on his scone. "Anything else to go on?"

"He had a strange tattoo on his right wrist. A sea serpent or perhaps a dragon, with Japanese characters alongside."

Clara had barely finished the description when Park-Coombs slapped the table with delight.

"I know who that is!" he grinned, ignoring the other diners who were looking across curiously at the noise. "I've had that fellow in my cells before now. Douglas Jones he calls himself currently? Last I met him, he was going along as George Cranshaw."

"He has worked in Brighton before?" Clara queried.

"He's a local lad," Park-Coombs elaborated. "But he spent a lot of time in London, where he became involved with gangs. That was his downfall. He started his life as a merchant seaman and, by all accounts, he would have made a good one and might have found his way to being a skipper with his own ship one day. But he couldn't take the stricture of life at sea. He fell in with some of the criminals who work the races in the summer. They were Londoners and he took a shine to their lifestyle and their seeming easy money. Since that day he has forgotten the sea and taken to a life of crime. His mother is most distressed about it all."

"His mother lives in Brighton?"

"Yes. She's about the only reason he comes back here. She is a good woman. Her son's dubious choices have caused her a lot of heartache."

"I think I will need to see her," Clara said. "George Cranshaw is involved in this burglary and might be able to tell me who hired him."

"He is involved with gangs, Clara," Park-Coombs tried to rein her in. "Even if he does tell you, you will be dealing with some very unpleasant people. Perhaps, for once, you will have to give up on this case."

"I can't," Clara insisted. "Not when I am getting so

close. In any case, I am not intending to cause these people trouble. All I want is the dragon back and I imagine Mr Jacobs would willingly pay for its return. I'll find the culprit behind it all and offer him money. Now no criminal will ever refuse money."

The inspector looked dubious, but he knew enough about Clara to realise that arguing with her was not going to succeed. He finished his scone.

"I wish people would take better care of their property," he sighed, mostly to himself. "This week alone I have had two reports of bicycle thefts, one of a missing dog, five house breakings and an armed robbery at a druggists' shop. Though, at least in the latter, I have a good idea of who might be behind it."

"You work hard, as always, Inspector."

"Theft is such a difficult one to solve," the inspector continued. "Rarely are there any clues left behind. And it can be such an anonymous thing. Still, we do our best."

"Would it be possible to have the address for George Cranshaw's mother?" Clara distracted him.

Park-Coombs gave her a long, hard look. Then he took a notebook from his pocket and, after a moment of thought, scribbled down an address.

"Mrs Pear is the recalcitrant lad's unfortunate mother," he said, tearing out the page and handing it to Clara. "I believe his real name is Albert Pear, but I could be wrong. He has used so many aliases in his time in my police cells. Mrs Pear is a nice woman, don't go upsetting her."

"Would I?" Clara asked.

· Park-Coombs merely huffed.

Their lunch finished, Clara insisted on paying their bill as a thank you for the inspector's time. He protested lightly, more for show than because he felt he should pay. They parted company at the door to the tearooms with Clara promising to try and find a suitable female candidate for Park-Coombs' police force. The inspector gave another of his solemn huffs and walked back to the station.

Clara went home. She wanted to collect her thoughts before going to see Mrs Pear. Despite what the inspector thought, she had paid attention when he had mentioned to her the dangers she could be facing. She was dealing with some very nasty sorts of people. There was no knowing what they might do to someone poking about in their affairs. Clara would have to take things carefully.

She found Tommy and Captain O'Harris in the dining room when she arrived home. They were going over some papers covered with drawings. There was a larger sheet which had been rolled up and sat to one side. They greeted Clara as she arrived.

"What is this?" Clara unfurled the large roll of paper and saw that it was the architect's drawing for O'Harris' house. While the captain had been absent, his large manor house had remained empty. One evening a tramp had found a way in and had started a fire in the dining room to warm himself. The fire had grown out of control and had gutted the dining room and left structural damage to the ceiling and rooms above. O'Harris was having the house restored before he moved back in.

"I have been making plans, Clara," O'Harris pushed a piece of paper towards her. It was another drawing of the ground floor of his house, but this time the rooms had been renamed.

"Why has the music room become a bedroom?" Clara pointed at the drawing.

"That is part of it," O'Harris grinned. "I have been wondering what to do with my life, now my adventuring days are behind me. Oh, maybe I will fly again one day, but that desire to be in the air all the time has been knocked from me."

O'Harris glossed over his flying accident which had come close to killing him and had resulted in him being missing for a year.

"It was while we were walking about London that it came to me. It was seeing that poor war veteran sitting on the pavement. Much has been done to treat the physical injuries of such men, but what about the mental damage? I know myself, as does Tommy, how debilitating those unseen wounds can be. My nervous breakdown was more frightening than my accident and it cannot be healed so simply as a broken leg. Yet, all about us are men who have come home from the war suffering just the same, and we are doing nothing for them.

"Which is when the idea blossomed. That horrid psychiatric ward in the hospital nearly finished me. But the generous Dr Cutt offered me a place in his house, a place in a home where I could forget I was ill and just concentrate on healing. I want to offer other men the very same."

O'Harris pushed another piece of paper towards her.

"I give you the O'Harris Hospital for War Veterans, specialising in the treatment of mental illness. It will be a place of non-judgement for men who can no longer cope with ordinary life, and will provide the latest, most progressive of treatments. All approved by myself."

Clara looked at the paper which showed a sketch of the three floors of the manor house, laid out as a series of bedrooms and communal rooms. There were offices set aside for doctors and rooms for the nurses and attendants.

"I estimate that the house could provide accommodation for six men at a time, that is taking into account the room required for the administrative staff and doctors and nurses. And naturally, I will have a suite of rooms too," O'Harris pointed all this out on his diagram. "Cost will be the greatest challenge. Which is why I must ask for my patients to pay for their treatment. However, I intend for there to be at least one room set aside for poor patients. The cost of the treatment for these men will be offset by the paying patients. And I shall also ask for donations."

"I am impressed," Clara nodded, looking at the drawings. "It is ambitious, but if anyone can pull such a scheme off, it shall be you."

Captain O'Harris smiled brightly at her. She sensed he had desperately wanted her approval and was relieved to receive it.

"Well, all I can say is that I am not doing the cooking," Annie declared, walking into the room with a tray loaded with teacups and teapot. "But I think it is a grand idea, nonetheless."

Clara looked around her at the three smiling faces and felt a wave of happiness come over her. She was so glad to see the captain making plans after his frightening ordeal and it filled her with a sense of contentment. She looked back at O'Harris, at the handsome face once more alive, rather than filled with the darkness and despair that had scared them all so. A gush of warmth flooded her chest. Clara tried not to over-analyse those feelings when they came upon her, but she knew they were growing day by day. She told herself she was just so glad to see her friend improving, she dare not admit to the real fondness that was blooming between them. She was not quite ready for that. Not just yet.

Chapter Twenty-two

Mrs Pear lived in a very respectable little cottage on the road that led from Brighton to Hove. She was a widow of some twenty years and had grown accustomed to living on her own, except for the occasions when her son visited her. She kept a neat vegetable garden that supplied most of her needs and was very fond of cats, having three of her own and often leaving out scraps for the local strays. Her neighbours found her pleasant and polite, no bother to anyone and always happy to help someone with a problem. Which made it seem all the more baffling that her son had turned to a life of serious crime. While Mrs Pear did not give much away, it was well known that her son, Albert, was part of a London criminal gang and only came down to see his mother when there was some crime afoot. Which was why everyone had been most careful to lock their doors when he appeared unexpectedly one weekend a month ago.

Clara hoped that Mrs Pear would be amenable to a little chat about her son. It was difficult to know what her response would be. While the woman had not cut Albert completely from her life, she certainly did not approve of his lifestyle or the company he kept. When Mrs Pear opened her door and saw Clara on her front step she was initially surprised. She rarely had visitors who were not already known to her. When Clara asked if it would be possible to have a chat about her son, Mrs Pear assumed he had caused the woman some trouble and felt the usual anxiety that accompanied all discussions about Albert.

"You best come in," she said.

Mrs Pear had just celebrated her sixty-fifth birthday, but the worries of life hung heavy on her and made her seem several years older. She shuffled about the house and her completely grey hair was kept swept back in a bun. There were birthday cards still sitting on the mantelpiece, though the one from Albert was half hidden behind a clock.

"Please sit, I could make tea?"

Clara had drunk enough tea in the last few hours to last a lifetime.

"No thank you," she answered politely. "I won't trouble you for too long."

"Will it be trouble?" Mrs Pear asked anxiously. "What has Albert done now?"

Clara thought there was little point in beating about the bush.

"I believe Albert to have been involved in a recent burglary," Clara explained. "Can I just confirm that he has a dragon tattoo on his right forearm?"

"Yes," Mrs Pear agreed. "Ghastly thing. I hate it. There are these weird symbols next to it which he tells me mean something. They just look a mess to me. Did he rob someone?"

"No. I believe he was involved in spying on a property to supply information to the thief."

"Oh," Mrs Pear was miserable. "I suppose it was during that weekend when he came home suddenly. He never visits without being up to something."

"Did he mention anything while he was here about what he was doing?"

"No, but then he never does," Mrs Pear sighed. "I shouldn't let him in the house, really. I just can't help myself. He is my only child, for all the woe he has brought me."

Abruptly Mrs Pear stood and went to a small table near the door. She returned with a framed photograph. A young man beamed out of the frame in black and white. There was nothing about him that suggested he was a criminal, he seemed very ordinary. This had to have been taken some years ago, since Mr Yaxley had described Albert Pear as being in his forties. Clara studied the picture for a moment, ingraining Albert's likeness to memory, then handed the picture back to his mother.

"A handsome lad," she said.

"He always was, and a bit of a charmer," Mrs Pear sighed. "I had such hopes for him as a boy. He was going to go to sea and become a captain of a steamer, like my dear old Henry had been. But when Henry drowned, Albert turned completely against the idea. He always blamed the ocean for the loss of his father. He and Henry were very close."

"Do you know anything about his criminal life?"

"As little as possible," Mrs Pear assured her. "I am sorry he has burgled your house, but I really can't help you."

"I was hoping to contact him," Clara said quickly, seeing that Mrs Pear was ready to dismiss her. "The item that was stolen has sentimental value. I would be willing to pay for its return, and I am not involving the police. That is assured."

Mrs Pear grimaced at her. Clara could not tell if it was a look of disappointment or one of disgust. Perhaps the woman was shamed to hear how Clara was prepared to bend the rules as well. Well, Clara was not ashamed. She knew the limitations of the police and arresting Albert Pear would do little good in the grand scheme of things. She had a task, to retrieve the jade dragon, and that was what she intended to do.

"I don't give out his address," Mrs Pear said firmly.

"I am not intending to cause him trouble," Clara

promised. "If anything, I am offering him money."

Mrs Pear began to speak again, when there was a shuffling of feet outside the door. Albert Pear appeared in the doorway of the room.

"It's all right, mother. I'll speak to her," he said, fixing Clara with his dark eyes.

The young man from the photograph was gone. He had been full of youthful enthusiasm and joy, what had replaced him was a sinister shadow. Albert Pear was now filled with suspicion, paranoia and anger. All these radiated at Clara.

Mrs Pear glanced from her son to her visitor. Then she made a noise, like a half-sob, and left the room. Albert Pear closed the door behind her and came to sit opposite Clara.

"You better speak quick," he said, his dark eyes full of menace.

"You helped in the theft of the green jade dragon from Mr Jacobs' house," Clara explained swiftly, there was no point messing about. "I want to get it back for him. So I need to know who has it now. Presumably that would be the person you work for?"

Albert Pear cracked his knuckles.

"Who says I was involved in that?" he said.

"A silent witness," Clara answered, then pointed to his rolled up sleeves and the tattoo on his forearm. "Your own skin ratted you out."

Albert glanced at the tattoo in blue ink. He laughed to himself.

"The butler fellow," he said. "Eyes like a hawk. He never left my side as I went about the place."

"It is distinctive," Clara told him. "The characters are Japanese?"

"No, Chinese," Albert answered. "They stand for luck, fortune and longevity. But you didn't come to talk about tattoos."

"No, I came to see if there is a means of getting the dragon back," Clara admitted. "I wasn't expecting to find you here, however. That was a stroke of luck."

"You think so?" Albert was amused.

"I would rather talk to you here than trying to track you in London. I have been up there twice already and train tickets don't grow on trees," Clara said. "I met Simon Clark, the thief."

"The only one of our party who was an outsider," Albert nodded. "The weak link."

"He was hardly that," Clara sighed. "He gave me very little, in fact, and most of what I got was by pure chance. Still, I owe him nothing and I don't much care if his employers find out I spoke with him. The only thing he really told me was that he was hired by a man called Mr Earling."

"I don't know about that," Albert shrugged. "I was just in charge of making a plan of the house and seeing where the netsukes were kept."

"Tell me, was the dragon stolen because of its value or for another reason?"

"Such as?" Albert seemed confused.

"It was just a thought, something that was mentioned to me," Clara did not want to give Albert any further ideas about the dragon. "Do you know if your employer still has the dragon?"

"You seem to think me very knowledgeable," Albert responded, cracking his knuckles casually.

Clara ignored the gesture of intimidation.

"You work for a criminal gang, and that gang will have a leader who decides what you will do. He was the one who orchestrated the burglary, who sent his people to watch the house, to learn the routines of its residents and to draw a plan of the interior. The only person he could not provide was a suitable thief," Clara paused. "So, yes, I do think you might be quite knowledgeable on the matter. You seem to have been with this gang some time, you probably know all its inner workings."

Albert gave that mirthless laugh again.

"And even if I do, why would I tell you?"

"I don't know," Clara confessed. "You don't have to tell me anything, but I hoped you might as I am offering money for the dragon. If the thing has already been sold, then I shall need to think again, but if not then I am sure Mr Jacobs will match any other offers for it."

Clara was not sure of that at all, but she was attempting to gull Albert and buy herself a little more time. If she walked away now she had nothing, and her only other lead looked even more hopeless.

"I don't speak for my employer," Albert told her.

"Then take him a message from me? Tell him, I want to buy the dragon."

"I'm not a messenger boy," Albert snarled. "I don't do things like that."

"And what, may I ask, will happen when you employer discovers he could have made a ready sum of money and you prevented it? Will he be delighted? I doubt it!" Clara leaned forward in her chair. "If you don't want to be the messenger boy, give me the name of the gang leader, tell me how I can get in touch with him and leave the rest to me."

Albert didn't instantly reply. Clara's implication that he might be in more trouble for refusing to put her in contact with his employer had worried him. Life in the criminal underworld was cutthroat and full of missteps. You might think you were doing everything you were supposed to be, only to discover that you had accidentally done something wrong. Gang leaders could be fickle, Albert knew that well enough. He had survived all these years because he was canny enough to know when to act against orders. Now might be one of those times, but he was not certain.

"Do I look like a great threat to your organisation?" Clara asked him. "I am just a woman, after all."

Normally Clara would revolt at being so self-deprecating, but on this occasion she felt it necessary. Albert sniffed haughtily, clearly giving Clara another good look and concluding that she was certainly no great threat to him.

"What will you do if I tell you?" he asked carefully.

"I will go to this gang leader and make my offer," Clara answered. "I only want the dragon back, nothing else."

Albert cast his eyes about the room thoughtfully.

"It was only a little green stone," he muttered to himself. "Why all the fuss?"

"Because of sentimental value," Clara said, not wanting to educate Albert as to the monetary value of the dragon. "Mr Jacobs was given the dragon by his late uncle. It was the last gift he ever received from him. A parting gift, except neither realised the parting would be so permanent. Shortly after, his uncle was killed in an accident. Mr Jacobs was just a boy, but the incident seared itself into his memory and the dragon became a vital link between him and his uncle."

Clara had a hunch that Albert might respond to such a story. He had his own tale of tragedy – the sudden loss of his father – which might make him understanding of Mr Jacobs' situation. At least that was what Clara hoped. It was difficult to know how much soul Albert had left after all these years with a gang of hardened criminals. Sentiment was redundant in such surroundings, it was something too easily mocked or lost. It could make a man vulnerable.

Clara watched Albert's face keenly. His eyes had turned to the photograph of him as a young man that Mrs Pear had accidentally left out on a table by the sofa. He was thinking – remembering.

"You won't go to the police?" he asked, his eyes coming back to Clara. She sensed he was weakening.

"Why would I? What would the police do?" Clara answered honestly. "My word alone is not enough to arrest your employer. They still need evidence of a crime and I imagine he is clever enough to avoid leaving any of that."

Albert was still dubious. He didn't like the idea of

getting into trouble for giving Clara a name. Clara tried one last attempt to convince him.

"You might earn yourself a cut of the money. For bringing me to the attention of your boss?"

Albert considered this suggestion. He seemed to like it. After a moment he conceded.

"All right. I'll give you his name," he said. "I work for a man called Brilliant Chang, I'll give you his London address."

Clara said nothing as he reeled off an address, her heart was sinking inside her. That was all she needed, to find herself involved with Brilliant Chang yet again. She managed not to sigh. She should have guessed he would be after the dragon. But she had his name now and that made her one step closer to restoring the dragon to Mr Jacobs. It was just a shame that doing so was going to take her back into the orbit of a man she had hoped never to see again.

Chapter Twenty-three

The last time Clara had found herself within the world of Brilliant Chang it had been as a result of police corruption. Chang had bribed a policeman to look the other way when it came to his nefarious activities and had caused the near murder of another constable. Clara had unravelled the mystery but Chang had eluded her. The wily Chinaman had slipped away with his freedom and a grin to Clara's failure. She had hoped never to meet him again.

Chang was dangerous; there was no doubt about that. He ran a criminal organisation in London, with his fingers in a lot of pies, though Chang was not interested in casual street crime. He had his mind set on greater and much more profitable adventures. Clara knew about only a fragment of the illegal activities he was involved in, but it was enough to know that he was a man with few scruples when it came to earning money.

Chang moved in affluent and important circles. His misdemeanours were not unknown to his society friends but they ignored them because he was charming, good looking and wealthy. Also, he had the sense not to bite the hand that fed him. He never caused his friends any harm.

Chang was ridiculously rich and you could just as easily find him partying the night away in a famous actress' mansion, as in some nightclub arranging his next heist. Chang owned people, just like he owned race horses and race cars, and a string of grand homes. He had made wise investments when it came to the world of high society. There were lords and earls across the country who owed Chang more than one favour – it might be because he had loaned them money at a desperate time, or because he had helped a wayward son or daughter out of a tricky and scandalous situation. Not to mention that he was at the heart of the drug trade in London, possibly in England. If you bought products from him you knew they were good stuff and not cut with other inferior goods like those from a street dealer. He charged well for these luxury highs, and he had clients who were attached to him forever more because of their addiction.

A man like that could pull strings to keep the police off his back. A man like that was very much out of Clara's league. But then, Clara never really took much heed of social status, just looking at her career choice would tell you that.

Clara would have to go to London and brave the lion's den. At the end of the day, if she could negotiate for the sale of the dragon back to Mr Jacobs, she would have fulfilled her mission and avoided losing face before the infuriatingly arrogant Chang. He had a committed a crime, yes, but it was the police's duty to arrest him for that. She just had to rescue the dragon.

Clara was planning her next trip to the capital, working out when Bob would be able to accompany her and which trains to catch, when the telephone in the hall rang. Clara began to rise but Annie, always on the ball, reached it first and answered. Clara listened to her half of the conversation.

"Hello… yes, she is here… may I say who is calling…"

Annie appeared in the parlour.

"Do you know a Mr McFry?"

Clara jumped up and ran to the telephone.

"Mr McFry," she said, hoping the businessman had news for her. "This is unexpected."

"Aye, well I have been doing a bit of poking around," McFry said placidly. "Thought you might like to know what I have learned."

"I would indeed," Clara said.

"Not that everyone wants to admit to paying for a robbery to be committed, but if you phrase things in the right sort of way and drop a few hints, well, it's surprising what people will talk about over a good lobster dinner," McFry was pleased with himself. He was a good negotiator, a man who had worked his way up from nothing by persuading people. He knew how to get people talking and saying things that common sense would normally suggest they shouldn't. "Do you happen to know the Ambassador for Japan?"

The question had been a genuine one. McFry often forgot that most people did not wander in his elevated circles.

"No," Clara said politely. "I haven't had the pleasure."

"Shame. Nice fellow. Good for a late night game of backgammon. And very keen on his country's cultural heritage being preserved in the face of modernisation," McFry continued without concern that Clara had no idea who he was talking about. "Japan is becoming a modern society, such as our own, but in the process they have been a little careless, on occasion, about their history. I think all societies are guilty of that, look at the great castles of England left to fall to ruin? Money can sometimes seem more important than culture."

"Especially when an ancient system of rule is being overhauled," Clara understood. "People might feel little compassion towards the objects of the past during such a time."

"You grasp my point," McFry sounded pleased down the phone line. "Mr Hokami, the Japanese ambassador in London, is most worried that Japan's heritage will be robbed away for the sake of profit, much like what has happened in Egypt, where the old pharaohs are sold as novelties to the tourists. Mr Hokami does not blame Englishmen for buying such goods when they are offered to them, but he does deplore his countrymen who are ransacking their country's history for profit. According to Mr Hokami, there is quite the trade in stolen antiquities from Japan."

"Might that include a certain jade dragon?" Clara asked.

She was certain McFry was smiling to himself as he replied.

"It would, indeed. Thefts from the imperial palace of Japan have been going on since the last century. The penalty for being caught thieving is death, but the rewards for a successful theft are high enough to counter the fear. Objects have been disappearing from the palace at an unhealthy rate. Things worsened during the war, because of the economic impact the conflict had on the country. Japan is an uneasy nation right now and their old ties with Great Britain and the Empire are looking frayed."

"That sounds ominous," Clara observed, "from a political point of view, but what about the dragon?"

"Mr Hokami knows I am a collector of Japanese antiques. He knows my interest in his nation's culture," McFry explained. "We play backgammon one evening a week. Finding a competent opponent is challenging and Mr Hokami and myself are very equal in our skill, so we regularly aim to outwit each other. Yesterday evening we met as usual for dinner and a game. During the course of the evening I brought up the news of a stolen netsuke, one that had been exhibited at the British Museum. Mr Hokami knew very swiftly the object I was describing, as he had been to the exhibition and seen the green jade dragon for himself. When I mentioned that the British Museum experts had their concerns about how the item ended up in England, he became quite talkative."

"He had his concerns too?"

"Not just concerns, he knew the dragon was a stolen item," McFry had that pleased sound to his voice again. "Mr Hokami had quite the story to tell, and I think it ties in nicely with the side of the story you told me. According to the ambassador, a few hundred years ago the then emperor of Japan was deeply concerned with his own mortality. As comes with such positions of power, he feared the prick of an assassin's blade and also the creeping hand of old age, that persistent and unavoidable assassin of men. The emperor did not wish to leave his life of glory to travel to the next world, despite ideas that the next was as grand, or even grander, than this life. The emperor was the sort of man who valued what he physically had, over an idea of what might be. So he became obsessed with preserving his existence eternally.

"The emperor commissioned all manner of objects and medicines to secure his immortality. Among them were items of rare jade, a precious stone that has been considered the key to immortality in the Orient. The Chinese emperor, for instance, would drink crushed jade in alcohol to increase his longevity. What is good for a Chinese emperor, ought to be good for a Japanese one, or so the Japanese emperor imagined. He became obsessed with having jade about him, believing it would preserve him indefinitely.

"Among the objects he had commissioned were two jade dragons. The dragon in itself is a lucky symbol, a symbol of power and fortune. The pair of dragon netsukes were made to hang on the emperor's belt and to offer constant protection. They were made by the best craftsman of the age, his name sadly now lost largely to time. It is said he was rewarded handsomely for the work, but was penalised a finger so that he might never craft something so fine for anyone else."

"That seems the fate of all too many master craftsman in antiquity," Clara remarked.

"You would think they would have learned by now,"

McFry chuckled. "Ah, but I should not mock the man's loss. Anyway, the jade dragons were made and were prized by the emperor. The flies in the ointment were the emperor's heirs who did not much like the idea of their father living forever. A plan was concocted. Fearing the jade dragons did truly carry a magical power, a concubine was sent to the emperor one night with the object of drugging him while he was engaged in her pleasures and then removing the jade dragons to a safe place. Once off the royal body, they could not wield their much-feared magic.

"That night an assassin, hired by the emperor's sons, was sent to his chamber and murdered him. The deed done, once the court had settled from the shock, the eldest son took to the imperial throne. But the power of the dragons appears not to have been as mitigated as the sons had hoped. Not long after he was made emperor, the eldest son contracted a fever and died. The next heir ruled barely a year before the great excesses of his lifestyle took him to the next life too, and the last heir slipped from his sedan chair at the coronation, fell out onto the paved road to the palace and cracked open his skull. The three murderers had all apparently succumbed to the jade dragon's curse.

"The new emperor, a distant relation and not involved in the assassination of his predecessor, had the jade dragons removed to a specially locked cabinet where he hoped they would cause harm to no one, especially himself. He ruled for nearly forty years and it seems the curse did not touch him. But the legend of the jade dragons' power grew. Mr Hokami explained that when the first western visitors came to Japan and heard the story they were curious about the dragons and were granted permission to look upon the magical creatures. Illustrations were made of them and Mr Hokami referred to one which I was able to locate in an old book written by a visitor to the country. The image tallied exactly with the dragon I saw at the British Museum, down to the craftsman's characters etched into the base."

"And then they were stolen?" Clara queried.

"One was," McFry answered. "At some point between one tourist being shown them and another asking to see them, one dragon disappeared. The servants at the palace naturally blamed the previous tourist, the officials at the court blamed the servants. The man who held the keys to the cabinet lost his head, by that I mean literally."

"Oh dear," Clara said, appalled at such drastic measures. "But, I take it, no one really knew who was responsible?"

"No," McFry agreed. "The dragon was lost, at least for a while. Then someone reported seeing it being sold to an Englishman. You have to understand, there were spies for the emperor everywhere in Japan and they often informed him of what foreign tourists were getting up to. The English were especially viewed with suspicion. The emperor sent men out to locate the dragon, but the trader who had sold it had already vanished. The Englishman, oblivious to having committed any crime, was easier to pursue. Mr Hokami did not know the whole story, but it seems agents were sent to track this man and retrieve the dragon. They failed and never returned to Japan. Until the exhibition earlier this year, no one knew what had become of the green jade netsuke stolen from the imperial palace."

Clara found herself sighing as the story concluded.

"What did Mr Hokami have to say about the burglary of Mr Jacobs' house?"

"I think he wasn't surprised. There are wealthy Japanese in this country who have as much concern for the heritage of their nation as he does. He thinks, like I do, that someone paid to have the dragon stolen so it might be returned home."

"That is a very noble idea," Clara pointed out. "And thieves are rarely noble. Someone might have stolen it because it was valuable."

Clara was thinking that Brilliant Chang was neither

Japanese nor much interested in heritage, but he did have an abiding fascination with money.

"Mr Hokami hinted that he knew who would go to those lengths for Japan," McFry explained. "I was unable to get the name, however."

"No matter, you have gone to great lengths for me already," Clara assured him. "What I can't fathom is why no one offered to simply buy it back from Mr Jacobs?"

"Oh, I can think of a lot of reasons. Pride, not wanting to pay for an item that was stolen, fear that Mr Jacobs would reject an offer and then suspect the person who made it when the burglary occurred. You must admit, the way the dragon was taken has left little trace and given the person behind the plan the chance to remain anonymous."

Clara could not disagree with that. But she knew something that McFry and Mr Hokami could not know. She knew that Brilliant Chang had orchestrated the burglary, either for his own personal benefit or at the behest of someone else. Tracing him was the key to retrieving the dragon, though Clara was as yet uncertain of who she was precisely supposed to retrieve it for. It was, after all, a stolen item that should be returned to Japan.

And then there was the question of Mr Jacobs' uncle and his unfortunate carriage accident. That was beginning to seem less and less likely to have been a chance mishap. And what of the agents sent after him who never returned home? Was it simply because they could not risk returning to Japan empty-handed? Clara knew there was yet more to this story than she had been told and London was likely to be the only place to find answers.

Chapter Twenty-four

They were once again a party of four as they set off for London the following Saturday. Tommy and Captain O'Harris were as insistent as before about accompanying Clara, and Bob was a natural addition to the party. The weather had taken a turn for the worse and they had to dodge puddles and people with umbrellas as Clara took them all first to Scotland Yard.

Clara had paid another call on Inspector Park-Coombs after her conversation with Mr McFry and had explained the story the Scotsman had told her, along with her concerns about the unfortunate death of Edmund Jacobs. The fact that her information had come from the Japanese ambassador himself, (via McFry) added credence to the possibility that Edmund Jacobs' accident had been less than accidental. Clara doubted it was important to her case, but wished to follow up the mystery, perhaps to bring justice to the poor man who had died all those years ago. It might lead her to the agents who were tracking him, but she doubted it. Those men had vanished long ago, they would be very old men now and it seemed unlikely they were still in pursuit of the dragon, though there was no telling, of course. Perhaps they were still pursuing their mission all these years later.

The story expounded, Park-Coombs agreed to arrange for Clara to meet with his counterpart in London. The same man who had offered information on the thieves. Park-Coombs would smooth the way and enable Clara to ask her questions. She might not get answers, but at least she would have tried.

There was, however, no room for four in the interview, and Clara persuaded her male companions to waste time at a nearby café while she spoke with Inspector Arran of Scotland Yard. After all, she was hardly likely to come to any harm within the confines of the police station.

So it was that Clara found herself awaiting Inspector Arran, friend and colleague of Inspector Park-Coombs, in a large tiled reception area that felt chilly on this damp and gloomy day. There were several people in the reception, and there was an air of discontent about the place. People were queuing to report crimes or nuisance affairs, without really much hope of anything being done about them. The London constabulary was as over-strained as every other constabulary about the country, only they had a city to police and all the complications that added.

Clara was relieved when a gentleman in a grey suit appeared in the reception and introduced himself as Inspector Arran. He was not very tall, about Clara's height and with pale eyes and a thin face that was etched with the lines of a life of too little sleep. He smiled readily enough, and his eyes crinkled up. He shook Clara's hand when she offered it.

"You must be Miss Fitzgerald."

"Yes, Inspector Park-Coombs rang ahead for me," Clara explained.

Inspector Arran merely nodded, too busy to worry about lengthy introductions.

"My office is this way."

He led Clara along a corridor and to a small room that was fractionally warmer than the reception. It was cramped because of the numerous filing cabinets and bookshelves propping up the walls. A desk just about squeezed into the middle and it was somewhat remarkable that Arran was able to move around it to reach his chair. He sat down nearly elbowing over a leafy plant growing in a large pot beside the desk, and motioned for Clara to do the same. Now facing each other, he rested his arms upon the desk.

"Park-Coombs says you are a private detective?"

"I am…" Clara said, but the rest of her statement was lost as Arran continued quickly.

"He says you are looking into an old case for someone. A Mr Jacobs, who lost his uncle several years ago?"

"It would have been the late 1860s or early 1870s," Clara added. "It was ruled an accident at the time."

"But you have reason to believe it was something else?"

Clara paused. Did she have a reason?

"Mr Edmund Jacobs was the unwitting recipient of stolen goods while travelling in Japan. The goods were from the Imperial Palace and agents were sent to retrieve them. This I have on sound authority from the Japanese ambassador. However, Edmund Jacobs died and the agents disappeared," Clara tilted her head a little to the side. "Coincidences bother me, Inspector, perhaps they bother you too. A man being pursued by dangerous agents of a foreign power suddenly dies and those agents vanish too? Such events cause me to pause and question."

Arran smiled at her.

"Park-Coombs said you had good instincts. He reckons that if you were a man you would be a police inspector yourself."

"Unfortunately, such an avenue is denied to me," Clara replied. "So I must dabble at the edges, and run the risk of being criticised as a nosy, interfering busybody."

"He said you were that too," Arran now grinned. "But he also said you were worth listening to, especially as you seem to be on the verge of solving a crime his own force has not the time or resources to investigate sufficiently."

"The Inspector is a very good policeman," Clara hastily added. "He has my full respect and it is truly not his fault that he is under-funded and under-staffed."

"I wasn't criticising him," Arran reassured her. "I know the limitations we police must face. You have the opportunity to step around some of those obstacles."

"And yet I am often faced with others," Clara added. "Which is why I value the relationship I have with the police."

"You need not convince me," Arran waved a hand at her. "I was convinced by Park-Coombs. We trained together, you know. Now, I pulled out the old file on the Edmund Jacobs' accident. It was investigated at the time and the file was rather interesting. It would appear that the police also had their doubts about the accident, but did not have the evidence to prove anything."

Arran pulled out a drawer and removed the file.

"It was 21 August 1871, nine o'clock in the morning. Edmund Jacobs was staying in his London flat and had informed his butler that he was going out to speak to his banker. He left the house alone and on foot around half past eight. By nine he was on one of the main thoroughfares waiting to cross the road. Witnesses remarked that he seemed agitated, one fellow who saw the accident said that Jacobs constantly kept looking behind him. Then suddenly, as if he saw something or someone who frightened him, he started into the road straight into the path of a coal cart. The whole thing was over in seconds. The horse managed to dodge him, but he slipped straight under the cartwheel and was crushed."

"It sounds as though Jacobs was not as unaware of his pursuers as I had imagined," Clara noted. "I had assumed he was oblivious to them, but now it appears he was alert to them."

"These Japanese agents?" Arran considered the possibility. "From what I gather, Edmund Jacobs paid a flying visit to his brother in Brighton before returning to London. I would suggest he guessed he was being followed and probably knew why. So he went to Brighton, ahead of his pursuers, hoping to briefly shake them while he placed the stolen dragon into his nephew's hands. Then he went back to London. That is my policeman's instinct. If Jacobs knew he was being hunted before leaving Japan, he would have made efforts to avoid being on the same ship as his pursuers. That would buy him time to hide the dragon. When they arrived in London, he would already be back and there would be no evidence of his hasty visit to his brother."

"And he was just an Englishman who they knew nothing about," Clara added to his theory. "They did not know if he had family. Even if they knew his name, the number of Jacobs in this country would have defied a search for relatives."

"And the funeral was private," Arran persisted. "Invited guests only. There were over a hundred of them, I might add. Private does not mean small, but it does mean the Japanese agents could not have attended and located family members. And, as it happens, the Jacobs clan is quite extensive. To have ascertained who precisely he gave the dragon to would have been quite challenging. I doubt they succeeded, just as I doubt they spoke a great deal of English. Trusted agents for the imperial palace would not necessarily be fluent with foreign tongues."

Clara agreed with all this. With the death of Edmund Jacobs, the agents for the emperor would have lost their one means of locating the dragon. Faced with this fact, they would have found themselves in a dreadful situation.

"Jacobs' flat was burgled shortly after the funeral," Arran continued. "It was one of the things that alerted the police to everything not being as simple as it seemed. That and the testimony of witnesses who said Jacobs seemed anxious."

"It all pointed to something being amiss," Clara could see that plainly. "But there was not enough to take the matter further."

"The police poked around, but resources are tight at

the best of times and there was no suggestion that Jacobs was pushed. He might have been frightened into stepping into the roadway, but that does not make for murder. It doesn't make for manslaughter. No crime had actually been committed."

Clara pondered over all this for a moment. Arran opened the file and showed her several witness statements. There was the one from the cart driver who had tried to avoid Jacobs and failed. There was the statement of the old man who thought Jacobs seemed agitated, and there was one from a nurse who was waiting to cross the road with her young charge, who also thought Jacobs seemed on-edge and constantly looking behind him. No one had expected him to step out into the road, however.

"I suppose it is too much to ask if anyone saw a Japanese man on the scene?"

Arran grinned and shook his head, that would have been too obvious. None of the witnesses had noticed such a man, though, on the whole, they were more worried about what was happening in the road than on the pavement. Edmund Jacobs had lived for around ten minutes after the cartwheel went over his torso. A heavy load of coal is easily of sufficient weight to crush a man, especially when that force is centred down onto a narrow wheel. But Jacobs did not die at once. He gasped and cried out. A woman bent down by him and held his hand while someone went to summon a doctor. A police constable was spotted and beckoned over. The road drew to a standstill as the aftermath of the tragedy emerged. Jacobs lay between the front and back wheels of the coal cart and the driver could not move his vehicle without further injuring the man. His horse was restless, upset by the incident and he had to drop from his cart seat and soothe the fretful creature. All in all, those ten minutes had been ghastly for everyone present and agonising for Jacobs as he tried to draw breath through his mangled chest, little guessing that his ribs had pierced his lungs in multiple places and each breath drew him unerringly towards his demise.

He did not live to see the doctor who was hastily brought to him.

"The one thing I conclude from all this," Arran remarked thoughtfully. "Is that Edmund Jacobs not only knew he was being pursued, but also why. He placed the jade dragon into the hands of his nephew for safe keeping, but none of his other treasures from Japan. Those were still in a steam trunk at the docks when he died. They were only delivered the day after."

Clara had also come to the conclusion that Jacobs had known the dragon was stolen, if not at the time he bought it, certainly afterwards. Why else would men chase him down? Ordinary thieves do not follow a man across the ocean. Jacobs could have saved himself by doing the honourable thing of restoring the dragon to the Japanese authorities.

"There is one other thing," Inspector Arran pulled a second file from his desk. "There is a reference note in Jacobs' file. My predecessor who investigated the case sensed a Japanese link to the affair and kept an ear open for any crimes he thought might be related. A few days after the burglary on Edmund Jacobs' house, where, in particular, his steam trunk containing Japanese antiques was ransacked, two bodies were dragged from the Thames. They were the corpses of two men, both Japanese by their clothing and appearance. They carried no English money nor anything that would suggest they had been in the country a while. One still had a ticket on him for a steamer. He had arrived a day after Jacobs returned home.

"There was not much to go on, but one of the men wore a shoe with a distinctive pattern on the sole. The same pattern had been noted in a muddy print found in the flowerbeds outside Jacobs' flat. The surmise was that this man had been involved in the burglary. But since nothing was taken, it would appear that whatever he was looking for was not there. Both men had drowned in the river."

"Because they had failed in their mission," Clara observed. "The Japanese take honour very seriously."

Well, at least Clara did not have to fear that the agents were still alive. So who was after the dragon? She had another man to visit, one she was much less looking forward to seeing than Inspector Arran. She thanked the policeman for his time and effort, and he made her promise to update him once the case was solved. He didn't seem to doubt she would find the dragon and his confidence in her was elating and unexpected.

Clara set forth from Scotland Yard with a new resolve in her stride.

Chapter Twenty-five

How to confront a master criminal in his own domain? As it turned out, Clara found making an appointment the simplest of strategies. Brilliant Chang operated a legitimate business as a front to his illegal activities. To many people Brilliant Chang was an aspiring entrepreneur who ran Chang Emporium, a large multi-level shop that specialised in exotic goods. People could wander into Chang Emporium and come away with a Japanese porcelain vase, or Indian fire screen or any number of foreign novelties for their homes. This friendly, respectable façade aided Chang in hiding his less salubrious activities.

Clara had telephoned Chang Emporium before leaving for London and had arranged an appointment with the man himself. Her excuse for the meeting was that she was seeking an unusual exotic object for a client and wanted to ask Brilliant if he could locate the thing for her. The girl who she had spoken with had tried to convince Clara that Chang Emporium sold absolutely everything, and if she only came down to see for herself she was bound to find the object she wanted. Clara had politely pointed out that this was hugely unlikely; the object was rare and expensive, but she hoped Mr Chang would be able to source it for her, if only she could meet with him personally to explain. Finally the girl conceded defeat and arranged an appointment.

Clara arrived at Chang Emporium with her entourage. She had made it very plain she would speak to Chang alone and would only call for them if she needed them. Bob had accepted this statement without question. Tommy had grumped about feeling useless, but had eventually agreed. O'Harris was the challenging one;

"He is a dangerous criminal!" he hissed in Clara's ear as they looked at a window display of Chinese fans and silk kimonos.

"Not here he isn't," Clara explained persistently. "Besides, I am no threat to him. In fact, I might be able to offer him a business proposition. He won't wish me harm."

"What if he doesn't trust you?" O'Harris demanded. "He might expect betrayal."

"I imagine Mr Chang always expects betrayal," Clara shrugged. "I shall have to convince him it is not in my interest to betray him."

Tommy could see the two were at an impasse, so he intervened.

"We will be nearby, old man," he told O'Harris. "Clara can scream loud if she needs too. Better he doesn't know we are there, else he will make arrangements to deal with us before Clara, if it comes to that. Which it won't."

The captain was not impressed, but he eventually backed down. Clara was not going to be dissuaded. The matter resolved, Clara went inside ahead of them to meet with Chang.

The Emporium was a glittery place of exotic oddities. Some were beautiful, some were ugly and others were downright strange. Clara wandered past a carved wooden elephant that stood as tall as her waist and found herself face-to-face with some growling Indian god with too many arms and a face like an irate mastiff. Dodging around these she found herself among a display of

Chinese silks in vivid blues, reds and greens. Cranes and deer were embroidered across the shimmering fabric, and danced among flowers and trees.

Clara finally removed herself from this attractive display and came instead to a long counter where a Chinese girl smiled at her brightly.

"I have an appointment to see Mr Chang," Clara explained.

"You see his secretary," the girl answered, then held up a finger to indicate Clara should bear with her a moment. She picked up a telephone from behind her counter, which was apparently an internal one that connected with the other floors in the shop. After a moment the girl spoke in Chinese to someone else. Clara could not understand a word.

"She come," the girl said with that same bright smile when she put down the telephone.

Clara moved to one side to wait and was intrigued to see how busy the Emporium was. During the brief time she was awaiting the secretary, several customers came to the desk with their purchases. Most of the people were English and Clara was mildly surprised at the strange oddities that seemed to attract them. One woman, a respectable looking matron who you might imagine an almost permanent fixture at her local church, came to the counter with a smaller version of the ghastly Indian god Clara had stumbled upon. She bought it without a glimmer of embarrassment or concern for what her neighbours might think. Clara was amused. London was so different to her little town.

A woman appeared. She was also Chinese and older than the girl. Clara found it hard to judge her age, but she was certainly mature. She was slender and wearing English clothing, and her hair was pulled back into a Chinese style bun.

"Miss Fitzgerald?" she asked Clara in perfect English.

Clara admitted she was.

"This way. Mr Chang is ready for you," the secretary

led Clara to a staircase that ran up the middle of the Emporium. They went up three floors and finally came to the private section of the shop, where the offices and storerooms stood. Clara was shown to a door with the name 'Chang' on a brass plate.

"Here," the secretary opened the door and showed Clara in.

The room was spacious, far more spacious than the cramped confines of poor Inspector Arran's office. Exotic art lined the walls. Everything from a giant Arabian decorated tile to Chinese parchment and Japanese watercolours. Clara found her eyes wandering all about the room as she walked from the door to Chang's desk. It was a surprisingly long distance, or so it seemed. When Clara finally dragged her eyes from the walls, she was looking at the man who had so confounded her the previous year and had escaped the hands of justice.

Brilliant Chang was good looking and charming. He had a large smile and seemed always amused. He slicked his hair back in the latest English style and wore expensively tailored suits. Clara had seen photographs of him mingling with the rich and famous. Landed gentry asked Chang to their dinner parties, politicians met him for a drink, celebrities hung off his every word. Chang was, right in that instant, the most wanted man in England – for a variety of reasons.

"Miss Fitzgerald, this is a nice surprise. Take a seat."

Clara sat in the chair at the far side of the desk. Her eyes dropped to an ivory tiger sitting on Chang's desk and roaring pointlessly at thin air.

"You want to buy something unusual?" Chang asked, leaning across the desk and grinning from ear-to-ear. "Or do you want to try and implicate me in some crime?"

"I was honest about my reasons for coming here," Clara promised. "I am looking for a rare item, and I do believe you are the best placed person to find it for me. Whether you will or not is another matter."

"You intrigue me," Chang leaned back in his chair.

"What might I be able to help you with?"

Clara studied his face. She was unconvinced that Chang was so ignorant of her purpose. She did not doubt for a moment that word had spread to him of a female private detective looking for a stolen jade netsuke. Even if Simon Clark had not spoken, there were plenty of witnesses to her enquiries, not to mention the other men she had talked to. And then there was Albert Pear, who was clever enough to think to warn his boss about the woman seeking him.

"The green jade dragon netsuke," Clara told him bluntly. "The one you arranged to steal. I want to arrange for its return. No doubt you will want a good price for it."

Chang's smile broadened, an almost impossible feat as he already seemed to have stretched his cheeks to the limit. He steepled his fingers before him, like he was contemplating a subtle chess move.

"I am a businessman. I don't go around stealing things," he said.

"I am not interested in the crime itself," Clara brushed aside his statement. "Only what it will cost to restore the dragon to Mr Jacobs. I have a feeling you did not steal it for yourself, but rather with a buyer in mind."

"Why would you say that?" Chang asked, dropping the pretence that he knew nothing about a burglary.

"You are not Japanese. What does their heritage matter to you? But the value of the dragon would not have escaped you. Perhaps you might consider adding it to your collection here, but I rather fancy you are too pragmatic for that. The dragon attracts some dangerous people."

Chang's eyes glimmered with intrigue.

"What do you know about all that? What dangerous people?" he asked, testing Clara.

"The dragon, from what I understand, was originally stolen from the imperial palace. When it was sold to Mr Jacobs' uncle two agents were sent to retrieve it. Neither succeeded, but I doubt that means the Japanese have simply forgotten about it," Clara paused. "A lot of people saw that dragon on display in the British Museum. Including the Japanese ambassador. He recognised it for what it really was. Who is to say someone else did not do the same? Should word have reached Japan, more agents might be sent, or diplomatic efforts made to retrieve the dragon. All too invasive for the quality of privacy you value, Mr Chang."

Chang was clearly delighted by Clara's knowledge and her perceptiveness. She half expected him to clap her for a good performance.

"You have been busy. And yes the dragon is too much of a nuisance for me to wish to keep it. The question you have to really ask is whether I have already sold it on," Chang watched her reaction, but Clara did not reveal anything. "I would hardly keep the thing on my person."

"Even if you have sold it on, I imagine you can get it back," Clara replied. "I think you are a cunning man."

"Maybe," Chang shrugged.

"I don't much care who hired you to steal the dragon," Clara persisted. "All I want is to find a way to restore it to Mr Jacobs. He will pay any reasonable figure for it."

"Are you not concerned that the item was already stolen by the time it fell into Mr Jacobs' hands?" Chang asked politely. "Is he the rightful owner?"

"I can't answer that easily," Clara admitted. "In fairness the dragon should be restored to Japan. It is an item of their heritage and one that was stolen. But that is not quite my decision to make, and a lot of years have passed since the crime occurred. Mr Jacobs is an innocent victim in all this, he is unaware of the artefact's origins. I will, however, explain this all in full to him and allow him the chance to decide what the fate of the dragon should be."

Chang was silent a moment, clearly considering all she had said.

"I might have already sent it on its way to Japan," he pointed out.

"You mean, the person employing you had honourable motives?" Clara said. "Wanting to restore a piece of their country's history?"

"Why not?" suggested Chang.

"That is possible," Clara observed. "Whether they would go through such criminal channels to achieve such a noble goal is questionable. Well, is the dragon back in Japan already?"

Chang toyed with her, letting her wait for his reply. He was beginning to irritate Clara immensely.

"No," he admitted at last. "The dragon is in a safe place. The person who commissioned its theft has yet to pay me for it. Their tardiness is beginning to irritate me."

"So you would be open to another offer?"

Chang folded his fingers together, his eyes narrowed, the smile dimmed.

"How can I be sure you are not intending to cheat me? Perhaps send the police after me the instant I agree to sell you the dragon?"

"What would I achieve?" Clara responded. "I have no direct evidence you were behind the burglary, other than the fact you possess the dragon, which you could state you bought in good faith off someone else. The only reason I know it was you behind all this is because I have spoken with some very dubious individuals. Individuals who will avoid the police and will not make good witnesses against you, for a start, they value your good graces too much. I could go to the police and say Brilliant Chang stole the jade dragon, but what would I gain?"

"You are beginning to understand the way the world works," Chang nodded. "You are not quite as naïve a little girl as I met last year."

Clara rankled at this assessment, but she did not say anything. Let Chang play his games, one day she would succeed in running him to ground and it would be his own arrogance that cost him.

"Will you sell my client the dragon?" Clara demanded.

Chang mused for a little longer, then his broad smile

returned.

"I will, Miss Fitzgerald. I shall write down a figure I am prepared to accept for it and you can take this to your client," Chang took a piece of writing paper from his desk drawer and used a fine fountain pen to write something on it. He folded the paper and handed it to her. "Now, I must owe you an apology."

"Apology?" Clara asked in surprise.

"When Albert Pear informed me that a woman detective was sniffing around the theft, I suspected you and imagined you were intending to turn me in to the police. I did not believe Pear that you had the sense to just bargain with me over the dragon," Chang shrugged his shoulders. "I was wrong and I did something I regret."

Clara frowned.

"What?"

"I sent a man to Brighton to frighten you. I sent him before I heard you wanted an appointment with me. I was not able to track him down and rescind my instructions. Clearly he has not yet arrived in Brighton and sought you out," Chang paused. "I shall write an extra note that you can give him should he appear on your doorstep. It will tell him to leave you alone."

Chang was writing again, but Clara had half risen from her chair, her mind whirring. Annie was all alone at home. If the man arrived today, while they were gone, she would have to face him.

"Does he know what I look like?" Clara asked fast.

"No," Chang answered. "I just told him to frighten the lady private detective in Brighton. He needed no other information."

Chang had written the paper and Clara snatched it from him. She glowered at him.

"If anything has happened to my friend back home…"

"You will do what Miss Fitzgerald?" Chang asked innocently.

They both knew there was not a lot she could do. Clara somehow managed to be polite as she concluded the meeting in haste. She had, after all, to think of Mr Jacobs too. But all she wanted right then was to race to the train station and get back to Brighton as swiftly as possible. She hurried out of the Emporium, trying to contain her anxiety for fear O'Harris or Tommy would do something rash (like attacking Chang) if she let them know the danger Annie was in. Instead she told them that she had what she needed and they ought to head home. No one argued. London was grey and bleak that day and no one wanted to stay.

They headed to the train station, Clara terrified that her activities had placed Annie in danger and desperate to get home as soon as possible.

Chapter Twenty-six

The train journey seemed interminably long. Clara's anxiety, increasing with each passing minute, finally attracted the attention of her companions and Tommy demanded to know what was wrong. He guessed that something had occurred during the meeting with Chang to cause Clara's unease. With London rapidly falling behind them, and no opportunity for the men to do something rash, Clara explained what Chang had told her about the goon he had sent to Brighton. Tommy only took a second to realise that Annie could be at risk. Now they were all willing the train to move faster and Bob was promising that whoever this fellow was, he would make mincemeat of him for daring to come near his friends. The rest of the journey he kept making fists with his hands and cracking his knuckles.

Brighton train station was a delightful sight. Clara hopped off the train and ran into the stationmaster's office to ask to use the telephone again. The stationmaster was still remembering the last time she had inconvenienced him, but the urgency on Clara's face persuaded him to allow her to use his telephone. Unfortunately, the call home went unanswered and Clara's anxiety was worsened by Annie's failure to pick up the phone.

They hurried for home as quickly as they could. No one spoke. As the house came into sight Clara was looking for signs that anything was amiss. One of her neighbours popped out of their front door and for an instant Clara thought the woman was coming to see her, to explain how something awful had happened while she was away. But the woman was only putting her empty milk bottles out. She looked up at Clara and gave her a wave, clearly mildly baffled by the haste with which Clara was running home. Because Clara was running now. Clara returned the wave and then jumped over her own doorstep and burst into the hallway.

"Annie? Annie?"

Annie appeared from the kitchen. She was drying her wet hands on a towel. She looked at Clara with concern.

"What has happened? You are out of breath," she came to her friend and rested her hand on her shoulder. "Did something go wrong in London?"

"Oh Annie!" Clara flung her arms around the girl and hugged her. "Why didn't you answer the telephone?"

"It rang while I was in the garden collecting the washing," Annie explained. "By the time I had heard it and rushed in, it had stopped. What is the matter?"

By now Tommy, O'Harris and Bob were also bursting through the door in various states of breathlessness. Annie was looking at them in astonishment.

"It's a long story," Clara said.

"Well, I just made a pot of tea and my fruit cake should be cool by now. Perhaps you ought to all come through to the kitchen and take a seat. You can explain to me then," Annie instructed firmly.

A short while later they were all restored to normality. Annie's cake was helping them recuperate and, as Clara explained her anxiety, the whole affair seemed far less frightening to them all. Annie was amused by their concern.

"I am sure he would have realised I was only your servant," she informed Clara when the tale was told. "I doubt he would have bothered me."

"There is still the problem that this gentleman might come to call," O'Harris remarked, looking worriedly at Clara.

Clara then explained Chang's note. They all relaxed again.

"I wish you had told me sooner, then I would have given Chang a piece of my mind," O'Harris grumbled.

"And that would not have helped me solve the dragon case," Clara reminded him. "No, it was best we did nothing. You don't gain anything by rash actions when it comes to Chang. He is too sly for that."

"Well, I am going to get dinner on," Annie rose from the table. "You'll stay, won't you Bob?"

"Yes, please," Bob grinned at Annie, who was close to being his most favourite person. "What are you cooking?"

"Lamb cutlets with bubble and squeak. And there is an apple crumble to follow."

With this information imparted, Annie went to her work.

Clara went upstairs and changed from her travelling clothes which seemed to have absorbed the smell of London smog and coal smoke from the train. She was beginning to feel quite like her usual self by the time she walked back down. She had just reached the hallway when the doorbell rang. Clara answered it.

"Clara!"

On her doorstep was Sarah Butler. Her red hair was flying wildly about her head and her face was crimson from crying. Clara was shocked by her appearance and quickly brought her into the house. Shuffling her through to the currently empty dining room, she shut the door and made Sarah sit in a chair.

"What has happened?" she asked in alarm.

Sarah was shivering from delayed shock. She had clearly been through quite an ordeal.

"It has been a bloody awful day!" she declared to Clara. "First, Mr Butterworth called at my office and yelled at me for helping his wife."

Sarah Butler pulled a handkerchief from her sleeve and blew her nose into it.

"He was so angry that I had revealed where he lived to his wife and that she had gone to see him."

Clara could imagine, having witnessed the man's ire herself. But Mr Butterworth was all hot air, she could not see how his bluster had reduced Sarah to such a state.

"What else?" Clara asked carefully.

"After I finally got rid of Mr Butterworth, another man called on me. He was horrible looking, mean and tall, with this scar across his face and beady eyes. He had a knife!" Sarah gasped at the memory. "He stormed in and asked if I was a private detective. I said I was and he proceeded to threaten me. Told me I was to back off from my case, because if I didn't horrible things would happen to me. He waved the knife about and said I was in over my head and I ought to stop at once or there was no telling how it would all end.

"I don't know how I kept calm as he spoke, because my heart was pounding and I was utterly terrified. Then he finished his speech, pointed the knife at me and with one last look left. As soon as I heard the door slam shut I burst into tears. I just couldn't believe Mr Butterworth would stoop to such things!"

"It was not Mr Butterworth," Clara explained, because she had guessed exactly who had gone to see the unfortunate Sarah Butler. "I'm afraid this is my fault. The current case I am involved in concerns a rather unpleasant criminal. I saw him today and he revealed that he had sent a man to frighten me off the case. He was unable to contact the man and rescind his order. I have been awaiting this thug myself, but obviously he mixed up his detectives."

"This was all your fault!" Sarah accused Clara. "This horrible day is all because of you!"

"I hardly sent him to your office on purpose," Clara countered, disliking the tone Sarah took with her. "Nor is it my fault your advertisement looked so similar to mine, causing confusion to such a person. The man who sent this thug is utterly unaware there is now a second detective in Brighton and had not bothered to inform his goon of my name. I am sorry this happened to you, but it is not really my fault."

Sarah started to argue, but thought better of it. She was after sympathy, not more heated words. She put the handkerchief to her face and breathed into it, for a moment finding peace in that pocket of nothingness.

"Would you like a stiff drink?" there was a drinks cabinet in the dining room and Clara mixed a gin and tonic for her guest without waiting for an answer. She stood it before Sarah. "These sorts of things happen in this line of work. I have been threatened a few times."

Sarah looked up at her sharply.

"Really?"

"Oh yes. I had a man break into the house and try to hurt me. I cracked him over the head with a poker in this very room. People don't like private detectives snooping about. You tend to make enemies."

Sarah Butler looked very glum.

"I had not expected that," she said. "I thought people would be glad of the help."

"People are," Clara assured her. "The ones you help, that is. But often there is a second party in these affairs and they generally don't appreciate your interference. Take your case, for instance, no doubt Mrs Butterworth is delighted with you, but Mr Butterworth has suffered as a result of your detection and is not so happy. With every case there will be such a person."

"And do they all come to yell at you?" Sarah asked, earnestly.

"Not all," Clara reassured her. "Just some. You develop a thick skin."

Sarah seemed unconvinced. She sipped at her gin and tonic, but was clearly not used to spirits and grimaced at the taste.

"I don't think I can do this," she said.

"I can get you another drink," Clara offered.

"No, not the drink. I mean... being a detective," Sarah stared across the room, looking at nothing in particular. "I thought it was just about solving puzzles and I like puzzles. I didn't think about the people involved. I thought I would stand aside from all that. I would just present my evidence, solve a mystery and step away. Instead there is all this complication. I was upset enough when Mr Butterworth shouted at me. His anger shocked me. I realised how difficult I had made life for him and I could not honestly say that he deserved it. He didn't seem to deserve it at all. I felt so awful."

"It is a complicated business," Clara agreed, sitting on the edge of the dining table. "People very rarely appreciate what you are doing, aside from your client. And even then, if you don't get the answers they hoped for, they can become nasty. I suppose I am just used to it."

"It doesn't worry you what people think of you, does it?" Sarah asked.

Clara thought about the question for a moment.

"Not really, at least, not most people."

"That is how we are different," Sarah sighed. "I care a great deal what people think of me. I don't like people taking against me or being angry with me. I have really made a fool of myself, haven't I?"

"No," Clara told her promptly. "You tried something new. That was a brave move. Just because it didn't quite go as you planned does not take away from the fact you tried. We can't always succeed at what we do."

"I never seem to succeed," Sarah said miserably. "Now I have nothing, yet again."

"You are going to stop being a private detective?" Clara asked tentatively, not wanting to show the delight this would give her. Having two detectives in Brighton was just too complicated and having the backlash from Sarah's cases fall on her was just as bad as thinking the consequences of her actions might fall back on Sarah.

"I… maybe…" Sarah tried a little more of the drink, but it was too strong for her and she pushed it away. "I don't know what else I can do though. I have to work, but what work is there for a girl like me?"

"You are an honest, hardworking person," Clara said. "That counts for a lot, and you have a good moral compass. Unfortunately, private detection can be a murky business. Sometimes our moral compasses have to falter. There is something else out there for you."

"I'll have to think about it," Sarah rubbed at her forehead. "I… I have to finish the Butterworth case first. Mrs Butterworth is at least happy with what I have done."

Sarah became forlorn again.

"I don't know who was right in that case," she said after a moment. "Mr Butterworth took the cat, but I am not sure if he didn't have some claim over it. And, in any case, all he wanted was to move on and be free. I know what it is like to feel trapped and just to want to break away. I lie awake at night and wonder if I have done the right thing."

"Don't," Clara told her. "You can't possibly know all the ins and outs of such a thing and you have to go by the information you have. It is best not to worry about what is right and what is wrong. That gets very difficult. Sometimes, whichever choice you make, none can be absolutely right."

"Then, I don't want to do this anymore," Sarah rose. "Thank you for listening to me, Clara, but this is not the life I want for myself. I want to be free, but not at the expense of others. You have reconciled this business with your conscience, I cannot."

Clara was hurt. Sarah made it sound as if she did not care about people, that she was quite content to hurt others if it solved a case. Clara did not consider herself so callous, she had just been trying to explain how there were often no perfect solutions to cases. Take the one she was working on at the moment; a crime had been committed, but it could not be resolved by the law. Instead she had to make the best of it.

Sarah wanted to go. Clara showed her out of the house, still feeling offended. She closed the door and wondered what the woman would do with herself now? Clara resolved that it was not her problem anymore and started to head for the parlour. Then she hesitated. Was that what Sarah meant about Clara reconciling her conscience to this business? Had Clara become too hard?

Chapter Twenty-seven

Clara paid a call on Mr Jacobs the following day. She wasn't entirely sure how to begin explaining the situation to him. There was so much to tell, and very little of it was pleasant. They sat in the parlour of his house, the noise of the workmen wiring his home for electricity a distraction in the background. Jacobs had suggested tea and Clara had agreed to buy her some time. When it finally arrived and there was no choice but to talk, she considered her words carefully.

"I know where the green jade dragon is and how it might be returned to you."

Mr Jacobs sat bolt upright.

"My word! I thought it almost impossible! Tell me, please."

"The dragon is in the hands of a rather unpleasant criminal named Brilliant Chang. You may have heard of him?"

Jacobs thought for a moment.

"I do believe his name has come up in the context of antiquities. I wonder if he was the gentleman who came to the Marquis of Surrey's luncheon the other year where I was a guest speaker? The name sounds Chinese, and this gentleman was certainly that."

"That is the sort of strata of society he moves in," Clara nodded. "However, while he masterminded the crime, he was not the instigator of it. That was a Japanese gentleman who has not been named to me. This gentleman has failed to pay Chang and he is now willing to sell the dragon back to you."

"Sell?" Jacobs gaped in astonishment. "The dragon is mine! Why, on earth, would I buy it back from the thief?"

"Because there may be no other way to retrieve it," Clara explained. "The police cannot touch Chang, even if we told them that he had your dragon. Chang is too clever for that. And he will have hidden the dragon well. Involve the police and the dragon will probably disappear for good."

Jacobs was unconvinced. Clara could understand his affront; being asked to buy the very thing stolen from him hurt not just the bank balance, but also a man's pride.

"And what price does this man demand?" Jacobs asked, trying to reconcile himself with the idea.

Clara took out the slip of paper Chang had written his offer on. She was biting her lip as she handed it over. She had, naturally, opened and read the details and realised that Chang was asking a ridiculous price. He had them over a barrel, that was the problem, and he was not stupid. He would have researched Mr Jacobs thoroughly before attempting the burglary and would know the sort of money the man could afford. And if he didn't pay it, well, Chang was quite happy to wait a while to find a more accommodating buyer.

Mr Jacobs opened the slip of paper and gasped.

"Preposterous!" he declared. "The dragon is valuable, but this..."

The paper trembled as his hands shook with rage.

"Miss Fitzgerald, this is unspeakable!"

"We might be able to negotiate," Clara mediated. "But Chang knows the position he has us in. He will bargain hard."

"This makes up my mind," Mr Jacobs said firmly, still

glowering at the figure on the paper. "I shall go to the police, insist they arrest Mr Chang and search his property for the dragon!"

"I don't think that will work," Clara told him gently. "Brilliant Chang is a very cunning criminal and he has avoided the law for a number of years. The only evidence I have for him being behind the theft of the dragon comes from other criminals. They owe their continued employment, even their existence, to Chang and will not betray him. In any case, a court of law would likely perceive them as unreliable witnesses. Chang did not commit the crime and the evidence of other thieves that he was the one who employed them is not going to be enough."

Clara gave a sigh.

"It is not how I want this case to be. But Chang is good at what he does. He will not have left a paper trail or any physical evidence to suggest he was involved. I must also warn you that Chang moves in influential circles and has powerful friends," Clara met Jacobs' eyes. "You said yourself, he was invited to the Marquis of Surrey's luncheon. Chang knows people, important people. He is the sort of man who cultivates powerful friends, and many of those people owe him greatly and will do all in their power to prevent him being arrested and convicted of this crime. I have to impress upon you that the police have their hands tied in this affair, as do I. I don't like it, but I can't change that fact for the moment."

"I believe in our justice system," Mr Jacobs replied, his tone firm. "I do not believe that anyone is above the law."

Clara thought that a very noble way of thinking, but hardly practical considering the situation they were in. The law was made and administered by people, and people were fallible. They could be greedy, corrupt or simply spineless. And Chang knew how to exploit all those features in a man.

"Brilliant Chang has policemen in his pocket," Clara explained, lowering her voice for fear of being overheard, though the clattering of the men upstairs drowned out most of their conversation. "I know this because last year I helped to expose one such policeman. I like this no more than you do, but I have to be blunt. Involving the police is unlikely to achieve anything but ensure the dragon is out of your reach forever. I appreciate that being made to pay for the dragon is a bitter pill to swallow. I don't much like that either, but life is not always simple. I suppose, the question you must ask yourself is, do you want to risk losing the dragon for good?"

Jacobs didn't know how to answer that. The dragon held a great deal of sentiment for him. It had been his uncle's parting gift, placed in his hand with the implication that he must take great care of it. The item was priceless to him. Yet, his principles made him want to crumple the piece of paper with Chang's insulting offer into a little ball and throw it into the fire. He wondered what his uncle would do, but the man had been so little known to him, just a memory of a man who Jacobs had idolised, that to try and imagine his response was an exercise in futility.

"There is something else you must consider before making your decision," Clara continued. "And this will, ultimately, be your decision."

"There is more about this Chang fellow?" Jacobs asked anxiously.

"No, there is more about your uncle," Clara hesitated. It was never easy to tell someone that the uncle they admired, hero-worshipped even, had dabbled in illegal activities. "My investigations have revealed that the dragon was originally stolen from the imperial palace. The Japanese have been looking for it for years."

If Jacobs had not looked astonished before, he certainly did now and nearly fell from his chair. The colour drained from his face and his mouth dropped open.

"Stolen?" his voice came out in a hiss. "By my uncle?"

"Oh no, I don't think that," Clara quickly reassured him. "The dragon was stolen by someone within the palace, and the scandal it caused quite literally resulted in heads rolling. Sometime later, your uncle was sold the dragon, and no doubt bought it innocently enough."

Clara was not certain of the last part, but she could not prove the situation either way and didn't see the need to upset Mr Jacobs further.

"However, the imperial authorities learned of the sale and sent two agents to follow your uncle and retrieve the dragon. My understanding is that before your uncle left Japan he became aware he was being pursued and also why."

Clara paused to allow the implication of this statement to sink in.

"My uncle left Japan knowing he had bought a stolen netsuke," Jacobs said steadily, the words not really hitting home just yet. He said them in a dull tone, as if talking about someone else.

"He ensured he reached England ahead of his pursuers and then came straight to Brighton to leave the dragon here," Clara was drip-feeding him the revelation. "Then he returned to London where his pursuers caught up with him once more and, it would seem, inadvertently caused his accident."

Jacobs was looking at the piece of notepaper still in his hand. The blue ink of Chang's fountain pen danced across the paper, the numbers he had written blurring. It would take him a long time to reconcile what he was hearing with the memories he had of his uncle.

Clara gave him a moment, then said gently;

"Were you to set the police on Chang, he would most likely reveal the origins of the dragon. There are people in authority who can confirm that such a dragon went missing from the imperial palace. Your claim on the dragon will be as void as Chang's."

"You mean, should I wish to keep a stolen item I must not cross the thief who stole it from me?" Mr Jacobs said in that same dull tone. He closed his eyes briefly, clearly struggling with all this information. "My uncle was a great adventurer. Daring, brave. He perhaps did not always play by the rules, but I never would have considered him a willing accomplice in theft. But, then again, what do I really know of him? I was nine when he died and he had visited my father perhaps once a year, usually just after one of his great adventures. He would tell such stories and I would hang off every word. Maybe, all these years, I have invented him in my mind, worked him up to being some great hero, when really he was just a man. Could it be that my uncle was not against appropriating stolen goods when he really liked them? Was the draw of the green jade dragon enough to overrule his conscience?"

"Those are questions I cannot answer," Clara replied. "We will never know what caused him to make such a decision, we can only know that he was aware that he was being pursued for the sake of the dragon."

"So," Mr Jacobs gave a sigh and pulled Chang's note into his lap. "I must make my own decision then? How much do I value the dragon?"

"You need not decide at once," Clara reminded him. "Give yourself time for the information to sink in. You can let me know what you wish to do when you are ready."

"On the contrary, Miss Fitzgerald, I know already what I want," Mr Jacobs tapped the notepaper. "Whatever its origins, the dragon means a great deal to me, it is the abiding link I have with my late uncle. Perhaps he was a less than honourable man, but he was my uncle. The dragon might be a piece of cultural heritage for the Japanese, but what precisely does that mean? Do they think of the dragon with the same emotion as I do? What will they do if it is returned to them? Seal it in some vault so it may never be stolen again? How can that be the right thing to do? I suppose, what I am saying, is that the Japanese can wait a little longer for their netsuke. Let me cherish it for the last years of my life. When I am gone, then it may be returned."

Clara listened intently. She had not made her own decision on the matter, thinking it best not to contemplate too hard how she would respond to such a situation. Mr Jacobs seemed to have found a compromise that suited his conscience. The dragon would retain its place in his collection, as a memento of his uncle, and when he finally passed it would be restored to its rightful home. In some regards, it could be imagined that Jacobs was merely borrowing it for a while.

"Does that mean you wish to accept Mr Chang's offer?"

Jacobs mouth had formed a hard, straight line. He clutched the paper a little tighter.

"I will have to eat my pride to stomach it, but yes, I shall accept the offer. Will you inform Mr Chang?"

"I will," Clara agreed. "And I shall arrange a meeting with him. Do you have a preference for a time or place?"

Mr Jacobs shook his head.

"Let him do the choosing. As you say, he has me over a barrel," Jacobs paused. "Do you think me a fool going to such lengths for a piece of jade?"

"No," Clara answered honestly. "Objects can become very precious to us, for lots of reasons. You are entitled to feel this way."

"Somehow I suspect this Brilliant Chang will not be so generous to my emotions. Tell him, I accept this written offer alone. Should he suddenly try to raise the price I will walk away. I might be a fool, but I can sometimes see sense."

Clara reassured him that Chang would be informed of all the details and would be made aware that they would not play any games. They both rose and Jacobs showed Clara to the door personally.

"May I just say, Miss Fitzgerald, I have found you very professional in this affair. You have acted efficiently and discreetly. Once the jade dragon is returned I will gladly pay what I owe you and with gratitude."

Clara was touched, she thanked him for his trust in

her. Mr Jacobs wished her well as she walked away from the house and through his immaculate garden. She was mulling over how best to arrange things with Chang. The meeting would be in London, naturally, and Chang would pick a place where he could have the advantage over them. He would have plenty of his men about in case of trouble. She knew that when it came to a match with Chang she was at a disadvantage, but she would have to make the best of it. She would have her own friends on standby – Bob, Tommy and O'Harris for a start. Should anything happen, Clara could be assured of their help.

Clara felt her stomach knot a little with anxiety. All this fuss for a jade dragon. Still, there was no reason to imagine things would not go smoothly. She headed for home, ready to brave Chang and set up a meeting.

Chapter Twenty-eight

It was yet another Saturday in London. They were in a square lined with houses and shops. A fenced garden stood in the centre, a lone statue of a man on horseback guarding its beds and borders. Soot was hanging low in the air, staining clothes and making you want to cough. The autumn was turning and the fires in the houses were being lit. Soon Londoners would return to a world of perpetual smog as winter took a firm hold.

There was a small restaurant on one side of the square. It had a long glass frontage with gold writing on the windows that indicated it sold hot cooked meals and spirits. Chang had named the place as his chosen venue for the sale of the dragon. Clara arrived with Mr Jacobs at the door of the restaurant and glanced briefly inside. She could not see Chang, but he was no doubt around somewhere. There was no telling how many of the men inside the restaurant were employed by him. He would no doubt have stationed several about to watch his back. Clara had followed suit. Bob, Tommy and O'Harris were masquerading as shoppers on the other side of the square. Mr Jacobs had brought his butler with him. Yaxley was sitting in the central garden reading a newspaper and trying to ignore the pigeons at his feet demanding breadcrumbs.

Clara glanced at Mr Jacobs. He nodded. They let themselves into the restaurant, ordered tea, and then sat down at a table near the window to wait.

"I thought he would already be here," Jacobs glanced at his watch. They were only five minutes early.

"He will be watching for us, somewhere," Clara promised ominously. "Chang is cautious, of that I am certain."

"I am actually quite nervous," Mr Jacobs toyed with his teaspoon. "I can't remember the last time I felt this way. But it will be over soon."

"Absolutely," Clara was nervous too, but trying not to show it. "Soon we will be heading back to Brighton with the dragon."

She was just finished talking when the restaurant door opened and the little bell over it rang. Clara had her back to the door, but Mr Jacobs was facing her and could see clearly who came in.

"I believe it is him," he whispered.

Clara turned in her chair and found herself staring into the smiling face of Brilliant Chang. He walked over, looking expensively dressed in a grey suit and silk tie.

"Miss Fitzgerald," Chang offered her a bow. "And this must be Mr Jacobs?"

The two men shook hands, though it was plain Mr Jacobs did not like being so close to Chang. Chang took a seat with them and waved his hand to a waitress to order a whisky and soda.

"Would you care for some?" he asked his companions.

"Too early," Clara shook her head.

Mr Jacobs said nothing.

"Shall we get straight to business then?" Chang pulled a small wooden box from his coat pocket and set it on the table. He flicked open its lid and there, on a velvet cloth, lay the green jade dragon. It was the first time Clara had seen it for real and she was stunned by its elegant beauty. The photographs from the catalogue had not done it justice. The detail was exquisite and almost defied belief. Clara shook her head, mildly astonished.

"A thing of beauty," Chang smiled at her, before quickly clicking back down the lid. "I can see why you value it so, Mr Jacobs."

"It is not just for that reason," Jacobs grumbled, but his eyes were still fixed on the box and any doubts he had retained about paying for it were now gone. He slipped his hand into his own pocket and removed a large brown envelope. "Please count this."

Chang took the envelope, gave Jacobs an apologetic smile, then set himself to the task of counting the money and ensuring it was real.

"Thank you, Mr Jacobs," he said once he was satisfied. Pocketing the cash, he pushed the box across to him. "Enjoy your dragon."

Mr Jacobs could not resist opening the box again and looking at the little netsuke. Chang's drink arrived and he sipped at it appreciatively, while Mr Jacobs feasted his eyes on the dragon. It was as if Jacobs had never seen it before, as if every detail was not already engraved on his memory. He gave a contented sigh.

"My uncle knew a treasure when he saw it."

"Hmm," Chang mused. "A man after my own heart, it seems. Not prepared to allow a little thing such as rightful ownership deter him from getting what he wanted."

Jacobs cast a withering look at Chang. Clara sensed that the atmosphere among them was rapidly deteriorating. It was time they got going. She rose.

"Won't you finish your tea?" Chang asked her pleasantly.

She looked into those viper eyes.

"We have done what we needed to," she said. "Why detain you longer?"

"Do you not appreciate my good company?" Chang asked her with amusement.

"I think we both know the answer to that," Clara

replied.

Mr Jacobs had risen too, Clara hoped to get him away from Chang before an argument began. She could see Mr Jacobs was barely keeping his temper in check. Unfortunately, Chang decided to rise with them. He drained his whisky and escorted them to the door of the restaurant. They stepped outside together. Clara desperately wanted to depart, but Mr Jacobs seemed determined to linger.

"Who did you steal this for?" he hissed to Chang.

Chang merely laughed at him.

"Why would I tell you?" he said.

Jacobs pressed the box with the dragon deep into his pocket and kept his hand upon it.

"Crook!" he declared loudly.

Clara was about to grab his arm and whisk him away when there was the shrill noise of a whistle and several men, previously standing around like idle passers-by, suddenly converged on the trio by the restaurant. In one horrible instant Clara realised that the men rushing towards her were the police. She recognised Inspector Arran among them.

"You betrayed me!" Chang growled.

"No!" Clara declared, but then her eyes went to Jacobs who was looking smug with himself. She gasped, the fool had double-crossed her too.

Everything began to occur too fast. Chang, his usual smile turned to an angry snarl, grabbed Clara from behind and pulled her to him. The next instant she realised he had drawn a knife from his pocket and it was pressed against her throat.

"Nobody come any closer!" Chang yelled at the plain clothes policemen fast approaching.

The policemen stopped. Inspector Arran was in the middle of them and called a halt. Mr Jacobs had staggered back when Chang grabbed Clara, now he was looking on in horror, for the first time realising the calamity he had caused. Clara briefly closed her eyes, took a breath and calmed herself. She knew Tommy, Bob and O'Harris would be racing over to her aid but, in reality, she would have to get herself out of this mess. After all, the knife was being held to her throat.

"I'll kill her if you follow me!" Chang snarled at the policemen, before dragging Clara back through the restaurant door.

The restaurant was now in chaos. The innocent diners were screaming or panicking at the sight of a man threatening to kill a woman — a woman he had just been seen dining with. Other figures, men in suits, were standing up and acting surprisingly calm. Clara guessed these were Chang's men.

"I didn't inform the police," Clara told Chang, being careful as she spoke not to slice her jaw on the knife. "I told Jacobs the police should not be involved. I thought he understood."

"You thought wrong!" Chang growled in her ear. He glanced at his men. "Go check the back door!"

Two men disappeared. Clara continued to remain as calm as she could. Panicking was not an option.

"I would prefer it if you didn't kill me," she said, hoping to ease the tension. "I have been double-crossed too."

"Miss Fitzgerald, I really do not care what happens to you," Chang hissed.

"I care!" Clara retorted. "And, I should point out, I have behaved honourably towards you. At least as honourably as such a situation can warrant."

"You are helping me get out of here, Miss Fitzgerald," Chang said, his voice low and nasty. "And when we are done, if I get away safely, I may let you go."

"That does not sound a great deal to my ears," Clara countered.

"What exact choice do you have?" Chang laughed at her, no humour in his tone.

His men had returned.

"They are at the back door too, boss," one informed

him.

Chang cursed.

"Then we might as well go out the front way," Chang hesitated even as he said this.

"You didn't see this coming, did you?" Clara remarked, not inclined to play nice. "I am actually disappointed you had not considered this as a possibility."

"Oh? And I suppose you envisioned yourself being held hostage, Miss Clever Boots Fitzgerald?" Chang snapped back, turning his head to her and letting the knife drop a bit as he spoke.

"Now you mention it," Clara answered. "I did come prepared for an emergency."

At that, Clara allowed the hat pin she had borrowed off Annie (just in case) which was concealed in her sleeve to drop into her hand. She stabbed backwards with it, catching Chang in his thigh. She rammed it hard and deep and Chang doubled with pain, the knife automatically dropping from her throat. Clara leapt forward. Chang grabbed for her hand and held her back. Instinctively she kicked out at him, not wanting to give him the chance to recover sufficiently to threaten her again. Due to Chang being bent double, the kick caught him in the throat and he gagged as he went backwards.

Clara was now free and wasted no time running for the front door. Some of Chang's men began to dart after her, others were going to the aid of their boss, but Clara had the advantage of knowing what she was about to do and made it to the door before anyone could grab her. She ran straight to Inspector Arran, who dragged her behind the police line, then blew his whistle again and sent his men charging into the restaurant.

For the next few minutes it was not plain what was occurring. Clara retreated to the garden with her friends. Mr Jacobs arrived there too, looking sheepish. Mr Yaxley took up a protective position between him and Bob, who was close to toppling the man for his foolishness. Clara put a hand on Bob's arm.

"I'm alive and well. No point in more violence," she told him. "I'll just add this inconvenience to Mr Jacobs' bill."

"I do apologise Miss Fitzgerald. I did not mean for such a thing to happen. I just wanted the fiend arrested," Mr Jacobs looked small behind his butler and was not quite able to meet anyone's eye. "I went to Inspector Park-Coombs and explained I was filing a complaint against the man I believed stole the dragon, and he gave me the name of Inspector Arran and said he would understand. I should not have gone behind your back."

"No," Clara told him angrily, "you shouldn't have."

"I apologise," Jacobs said meekly.

But the deed was done. Clara rubbed at her throat, relieved it was unscathed. She did not like to think what Chang's reaction would be to this skirmish. He was not a man you wanted to make enemies with. She would have to be even more careful.

Eventually the chaos died down. Inspector Arran appeared from the restaurant with his troops. Several were injured; bruised faces, slashed arms and bloody noses seemed the order of the day. A handful of Chang's thugs had been arrested, but as the prisoners were paraded out of the restaurant, Clara was disheartened to see Chang was not among them. Chang had slipped away despite everything. But perhaps that was just as well. What could the police do to Chang, after all?

Inspector Arran approached Clara, trying to get a statement off her, but she refused to say anything other than that she had met Chang in the restaurant by coincidence. She would not press charges, she had no desire to arouse Chang's ire further. All she wanted now was to get home and forget this ever happened. Jacobs looked in a similar state. He had the dragon safe and it was plain he was now regretting his insistence on summoning the police. What had he achieved? Not a great deal and Clara could see he was now wondering what revenge Chang might take for his rash decision.

Jacobs would be upping his security again.

Bob sat next to Clara on the train home, while Tommy and O'Harris sat opposite her. The first part of their journey their compartment contained two other passengers, so they said nothing about the incident in London. Halfway home, the other passengers departed and Clara was soon assailed by questions. The obvious one was how she had slipped away from Chang. Clara explained about the hat pin.

"And what made you take that with you?" O'Harris asked curiously.

"I suppose it was my natural cynicism," Clara shrugged. "I didn't trust Chang to play fair."

"So you armed yourself?" O'Harris said in amazement.

"This is Clara, old man," Tommy laughed. "She expects the worst in people. I'm just surprised she didn't hide the dining room poker up her sleeve."

"The hat pin was more convenient," Clara said demurely. "I thought it might come in handy. Actually, I had one up both sleeves."

With that Clara shook her left sleeve and the second hat pin fell out. She shoved it into her hat. Tommy laughed. Bob grinned. O'Harris just looked on in a daze.

"Chang won't forget this lightly," Tommy suddenly stopped laughing and his tone became sombre.

"And I won't forget lightly," Clara replied. "No, I shall write him a letter when we get home suggesting we call this one a draw."

"This one?" O'Harris asked.

"I have a nasty feeling Chang will pop up in my affairs once again before long," Clara replied. "He is challenging to avoid."

"What about Mr Jacobs?" Bob rumbled, his voice like mountains crashing together in its low tone of anger.

"Mr Jacobs will pay my bill, with the extra I shall add to it for my own inconvenience. And then he can spend the rest of his days worrying whether Brilliant Chang is out for revenge," Clara paused for a moment. "I suppose I understand why he did it. It rankled his ethics and his pride to think a thief would go scot-free for the crime he committed. But he acted rashly, as did Inspector Arran. There will be a time when we can catch Chang and have him warming a prison cell, but this was not it."

"As long as you are all right," O'Harris said.

"I am," Clara smiled. "And one day I shall have my own revenge on Chang."

Clara smiled at them all.

"And it won't just involve a hat pin."

Chapter Twenty-nine

Inspector Park-Coombs knocked on Clara's front door. Annie let him in and he found Clara in the parlour just finishing her breakfast. Clara put aside the last bite of toast.

"Inspector?"

"I'm feeling rather guilty," Park-Coombs stood before her looking surprisingly abashed.

"Oh dear, Inspector. What could have possibly brought that on?" Clara asked him.

"Inspector Arran has just been in touch with me on the telephone. He informed me of the events of yesterday. I didn't realise, when I gave Mr Jacobs Arran's name, what would occur. I placed you in danger."

"Hardly your fault," Clara said, pushing out a chair to try and get him to sit down. "I suppose I should tell you that I instructed Mr Jacobs not to involve the police in this matter. I knew how tied your hands would be."

"Brilliant Chang is a pest," Park-Coombs grumbled, finally sitting down. "A thorn in my side, just like he is a thorn in Arran's side. But there will always be men like him around and, as long as there are people in power helping them, I will have to bite my tongue and watch on. I understand why you suggested the police not be involved."

"My task was to restore the dragon to Mr Jacobs. Had this been a murder case I would have been less pragmatic and insisted we find a way to achieve justice. As it was, I thought it best we simply arrange for the return of the dragon," Clara shrugged her shoulders. "And Chang caused me no harm, in the end. Though I wait to see what he will do next."

"If you are fearful, I shall offer police protection," Park-Coombs declared immediately.

Clara merely shook her head.

"I will be fine. And your police constables have better things to do."

"Don't remind me," Park-Coombs became morose again. "The Superintendent is still badgering me. He wants more constables patrolling the streets. All very well, except he is not offering extra money for them! And he still wants me to hire a woman constable."

"No luck with that?" Clara asked.

Park-Coombs hefted his shoulders with a sigh.

"I might have an idea for you," Clara said. "Come with me."

Clara took the inspector across Brighton and to Sarah Butler's offices. She wasn't sure if the woman would be at work after her recent misadventures, but she hoped so. She also hoped that Sarah was still interested in improving the world she lived in and helping others, despite her setbacks. They were in luck. Sarah Butler was in her office, writing a letter.

"I have paid the rent for the week," she said, as Clara explained how she had hoped she would be there. "I might as well use the space."

"Have you made any plans?" Clara asked.

Sarah shook her head.

"Not yet."

"Then may I suggest that Inspector Park-Coombs here might have just the opportunity you are looking for?"

Sarah glanced at the inspector cautiously.

"What sort of opportunity?"

"The inspector needs a female police constable," Clara explained. "I thought the role might suit you?"

"I don't have the resources to volunteer for such a role," Sarah shook her head.

"It isn't voluntary," Park-Coombs interrupted. "You will be paid."

Sarah's face lit up with interest, but she was still uncertain.

"I didn't intend to work for anyone…" she mumbled.

"Sometimes working for someone else is not a bad thing," Clara told her. "You wanted to help people, did you not?"

Sarah gave a slight nod of her head.

"This way, you will be helping people, but you will have the back-up of the entire police force. No one will come barging into your rooms to shout at or threaten you again," Clara pointed out. "Not only that, but you will be doing something that few women have ever done before. Certainly not in Brighton. You will be a pioneer for women!"

"Steady on," Park-Coombs frowned at Clara. "It's mainly about talking to women and girls, providing a friendly ear for their troubles."

"A pioneer," Sarah whispered to herself, then she looked at the inspector directly. "Do I get a uniform?"

"Naturally," he agreed. "I should warn you, as I would warn any woman taking on this role, you will face prejudice and resentment. From your fellow constables as much as the general public. I know my men, I picked many of them, they are good constables. But some of them are very old-fashioned."

Clara had visions of the desk sergeant, her nemesis. What would he make of a female police constable? It could finish him off.

"I can handle prejudice," Sarah replied. "I am use to it. Just not the threats or danger I faced alone as a private detective."

"You won't be alone," Clara reassured her. "You will always have the other constables to rely on, and the Inspector."

Park-Coombs smiled at Clara, appreciating her trust in him.

"Well, Miss Butler? Would you like to give it a try?"

Sarah Butler considered all this for a while. Finally she turned her tough gaze on the inspector.

"I think it might be worth my consideration," she said to him. "I'll give it a go."

The relief that came over the inspector was palpable. He grinned at both Sarah and Clara, which was unusual in itself.

"That is very good news," he said. "Very good."

Clara was delighted. She thought Sarah Butler would make a good police constable. She had the presence for it, but also the ability to be sympathetic. She didn't say it aloud, but she also suspected Sarah would be a match for the inspector, should the need arise. It was a very good arrangement on the whole and Clara was pleased she had thought of it.

On the way home from Sarah's offices, Clara dropped by Mr Jacobs' house to supply him with her bill. For once Yaxley the butler let her in without a fuss. He couldn't quite meet her eyes, as if he too felt guilty for the mishap of the previous day. Mr Jacobs was in his usual sitting room. The workmen were also present, installing a new light fitting in the ceiling. When Jacobs saw Clara he flushed red.

"I have come to submit my bill," Clara informed him, her tone rather cold. She was still upset by what had occurred.

"Thank you," Mr Jacobs took the envelope she offered him without meeting her eyes. "I thought I would let you know, I have been thinking everything over and I have decided to offer the green jade dragon to the Japanese ambassador, so he might return it to its rightful home."

Clara was mildly surprised.

"I thought you intended to keep the dragon?" she said.

"I had intended that," Jacobs agreed. "But, after what occurred, I started to think again. It is an object, after all. A thing. It is not a person. People have died over this lump of stone, including my uncle. You came into harm's way because of it. I keep thinking that people are worth more than this dragon. In any case, now when I look upon it, it stirs thoughts of my uncle's misdeeds. I don't want to remember him that way."

Mr Jacobs moved to his netsuke display case and stared at the dragon, where it sat once more restored to its place.

"My uncle would still be alive but for this dragon," Jacobs murmured. "I would rather he had lived. This memento cannot replace him."

"I think you are making a wise decision," Clara told him. "The dragon will only bring you anxiety while it remains here. Let the Japanese have that worry."

"That is what I thought," Jacobs nodded. "And, if there is anything I can do for you... perhaps a letter to Chang to explain you were not involved?"

"Do not worry about it," Clara brushed aside the offer. "I will sort it all out."

Mr Jacobs nodded.

"Thank you, Miss Fitzgerald. I put you to a lot of trouble to retrieve an object I no longer want in my house. I was a fool."

"No, Mr Jacobs, you were just trying too hard," Clara sighed, deciding forgiveness was the order of the day. "Just take care of yourself from now on."

Mr Jacobs managed a smile.

"Thank you."

Clara strolled home, thinking. She had one final task before she could rest easily.

Back at home, Clara used the telephone to ring the Chang Emporium. She asked to speak to Mr Chang, insisting it was urgent. There was a long delay, the phone receiver at the Emporium must have been placed to one side as Clara could hear the noises of people bustling about. Eventually she was allowed to speak to Chang's secretary, and through her she was finally granted an audience with the man himself.

Brilliant Chang sounded gruff on the telephone.

"Miss Fitzgerald," he growled down the line. "You know you broke a tooth when you kicked me?"

"You were holding a knife to my throat," Clara replied. "I wasn't feeling merciful."

"Why are you ringing me?" Chang demanded.

"Because I want to agree to a truce, for the moment, at least," Clara explained. "You are angry with me, but I swear I was not aware of the police presence yesterday. Had I been, I would have made jolly sure I was not near enough to you to let you grab me."

"That did seem unusually lax for you," Chang admitted grudgingly.

"I won't hold a grudge over the knife you held to my throat, as long as you won't hold a grudge over the police," Clara bargained.

"What about the hat pin and my tooth?"

"I rather felt you deserved both of those," Clara answered. "By the way, do you still have the hat pin? It wasn't mine, you see."

Chang gave out a chuckle down the phone line.

"You are quite something Miss Fitzgerald! I have never known a woman like you!" his tone sounded less aggressive. "You stab a man with a hat pin and then politely ask for it back! If you were not so conscientiously moral, I would invite you to work for me."

"I'm afraid our personalities would clash," Clara informed him. "So, can we call this one a draw?"

Chang was silent a while, then he let out a long breath.

"I really have no desire to be chasing you about. In any case, you make my life miserable every time I get caught up with you. All right, I'll let this one be counted as a draw, but next time we meet Miss Fitzgerald, I won't be so generous."

"Nor will I," Clara promised him. "I was very careful with my aim of the hat pin, though you might not credit that."

"I don't," Chang muttered.

"Take care of the tooth," Clara said breezily down the phone. "I hear dentists can work wonders these days. And I hope your thigh is well again soon."

"Don't push your luck," Chang grumbled.

Clara was smirking to herself and very glad Chang could not see her face.

"Goodbye Mr Chang."

"Goodbye you infernal woman," Chang griped down the phone. "Stay in Brighton."

"Stay in London," Clara replied and then the line went dead.

Clara returned to the parlour feeling that her case was finally wrapped up. The dragon would go home to where it belonged. Chang would leave her alone, for the time being, and Mr Jacobs would slowly pick up the pieces of his broken memories. Perhaps he regretted involving Clara, but that was hardly her fault. She had only gone after the truth, and sometimes the truth was not pretty.

Captain O'Harris wandered into the parlour, he had a big scroll of paper under his arm.

"I'm heading to the house," he said. "Going to go over my new plans with an architect. Would you like to come?"

Clara looked up, pleased to see the eagerness in his face. He was finally coming alive again.

"Of course," she said gladly.

Holding out his arm, so Clara could loop hers through his, they headed together for the door. Clara reflected that as one adventure came to its conclusion, so another was just waiting to begin. That was what made life so exciting.

Clara Fitzgerald walked out into the autumn sunshine and looked up to a blue sky. She was very content with her life in that moment, very content indeed.

28816900R00149

Printed in Great Britain
by Amazon